...TTER
...OFF DEAD

"Small-town charm and big-time chills. Jewel Bay, Montana, is a food lover's paradise." —Laura Childs, *New York Times* bestselling author

LESLIE BUDEWITZ

AGATHA AWARD–WINNING AUTHOR OF *CRIME RIB*

BERKLEY
PRIME
CRIME

$7.99 U.S.
$10.49 CAN

S EAN

ISBN 978-0-425-25956-6

9 780425 259566

5 0 7 9 9

PRAISE FOR
THE FOOD LOVERS' VILLAGE MYSTERIES

Crime Rib

"Budewitz's latest is deliciously appealing . . . Cozy mystery lovers and foodies alike will enjoy this story of good neighbors, luscious food, and a bad egg (or two) who is capable of murder."
—*RT Book Reviews*

"Mouth-watering descriptions of food are just as enjoyable as the characters . . . The unpredictable ending is the perfect dessert course for a well-planned menu of murder."
—*Kings River Life*

Death al Dente

"Small-town charm and big-time chills. Jewel Bay, Montana, is a food lover's paradise—and ground zero for murder! A dizzying culinary delight with a twisty-turny plot! I'm totally enamored of Leslie Budewitz's huckleberry chocolates, Shasta daisies, and Cowboy Roast coffee."
—Laura Childs, *New York Times* bestselling author of the Cackleberry Club Mysteries and the Tea Shop Mysteries

"The first book in a delicious new series. Leslie Budewitz has created a believable, down-to-earth heroine in Erin Murphy, who uses her sleuthing skills and the Spreadsheet of Suspicion to catch a killer. The supporting cast of characters, from Erin's mother, Fresca, to her cat, Sandburg, are charming. I'm looking forward to my next visit to Jewel Bay."
—Sofie Kelly, *New York Times* bestselling author of the Magical Cat Mysteries

continued . . .

"An intriguing sleuth who loves gourmet food, family, and her hometown, plus recipes to die for, distinguish a delectable mystery."

—Carolyn Hart, *New York Times* bestselling author of *Don't Go Home*

"Seldom does a new author hit all the right notes in a first book, but Leslie Budewitz does. Convincing characters, a believable plot, the right dash of romance, and a deft use of words all come together to create a seamless and satisfying read."

—Sheila Connolly, *New York Times* bestselling author of *Picked to Die* and *An Early Wake*

"Clever, charming, and completely yummy. Leslie Budewitz cooks up a delectable mystery! A tempting concoction of food, fun, and fatalities that will have you racing through the suspenseful pages . . . then heading for the kitchen to try out the irresistible recipes. More please!"

—Hank Phillippi Ryan, Agatha, Anthony, and Macavity award–winning author

"A great mystery. There were clever twists that keep me engaged. It is hard to delve deep into a whodunit and lay the proper foundations for stories going forward but [Budewitz] has pulled it off. I can't wait to shop again at The Merc!"

—*Escape with Dollycas Into a Good Book*

"Budewitz writes with command and with a purpose. Her writing is straightforward and her characters are full of surprises. Budewitz serves up mouth-watering treats as well as murder in this first in a series book that readers will find simply delicious!"

—*Debbie's Book Bag*

"[A] new culinary mystery that offers a unique taste of Montana. Author Budewitz has created an engaging character, a charming town, and a whole new perspective on the state."

—*Mystery Scene*

...✿...

BUTTER
OFF DEAD

Leslie Budewitz

BERKLEY PRIME CRIME, NEW YORK

An imprint of Penguin Random House LLC
375 Hudson Street, New York, New York 10014

BUTTER OFF DEAD

A Berkley Prime Crime Book / published by arrangement with the author

ISBN: 978-0-425-25956-6

PUBLISHING HISTORY
Berkley Prime Crime mass-market edition / July 2015

PRINTED IN THE UNITED STATES OF AMERICA

10 9 8 7 6 5 4 3 2 1

Cover illustration by Ben Perini.
Cover design by Rita Frangie.
Interior text design by Kelly Lipovich.

Penguin
Random
House

For those who create the work that deepens our experience of this life:
those who paint; work fabric, clay, and metal; plant gardens;
write poems, plays, and stories; cook great food;
make music; make movies;
and so much more.
Your pursuit of your passions
brings this world—and all of us in it—alive.

Acknowledgments

As always, my thanks to my friends and neighbors for allowing me to wreak havoc on a community so much like the one we know and love. Thanks also for understanding that I have played with the map, changing names of streets and roads, and moving buildings and businesses to suit the story. Forgive me for torturing you by imagining a bakery that does not exist; I, too, wish it did.

It takes a village to catch a killer, and to support a writer. Thanks in particular to Derek Vandeberg of Frame of Reference, who throws the best launch parties ever, with help from Chef Dan Solberg, who brings my recipes to the table; Marlys Anderson-Hisaw of Roma's Kitchen Shop; and Annie Leberman and Kim Crowley of Imagine IF, the Flathead County Library system.

Mark "Mister" Langlois, barkeeper extraordinaire, once again let me rechristen his place as "Red's Bar." Julie and Joe Cassetta, aka the Pinskys, lent me their home and their collection of Montana movie posters. So sorry about—well, no spoilers. Several readers bought character names at charity auctions: thanks to Dana Grant for supporting the Safe Harbor domestic violence shelter and education program, and Donna Lawson and Dean and Jamie Beckstead for their contributions to the Crown of the Continent Guitar Festival.

A note on two characters who first appeared in *Crime Rib* and are based on much-loved real-life counterparts. Both the real and the fictional Christine Vandeberg are redheaded painters and former framers who work in bright acrylics, were raised in Vermont, and wear glasses of many colors. Everything else, I made up. Thank you, Christine! (See her paintings at Frame of Reference and online.) Iggy Ring bears the childhood nickname of my late mother-in-law, Louise Raff, as well as her physical appearance and style, her New England upbringing, and her love of art. Iggy's personal story as told here is completely my invention. My mother-in-law, who played a part in founding the Charles M. Russell Museum in Great Falls, cherished a small collection of Western bronzes and paintings, and would have greatly enjoyed her fictional namesake's treasure trove.

All art in the book is authentic, except for the pieces attributed to Iggy, Erin's purchase from Christine, and the item tied with ribbon. (No spoilers!) Readers who have toured the Russell studio and home may be surprised to hear that the home once contained several Asian pieces, including the gong and tapestry—perhaps gifts to Nancy Russell. The stone chop does exist, but did not come from the Russell collection.

The problems Erin and her friends uncover here are very real. Next time you visit a small art museum or historical center, please tuck a few dollars into the donation box.

I came across the essay "Pie" by Susan Bright, from her collection *Tirades and Evidence of Grace*, more than twenty years ago when it was reprinted in *Utne Reader*. A yellowed copy still marks the Pies section of my recipe binder. The poem "Making Tortillas" is by Alicia Gaspar de Alba, and appears in *Claiming the Spirit Within*, edited by Marilyn Sewell.

Thanks to Mary Jo Naive, board member of the Bigfork Center for the Performing Arts, and Dwayne Ague, Bigfork Summer Playhouse stage manager, for the backstage tour and the stories of what can go wrong when you entertain four hundred fifty friends two hundred nights a year. (And by the way, despite having once run a delightful children's shop, Mary Jo is *not* the model for Sally Grimes!) Sharon Woods Hopkins shared her classic sports car expertise. Emily Budewitz, Paige Wheeler, and Bella McGuire contributed to Landon's costumes. My friend and neighbor, wildlife biologist Cristina Eisenberg, has taught me much about wolves and their role in our ecology. If wolves intrigue you, dive into her books, *The Wolf's Tooth: Keystone Predators, Trophic Cascades, and Biodiversity* and *The Carnivore Way: Coexisting with and Conserving North America's Predators*. I also recommend *Decade of the Wolf: Returning the Wild to Yellowstone*, by Douglas W. Smith and Gary Ferguson.

Of course, I made all the mistakes myself.

As a kid, I always wanted a sister. As an adult, I've found more than I can count in Sisters in Crime, across the nation and in the Guppies chapter. The first third of this book was written in January 2014 at the Sisters in Crime retreat in Charlotte, North Carolina, during weather that made me feel write—er, right at home. Thank you, Beth Wasson, Cathy Pickens, and my sisters and brothers of ink, for a week of nurture, of being valued as a writer, of being in the midst of what my friend Lita Artis calls "intentional creativity."

Thanks to my agent Paige Wheeler of Creative Media Agency, Inc., my editors, Faith Black and Robin Barletta, and their colleagues at Berkley Prime Crime, and everyone else—including the readers, book clubs, libraries, and booksellers—who have helped make the Food Lovers' Village Mysteries spring to life.

And finally, my husband, Don Beans, aka Mr. Right, watched enough foodie movies to keep the Food Lovers' Film Festival rolling for years. He is always willing to brainstorm over dinner, in the car, and on walks as if my characters were real. Thanks to you, babe, they are.

"*Once upon a time there was a quiet village in the countryside whose people believed in tranquility.*"

—*CHOCOLAT*, SCREENPLAY BY
ROBERT NELSON JACOBS

"*It's a good thing it takes all kinds—because there are all kinds.*"

—ALICE BUDEWITZ

The Cast

THE MURPHY CLAN:

Erin Murphy, manager of Glacier Mercantile, aka the Merc

Francesca "Fresca" Conti Murphy, Erin's mother and the Merc's manager emeritus

Tracy McCann, salesclerk and budding chocolatier

Chiara Murphy Phillips, Erin's sister and co-owner of Snowberry Gallery

Landon Phillips, age five, Chiara's superhero son

Nick Murphy, aka Wolf Man, Erin's brother and a wolf biologist

FESTIVAL CREW:

Christine Vandeberg, painter and chief organizer of the Food Lovers' Film Festival

Larry Abrams, retired Hollywood lighting director, Film Club advisor

Zayda George, president of the Jewel Bay High School Film Club

Dylan Washington, future filmmaker

VILLAGERS AND FRIENDS:

Kyle Caldwell, head chef at Caldwell's Eagle Lake
Lodge and Guest Ranch, and car nut

Sally Grimes, owner of Puddle Jumpers Children's
Clothing and Toys

Danny Davis, Kyle's high school buddy and fellow
car nut

Rick Bergstrom, aka Farm Boy, hunky grain
salesman

Adam Zimmerman, hunky Wilderness Camp
director and Erin's college classmate

Jack Frost, aka the Junkman, Christine's feisty
neighbor

Ned Redaway, longtime owner of Red's Bar

J.D. Beckstead, Ned's grandson and a sign of
change at Red's

Wendy Taylor Fontaine, baker extraordinaire

Mimi and Tony George, Zayda's parents and
proprietors of the Jewel Inn

THE LAW:

Kim Caldwell, sheriff's detective and Jewel Bay's
resident deputy

Ike Hoover, undersheriff

FOUR-FOOTED FRIENDS:

Mr. Sandburg, Erin's sleek, sable Burmese cat

Pepé, Fresca's lively Scottish terrier

Pumpkin, Christine's full-figured orange tabby

Bozo, Tracy's Harlequin Great Dane, a rescue dog

· One ·

"**I** need to talk to you."

One hand on the aluminum stepladder, I peered out the broom closet door, wondering who needed me and why she whispered about it so urgently.

A blond teenager in gray leggings and purple running shoes, hair in a ponytail, stood at the open door to the Playhouse control room, her fleece-clad back to me.

"Later," came the reply. Older, male, firm.

"Now," she demanded, and I recognized Zayda George— high school senior, track star, president of the student Film Club.

"Coming through," I called, and wriggled my way out the door and into the wide passage leading to the lobby, both hands gripping the six-foot ladder. In the shadows, Zayda froze. I didn't need bright lights to know she'd been pleading with Larry Abrams.

Half a dozen kids from the Film Club who were running the projectors, lights, and sound for the weekend mingled in the Playhouse lobby. Christine Vandeberg pointed to a spot on the tile floor and I set up the ladder. She whipped a plastic bag off a five-foot-long hand-painted sign leaning against the wall.

"Like it?" Christine clasped her hands, squeezing her fingers as she waited for my opinion.

"Perfect." For our first Food Lovers' Film Festival, we'd rechristened the Playhouse in Jewel Bay, Montana, taking it back to its roots. You can't go back again, not really. Times change. The places you love change. You change.

But the right sign can transport you anywhere.

"Perfect," I repeated. "Like an old-time theater marquee." Flamingo pink stripes emulating neon tubes ran across the top and bottom. On each end, faux diamonds, rubies, emeralds, and sapphires sparkled. And in the center, three-dimensional gold script read THE BIJOU. Literally, the jewel. Figuratively, the Jewel Box.

"You're too young to talk about old-time, Erin." I hadn't seen Larry Abrams approach. Not quite movie-star handsome but close, with white hair and chiseled features just beginning to soften. "It's Brooklyn, 1955, decades before you were born. I went to the movies every Saturday afternoon, sometimes twice."

The red hair coiled on top of Christine's head in a tribute to Marge Simpson bobbed like a buoy in a windstorm. "I used Larry's movie poster collection and a picture of our original theater as inspiration. Larry, hold the ladder while we hang this."

The longtime Hollywood lighting director forced a helpful expression. In his post-retirement volunteer work, he enjoyed being in charge.

I could relate. But this Festival was Christine's baby, and to tell the truth, being the gofer made for a welcome break.

Larry steadied the ladder and Christine clambered up the rungs. I handed her the chain attached to the sign. She slipped the top link over a hook barely visible in the shiny tin ceiling and climbed back down. As I juggled the weight of the sign and Larry scooted the ladder over, I caught sight of Zayda a few feet away, one arm folded across her torso, absently biting the tip of her little finger.

Moments later, I stepped back. "What do you think, Zayda? Right height?"

"Um, it's good. Sparkly." Her voice lacked its usual zip, and she blinked rapidly as she glanced at Larry. His own eyes lit on her briefly before refocusing on the sign.

"Seriously, old man. You kept the posters from when you were a kid?" Zayda's boyfriend, Dylan, ran a hand through his dark blond hair. I'd spent enough time with the kids to realize that while she adored the movies, it was the technology that fired him up.

"They came later," Larry said. "Took me years to build that collection."

"What's the deal about collecting?" Dana Grant, another Film Club member, tilted his head. "I don't get it."

"Think of Barbies or Legos you're too old for, but you still love," a girl with hair in shades of red from strawberry blond to cranberry replied. Her parents ran the pizza joint. "Or tickets from a concert. You keep them to remind you how you felt."

"Zayda's got her number bibs from every race," Dylan said. "Plus all her ribbons. They cover the back of her bedroom door."

"'Cause she always wins," the redhead said.

"Yeah, but buying stuff just to hang on to it . . ." Dana's voice trailed off. Clearly, he was not in possession of the collector gene.

"Enough jabbering. Gotta make sure all this new gear runs like it's supposed to." Larry pointed toward the control room.

"Yessir." Dylan gave a mock salute, and the kids swarmed out of the lobby.

Zayda trailed behind. "Larry, you promised . . ." she said in a low voice.

"Soon as the job is finished," he said. Zayda bit her lower lip and followed the other kids. Larry headed for the men's room.

"What was that all about?" I asked Christine.

Face raised, her gaze darted from one end of the sign to the other, measuring whether it hung straight and level. Years as a professional framer gave her a sharp eye for details.

The sign sparkled. Which was the point: To bring a little color and light to a village mired in the deep midwinter. Let other towns break the monotony of February with hearts and flowers. But a town that calls itself the Food Lovers' Village and boasts first-class summer stock plus a vibrant community theater? Food and film, a natural combination.

"What? Something happen?"

I reached for the ladder. "No. But Larry may be a little too directorial." Zayda was a good kid, eager to prove herself. Eager, too, to get on a pro's good side and make contacts in the industry. Her mother, Mimi, had told me she had her heart set on film school in L.A. She'd work lights and sound, almost any job, biding time for a chance to get behind the camera. Let other girls crave the spotlight. Zayda George wanted to be the one telling them what to do.

Christine squinted at the sign through turquoise glasses frames. "Yeah. But without the money he raised for the screening equipment, we wouldn't be having a film festival, so . . ."

"Did you convince him to display his poster collection in the lobby?"

"Your sister figured out some kind of insurance thing, so he finally agreed." She scooped up the bag from the sign.

"Are all his posters for movies about Montana?"

"Just the ones he's lending us—Jane Russell in *Montana Belle*, Gene Autry in *Blue Montana Skies*, a dozen others. I guess some are pretty valuable."

"Speaking of collections," I said. "Have you decided

what to do with Iggy's? I still can't believe she had all that amazing art." Iggy Ring, painter, collector, teacher, mentor, and a fixture in Jewel Bay, had died over the past winter. A tiny woman who'd left a huge hole in the community, and in my heart.

The red-haired buoy wobbled dangerously. "A few legal details to work out, but most of it's going to the Art Center. What they can't keep, we'll sell to fund education programs. Art classes for teens, I'm thinking, and a business training course for artists. I've got to finish Iggy's inventory, then get an appraisal."

"Good work, ladies." Larry crossed the lobby to join the kids.

"Thanks," I called to Larry. To Christine, "good choice." More than a century ago, settlers began floating logs cut from the surrounding mountains down the Jewel River to a mill beside the bay. Around 1900, construction of a small dam and power plant, and a new road for lumber wagons and trucks, spurred more growth. By the 1970s, the mill had closed, lights had dimmed, and the town needed a new spark. Locals— including Old Ned Redaway and my family—fashioned Jewel Bay into an arts village, and in recent years, cooked up a reputation as a food lovers' haven. Others built up the area's recreational assets.

Now those passions bloom side by side, making Jewel Bay, Montana, a most unexpected place. It melds mouth-watering food, eye-watering art, a golf course designed by Jack Nicklaus, tummy-churning whitewater, and the most dedicated volunteer force on the planet. The result? A village chock-full of charm. Not to mention that it sits on a bay of the largest freshwater lake west of the Mississippi, with a backyard wilderness stretching more than a million acres, and Glacier National Park half an hour's drive away.

Since moving back home nine—nearly ten—months ago to take over the Merc, my family's hundred-year-old grocery, I'd come to understand the power of local in a whole new light. My mother and I converted the Merc into a market specializing in foods grown or produced in the region. Wine to wash them down, pottery to serve them, and soap to wash up, all of it locally made, too. We also created a commercial kitchen in the back of the shop, so vendors can cook and pack their products in a facility that meets health department specs.

But while I love my vendors dearly, it took about ten seconds to realize that knowing how to make fabulous pasta and pesto, cure award-winning salami, or cook huckleberry jam that makes grown cowboys tear up is a far cry from knowing how to market those skills. A whole 'nother kettle, as my grandfather Murphy would have said.

So I'd put my decade of experience as a grocery buyer for SavClub, the international warehouse chain based in Seattle, to work mentoring my vendors in the fine arts of inventory control and cost management, giving an occasional lesson in sales and marketing.

And after watching my sister, Chiara, launch a successful co-op gallery while other artists struggled to pay the bills, I firmly believe every working artist needs a crash course in business savvy.

As a painter and framer, Christine had seen plenty of artists fight that same battle. She gave the sign a long, loving gaze. "This weekend is going to be a hit, isn't it?"

I folded the ladder and hoisted it onto my hip. "Everything's falling into place perfectly."

Famous last words.

The first Friday in February and the Merc was quiet as a cloud. I minded—cash flow trickles this time of year—but it's kinda nice to catch your breath once in a while.

Happily, Tracy McCann, my shop clerk and sole employee,

is a display whiz. The plate glass windows on either side of our front door boast deep bays that present a constant challenge. To me, anyway. To Tracy, changing the product mix and finding the right theme and accent pieces is the best part of her job.

Second best, after a seriously fine talent for making truffles.

One window celebrated Valentine's Day: wine and roses, chocolates, scented soaps and lotions, red-and-white dishes. A picnic basket—one of our year-round specialties—brimming with ingredients for a romantic dinner for two.

In the other window, the movies held center stage. The Festival poster. Popcorn poppers in the newest, grooviest styles, from Kitchenalia, across the street. Saltshakers in two simple designs: clear quilted glass with a metal screw top, and an aluminum canister with a curved handle. And from my favorite NFL player-turned-potter: a serving bowl in a poppy red glaze and four small bowls, each bearing a distinctive red-and-white pattern. Red-and-white popcorn cartons and boxes of Junior Mints and Dots continued the theme.

Not to mention the bags of organic white popcorn, grown in Montana and sourced for us by Montana Gold, a family-owned wheat and grain farm and distributor headquartered on the Hi-Line, the state breadbasket.

"Now for the pièce de résistance, or whatever it's called."

"Great find." I picked up one end of the antique movie projector. "Woof. Heavy."

The red enamel hearts that hung from Tracy's earlobes swung drunkenly as we hoisted the projector carefully into place. She stepped back to catch her breath. "Borrowed it from the tuna tycoons."

Jewel Bay is home, at least part-time, to all kinds of folks who made all kinds of fortunes in all kinds of ways. We've got our coaster king and queen—Bob and Liz Pinsky, the family friends who own the property I take care of in exchange for rent. We've got our mattress million-aires, our software squillionaires, our baby-wipe barons.

And our tuna tycoons. Tracy and Mrs. Tuna bonded over their love of rescue Great Danes—Tracy's baby is a black-and-white Harlequin called Bozo. Major movie lovers, the Tunas had joined forces with a dozen other businesses and individuals as Festival co-sponsors. Winter events are for fun and friendship, not profit, though we seriously heart any and all mid-winter vacationers who stray our way.

"And the final touch." She cleared a space on the front counter for a red-and-white popper, a replica of a theater-style machine.

"It even smells like popcorn. Plus it's the perfect color." Like other businesses—both in the village, aka downtown, and on the highway—we fly red and white on weekends, in a show of school spirit.

"The big popper they salvaged from an old theater is going in the Playhouse for the weekend," she said. "We can use this one to get people in the movie mood."

"Mood, I like; the mess, I don't like, but it's all for a good cause." During my SavClub years, I worked a day or two a month in a Seattle warehouse to stay current and get real-time customer response to our products. That meant an occasional stint cloaked in white, my dark above-the-shoulder bob in a hairnet, serving hummus on chips or chicken cacciatore. Those little white pleated paper cups and napkins end up *every*where.

We have a similar problem here whenever we offer samples—one of the few similarities between slaving for an international food giant and sweating over a small-town specialty shop.

"What are we waiting for?" I said. We plugged in the popper and poured in the corn. Suddenly, we were ten again, going to the movies.

Tracy glowed, and not from the light sweat we'd worked

up. Or from the mouth-watering smell of the kernels popping.

No, I suspected her glow came from thoughts of Rick Bergstrom, the Montana Gold sales rep. He and I dated briefly last summer, but quickly discovered that a shared passion for the food biz was not enough to overcome a clash of temperaments. "Farm Boy," as Tracy dubbed him when he first came calling on the Merc, is a great guy. Just not the right guy for me. I'd been delighted to see him and Tracy get together.

My own love life had taken another twist, one that still took me by surprise.

"What are you girls doing?"

"Mom." Even after working with my mother most of a year, I don't always remember to call her "Fresca," short for "Francesca," at the shop. I licked butter and salt off my fingers. "Try some. It's really good."

"With one of your special seasonings?" She scooped about six kernels into a red-and-white paper boat. "The secret is portion control," she always says when I worry about my weight, but clearly I had not inherited her metabolism, or her flawless olive skin, oval face, and perfect features.

"We went classic for the first batch."

"Classic is good." She licked a finger, her Coral Sunset nail polish complementing the fluffy yellow-white kernel and golden butter. She makes fresh pasta, sauces, and pestos in the Merc's commercial kitchen on Mondays and Tuesdays, and gets a manicure every Wednesday.

"We tested them all," Tracy said, settling onto a red vinyl stool at the stainless steel counter separating shop floor from kitchen, her second sample in hand. "Cajun, dark cocoa, bacon salt." She made a face at that one.

"And everyone's favorite"—I paused for effect—"cheesy garlic," as Tracy sang out "caramel marshmallow."

"They sound divine. I popped in—no pun intended—the

day you tried truffle salt, but I didn't hear that on your menu," Fresca said.

"Too expensive. We need to keep every variety the same price."

Her coral lips tightened. She thinks I pay too much attention to cost of goods sold, inventory on hand, turnover rates, and price point—"all that business blah blah blah"—but we were finally making a profit. Not a lavish one, but trending up. The Merc had not turned a profit under her care, though she established a tradition of great food with a local emphasis. I thought we could have it all. So far, so good.

It's particularly important to keep costs down on "adventure food" or "splurge snacks"—foods people don't need, but think would be fun to try. We managed by packaging the blends in clear resealable bags dressed up with labels my sister designed.

"Speaking of divine, Candy's bringing in a special taste treat." Candy Divine—Candace DeVernero on the checks I write her every month. "Jewel Bay Critter Crunch."

"You love Critter Crunch but can't stand caramel marshmallow popcorn. What's the difference?" Tracy said, laughing.

"One has chocolate and nuts and the other has marshmallows," I replied. She rolled her eyes at my food quirks. Not that I think anyone who drinks Diet Coke for breakfast has a leg to stand on in Taste Wars.

"It all sounds wonderful, darling." My mother kissed my cheek. "And Tracy, the shop looks so festive."

Tracy beamed. "See you tomorrow, Erin. 'Night, Fresca."

Last spring, when my mother asked me to come home and run the shop, Tracy worried that she'd be fired or forced out when the Merc once again became a family business. But while we have our moments, on the whole, we make a good team.

"And I'm off as well. Bill and I are going to Paris for the evening."

One of the many advantages of my mother's involvement with Bill Schmidt, the town's only ex-lawyer herbalist, is that she now has someone besides me to drag along to festivities, this one a French-themed fund-raiser for the community college in Pondera. We'd been so focused on the displays that I'd barely noticed my mother's flapper dress, seamed stockings, and wool felt cloche. And the dead fox draped over her shoulders, beady black eyes and all.

"Where did you find that thing?" I wrinkled my nose. "Oh, geez. It's nearly six. I meant to fix that inventory glitch before Pool Night."

"It belonged to your grandmother Murphy," she said. "Don't you remember, Nick used to scare you with it when you were little?"

I remembered. The only thing Nick liked about having two little sisters was terrorizing us. "And you wonder why he became a wildlife biologist? Have fun."

"You, too, darling. Stay out too late." She sashayed off into the night.

I locked the front door, switched off the lights, and carried the iPad and the vintage metal sewing box we use as a cash register up the half flight of stairs to the loft.

The office finally felt like my space. Fresca's collection of cookbooks and food magazines had migrated, stack by stack, to shelves we'd installed in the basement—given a thorough cleaning and spiffing after last summer's misadventures. We'd swapped the old green-and-gold linoleum for a slate look and painted the walls Roasted Red Pepper, a name that always makes me hungry. I'd begun sprinkling in personal touches, including a painting I bought from Christine last summer at the Art and Food Festival.

I sank into the fancy desk chair Tracy had scored second-hand, remembering what I'd rather forget. Murder and mayhem. Threats to my family, my friends, and this marvelous, maddening pile of bricks.

And to me.

My right hand circled automatically around my left wrist, my thumb massaging the three colored stars tattooed there.

Thank goodness for winter. Cold, calm, peaceful winter.

· Two ·

"Four in the corner pocket," Kyle Caldwell said, and I knew we were sunk.

If you had told me a year ago that the highlight of my week would be a burger and a beer at Red's followed by hours of good-natured but competitive pool shooting, I'd have asked what you'd been smoking.

Well, everyone else is competitive. My run of beginner's luck was screeching to a halt.

Adam leaned his long frame against the paneled wall, fingers wrapped loosely around a cue, a bottle of Moose Drool brown ale dangling from the other hand. A neon sign for Pabst Blue Ribbon glowed above him, giving his dark curls red and blue highlights. He has a natural detachment, an ease that rarely fails. "Unflappable," my mother says. Good trait in a man who runs outdoor programs and a summer wilderness camp for kids.

Also, a nice balance for what my mother calls my "energy."

His black-coffee eyes met my brown ones. He winked.

"Five in the side." Kyle tapped the cue ball with a soft

touch, the cue ball hit the five with a heavy clonk, and the solid orange ball slid down the hole and rattled down the rail to join its littermates.

"He's running the table," Christine said. She'd wrapped red and white ribbons around her coil of hair, making it look like a drunken candy cane.

When he was on it, and we gave him half a chance, Kyle often ran the table. As the last shooter, I'd given him more than half a chance. Three-quarters, at least.

Nick crept up behind Christine and leaned in to kiss her neck, her short sturdy frame a contrast to his slender height. When we started playing a few weeks ago, after Christmas, he'd sworn they were just friends.

That was then; this was now.

The game ended. Kyle racked and his teammate and cousin, Kim Caldwell, broke with a sharp, satisfying crack. This round pitted them against Nick and Christine, so I two-stepped across the room, in time to the music blaring through the speakers. Satellite radio.

"Hey, good-lookin.'"

"Hey, yourself." Adam set his cue aside and drew me close. He tasted like chocolate and hops. "Your brother and Christine are having fun."

"I like her," I said. "A lot. But she dumped him once, a couple of years ago, and it hit him hard. I hope she isn't using him because she's lonely."

"You mean after Iggy died."

"Yeah. Not that one relationship is anything like the other, but . . ." Despite a fifty-year or more age gap, Iggy and Christine had been fast friends as well as studio mates and painting partners.

"But Nick came back to town right about the time Iggy died, and you can't help wondering if Christine latched onto him for the right reasons."

Adam's astute observation made me wonder if my

boyfriend and my brother had been talking. "I guess I should let him figure that out," I said.

He squeezed my shoulder in agreement. "Hey, we're invited for a snow barbecue Sunday, after skiing."

The front door opened and a blast of arctic air blew in, ruffling the red-and-white bunting Red's leaves up all year. A stocky man in grease-worn Carhartts and work boots, a ball cap pulled tight, shoved the door closed.

"Jack Frost," the crowd yelled.

Not some magic winter incarnation, but his name. A Friday night regular, also known as "the Junkman." He waved nicotine-stained fingers and stomped to the bar.

And as he stomped, Christine gave him the evil eye.

A few minutes later the last game ended, the Caldwell cousins still the champs. We ordered a plate of nachos and a basket of Red's waffle fries and settled around a scuffed wooden table. The smells of hot cheese and jalapeños mingled with the scents of hot potatoes, salt, and spicy mustard.

The front door flew open again. Two men headed for the bar, passing our table on the way.

"Look who the cat dragged in." Kyle stood, tall, slender, and blond like all his family, and extended a hand toward a man about his own age—mid-thirties—but his opposite at about five-seven and two hundred pounds. Opposite in dress, too: Kyle had traded the chef's duds he wore by day for jeans, boots, and a collared gray knit pullover. The other man's royal blue parka hung open, exposing pleated khakis and a navy tie dotted with green sailboats loose at the neck of his pink button-down.

"Caldwell," the man said, squeezing Kyle's hand in his own plump mitt. "Haven't seen you in ages." The sight whisked me back to a hot August day. Danny Davis, manager of the rental car agency in Pondera. *PON-duh-ray*, the big town—all of thirty thousand—thirty miles away. He'd given me the evidence I'd needed to persuade the undersheriff to probe a little deeper. Evidence that proved a man a liar and a killer.

"You know some of these folks, don't you?" Kyle gestured around the table. "Christine Vandeberg, meet Dan Davis. My high school buddy and fellow car nut. Nick and Erin Murphy, I think you know."

Nick stood and they shook hands. Four years my senior, he may not have known Danny. Kyle and Danny had been a year ahead of me, though Danny had barely been on my radar screen. As their hands dropped, Danny's eyes settled on me and I wasn't sure if they were friendly or not.

"Adam Zimmerman." Adam's chair leg hooked mine as he pushed it back, forcing him to an awkward half stand.

"And you know my cousin Kim," Kyle said. "Don't get on her bad side. She's a pool shark."

Not to mention a deputy sheriff. Danny rubbed his face and his eyes flitted around our table, chased by a hearty bellow. "So this is where the action is in Jewel Bay. Red's never changes."

"What brings you down here on a Friday night? You live in Pondera, don't you?" Kyle reached for his chair. "Sit. Have a beer."

"Dropping off a rental car." Danny grabbed an empty chair from the next table, spun it around, and sat, arms folded over the chair back. An "I'm not staying" gesture. "Thought we'd grab a drink before heading home."

"We were talking about the film festival these two"—Kyle pointed first at Christine, then at me—"cooked up."

"The Food Lovers' Film Festival," Christine said. "Next weekend. Five great films, classic movie food. An Oscar feast to wrap it up on Sunday. You should come over."

"I do love food." He reached for the nachos.

"Six great films," I said. "Don't forget the kids' documentary. World premiere."

Kyle set his bottle on the table and leaned back. "Right. High school Film Club, Video Club, whatever they call it now. They shot a piece on classic cars and their owners—serious collectors. And a few basic car nuts like you and me."

Danny frowned and tugged a wad of chips, cheese, and peppers off the platter. "What's that got to do with food and the Oscars?"

I slid the napkin holder toward him. "Nothing. It's just a way to showcase the kids' project. Last summer, a rally came through town. A dozen pre-war Rolls-Royces, including a Silver Ghost from 1910, same year as the Merc was built. The owner and I got talking, and the kids got out their cameras. Shot some footage, realized they might have a story."

"The story of horsepower and obsession," Nick said.

"They even filmed me," Kyle said. "Remember that old 1970 GTO Judge? You and I spent every spare hour in the barn. We tuned that engine till it purred."

In the dim bar light, I saw the other man shift on the hard chair, wincing at its discomfort.

"You don't still have that old wreck?"

"Yeah. Parked it when I went in the Army, and there it stayed. I go pet it occasionally. Still in good shape—some minor body damage." Kyle had enlisted after graduation. Became a cook. Went to Iraq. Came home and worked his way up to head chef at Caldwell's Eagle Lake Lodge and Guest Ranch, the family biz. "Drove it around for the kids. Been too busy to work on it, but I'm getting the bug again. Might turn it into my summer car."

Beside me, Kim scraped her boot on the wood floor. I had the feeling she hadn't quite forgiven her cousin for his part in the Art Festival tragedy, though they'd buddied up for Friday night pool. His had been a bit part, stemming from an old mistake, but as I knew too well, Kim does not let resentments go easily.

J.D., the new man at Red's, cleared our empty beers and brought a new round. He gave Danny a questioning look.

"Gin and tonic, at the bar," he said, his hands in push-up position on the chair back. "Been some changes around here after all."

"J. D. Beckstead. Old Ned's grandson," I said. "So there's still a Redaway behind the bar at Red's, despite the last name. And a redhead, to boot."

"It'll be good for Ned to have family around, after what happened in June," Christine said. "Not to mention what happened at the Art Festival. After a run of crime like that, you start to wonder, but thank goodness the system worked."

Amen to that. My own father's death in a hit-and-run nearly fifteen years ago had never been resolved. I was grateful that another family had gotten justice, or some semblance of it.

Kyle picked up his fresh beer. "The guy had to know they'd figure it out. Somebody always sees something."

Danny stood abruptly, the wooden chair creaking. For a bulky man, he moved with grace. I had an idea he'd been one of my father's basketball players. In small towns, kids of all sizes play all kinds of sports.

"Good to see you, Kyle, Kim." His quick glance around the table took in all of us. "Don't have too much fun tonight." He winked and headed for the bar.

"You know, little sis, you guys ought to put on a wildlife film festival," Nick said.

Christine snickered and stood. One of the few visible changes since my mother bought the building from Ned last summer had been to make the women's room a place a woman no longer cringed at the thought of visiting.

As soon as she was out of earshot, I leaned across the table to my brother. "So, you guys back together or what?"

Nick played with his beer. "Christine isn't the kind of woman you cut out of your life, just because you don't want to spend the rest of it with her."

"Because you're not that kind of guy," I said.

Sharp words spoken near the bar caught my ear. Red's

was still Ned Redaway's business, not my family's, but the tone was hard to ignore.

Christine uttered an equally sharp reply I couldn't decipher, her pale skin flushed. Jack Frost spun his barstool, showing her his back, and barked an order at J.D.

But she was all smiles when she returned. We drank our beers and ate our nachos and fries—Red's makes the world's best waffle fries. We chatted about the film festival, the winter slowdown, business, art, food. How much fun it is to hang out and play pool, even though the Caldwells usually win.

"They must be cheating," Nick said, "but I can't figure out how."

"That," Kim replied, pointing a nacho at him, "is because you are too lame a player to recognize masters at work."

Fighting words.

"Hey, Caldwell," Danny Davis said on his way out. "Let me sell that rust heap GTO for you. Get you in a real ride."

Kim looked at him sharply, jaw tight. Kyle turned in his seat. "You faker. Half an hour ago, you called it a piece of junk. You trying to con me?"

"Your choice. You want to drive around like some old fart trying to hang on to his youth, or grow real balls."

Men and car talk. One more thing I'll never understand.

· *Three* ·

Months before Christine roped me into helping launch the film festival, I'd started my own winter project: developing the Merc's signature drink line. "You need another project like the proverbial hole in the head," Fresca had said. Just when I thought she understood that a business has to keep reinventing itself to stay current.

So instead of my usual double latte and *pain au chocolat* from Le Panier, I started Saturday off with a chai mix taste test. Unlike the popcorn seasonings, we hadn't created these ourselves. Instead, we'd put out a call inviting home cooks, restaurateurs, and other entrepreneurial types to submit their blends. We'd credit the winner on the label, and handle marketing, sales, and distribution. They'd also get to use our commercial kitchen for a reduced fee.

We already had our own custom coffee, Cowboy Roast, roasted and blended to our specs in Pondera. We also sold Montana Gold's Wheat Coffee, a whole-grain substitute. This spring, the women of Rainbow Lake Garden would plant mints, lemon balm, and other herbs, and come summer, harvest the herbs, dandelions, and raspberry leaves for the Merc's line of Jewel Bay Jewels, refreshing herbal teas.

But no black teas for the time being. Not exactly a made-in-Montana product. My neighbors and I hoped to recruit someone to open a tea shop in the village, serving high tea, low tea, and all kinds of tea in between. Huckleberry scones, huckleberry creamed honey, huckleberry clotted cream. The Village Merchants' Association and the Chamber of Commerce had joined the effort. One prospect had turned us down. A second had toured the village earlier in the week but had yet to give us her decision.

I measured out chai mix, created by a local woman after a visit to a friend in India. Added hot water and stirred. Sipped.

Not bad. A touch sweet, but then, while I adore chocolate—the darker, the better—I don't have the sweetest tooth. That, I leave to Tracy and Candy Divine.

I rinsed my mouth and tried the second blend. Both had impressed the first-round judges: Tracy, Fresca, and Heidi Hunter, owner of Kitchenalia. Sweetened with stevia, this one would score well with the calorie-conscious, an important factor in product development. A less traditional flavor combination than the first. Pepperier, if that's a word.

"Yoo-hoo, Erin!" A voice rang out over the sound of the front door chime as two women entered. Mimi George, Zayda's mother and the owner—with her husband, Tony—of the Jewel Inn, the chalet-style restaurant at the north end of the village. Best breakfast joint around. Dinner service would resume in the spring, when the new chef arrived.

Mimi sat at the counter, and I set out cups of chai. "Sit," I told Wendy Fontaine, dressed in her white baker's jacket, colorful cotton pants, and cherry red rubber clogs. "I need your professional opinion."

They tasted, debated, retasted, and opined. The verdict? Different enough to offer both.

"So. Now," Mimi said. "Let's see the film festival menu." The reason for our meeting.

Wendy opened her three-ring binder. "Thursday night is the reception in the Playhouse lobby for donors and sponsors, followed by the kids' documentary. It's an upscale night, so the appetizers and desserts will be fancier than our usual fare. Paddlefish caviar on crostini—Max cures the roe himself. Goat cheese on salted olive crisps."

I love it when Wendy talks dirty.

"Vegetable platters—fresh, roasted, and pickled," she continued, "Crostini of zucchini, *scamorza*—that's smoked mozzarella—and bacon."

I groaned.

"Chocolate *mollieux* and raspberry panna cotta for dessert. Sparkling wine, and the usual other beverages."

Heavenly.

"If there's a movie theme in there, I don't get it," Mimi said.

It doesn't take much to get Wendy's Jell-O up. (As kids, we called her Wendy the Witch, conveniently forgetting that cartoon Wendy was a good witch.) And for all Mimi's experience in the restaurant biz, tact does not top her talent list.

"We did agree to go for a bit of glamour Thursday night, and focus on the classic movie theater experience the other nights. Then Sunday, by reservation only, the Oscar-themed dinner at the Inn." I laid my hand on Wendy's notebook. "Lovely as all this sounds, I think we can figure out easy appetizers with a movie tie-in."

After several more rounds of chai and debate, we had a plan. To honor *Julie and Julia,* canapés au Camembert. For *Ratatouille*, crostini topped with what else? A ratatouille of eggplant, peppers, and tomatoes. And for *Chocolat*, oh, the options! We settled on éclairs, for fun and ease of service—no forks required.

"But what about *Tampopo*?" Another challenge, and

another debate. Ramen bowls were the obvious choice for the noodle Western, and impossible.

"Wontons," Mimi suggested.

"Those are Chinese," Wendy reminded her. "Chicken satay skewers are always popular."

"Thai," I said. "I know—sushi!" We settled on two varieties of rolls: tuna, and crab and avocado.

"And for *Babette's Feast*," Wendy said, "we can make the crostini with paddlefish roe."

"Uhhhh, sorry. Christine decided we had too many French films, so we switched to *Big Night*. Two brothers from Italy try to save their failing restaurant in New York." I had to hurry before Wendy exploded. "How about *arancini*? Fried rice balls are easy and popular, and if you add sun-dried tomatoes to the filling, they won't need a sauce."

Mollified, she made a few notes and we wrapped up the menu. I'd already talked to Donna Lawson, the liquor store owner, who'd agreed to supply the drinks. Friday and Saturday, we'd offer free movie popcorn. In the concession stand, the kids would sell cookies donated by Le Panier: Junior Mints sandwich cookies, already a hit in the bakery, and Wendy's and her assistant's latest obsession, iced cookies.

"I picked shapes to go with the movies. Old cars. The Eiffel Tower. A cowboy hat—that ties *Tampopo* to Montana. And Oscar—the statue, not the grouch—iced in gold." She opened a bakery box and laid out samples.

"Almost too amazing to eat." *But not quite*. I nibbled a wheel off a race car.

"It's practice for the Sugar Show, at Cookie Con. My assistant's teaching a class on icing, and I'm giving a workshop on presentation. You know, cookie baskets, platters, bouquets."

"Perfect. The grocery store is donating snack-size boxes of Dots, Milk Duds, and Hot Tamales," I said. "Zayda and I are meeting Christine this afternoon at her studio to go over a few details."

"She's been so wrapped up with this Film Club thing." Mimi downed the last drops of her chai. "She takes everything so seriously—I almost wish it were over. And there's her college applications. Can you believe they need written references?"

Zayda reminded me of my teenage self: intelligent and determined. Sensitive? Yes, but often that's what exasperated parents call kids who care deeply about things the adults think—or know from experience—don't really matter.

Tracy arrived moments after Mimi and Wendy left. Today, the Queen of Cheap Chic wore a black knit skirt that hit her mid-calf and a scarlet tunic, a black-and-white geometric print scarf tied around her hips like a belt. She'd drawn her thick chestnut hair back in a black scrunchie to show off her mother-of-pearl earrings. Great look, and I doubted she'd spent more than twenty-five dollars for any of it. Except the low-heeled black harness boots.

I made a strong cup of coffee to wash down the sugar and spice of the chai and headed upstairs to tackle the project I'd skipped last night.

I ran the figures for our new Jam Club, begun just before Christmas. After a purchase of ten jars, the club member gets a free six-ounce jar, any flavor. Sales and net revenue had already skyrocketed. *Yes!*

Then, time to tend the shop floor. Even in February, Saturdays are our busiest days. We've worked hard to position ourselves as a local foods market, not another trendy, high-end shop, so when the dentist's wife bought our last eggs, sausage, and organic cheddar, I cheered and called my producers for more.

"Have you decided about Treasure State Olive Oil?" Tracy asked.

"I'm still not convinced," I said.

"It's as local as the chocolates," she said. "They use California oils and the balsamic vinegar comes from Italy.

But they blend the flavored vinegars themselves, and bottle everything in Montana."

The owners had pitched the health benefits, the taste benefits, the profit benefits. "It's a good product, but I can't justify the investment. Not at that price point."

"Why do you care about their price so much? You don't mind the price of chocolate-Cabernet sauce." Tracy's voice hovered between a challenge and a pout. "And you don't have to invest anything. They're willing to consign."

"It means an investment in space, especially for an entire line, and in your time and mine explaining the products to customers. Chocolate-Cabernet sauce practically sells itself."

Tracy mopped up a customer's snowy footprints a tad too forcefully.

That reminded me to shovel the front walk, a first-thing chore I had put off to meet Mimi and Wendy. The downside of an unincorporated town—no town services.

I piled snow on the berm between sidewalk and street, careful to leave cuts for access, then perched on the window ledge to catch my breath and savor the sights and sounds of a sunny winter morning in Jewel Bay.

A flash of light across the street drew my eye. Larry Abrams stood in Puddle Jumpers' open doorway. Sally Grimes's hands flew, gesticulating dramatically. Sally always speaks dramatically. Fresca calls her "the Queen of the Againsters," the folks who oppose any new idea. They're convinced what works in other towns can't possibly work here. First words out of their mouths are always "the problem is . . ." Sally wears a deflector shield worthy of a starship.

Had Larry broken through her defenses? His white head leaned in closer, his hand lightly touching her upper arm. And then, to my utter astonishment, he kissed her and strolled down Front, whistling.

Why not? Larry seemed eligible, and Sally Sourpuss is

attractive when she smiles, which isn't often. At least not at me. She does not like me. She tolerates my mother and my sister, barely knows my brother, and absolutely cannot stand me.

I must have stared a moment too long. She turned and glared, as if to say, *What's it to you?* Then she spun on her heel, almost losing her balance on the frosty concrete, and tugged the door of her shop tight behind her.

At half past twelve, while I straightened Luci the Splash Artist's soaps and lotions, the front door chime rang.

The tea shop prospect hitched her bag high on her shoulder and gave me a this-hurts-me-more-than-you look that I didn't quite believe. "Jewel Bay is adorable. But your downtown is built on restaurants and retail. That gives you ninety days to make a living off the tourists."

"Small towns are short on office workers," I admitted. And it's easy for the few we have, along with the bank tellers and retail employees, to run home for lunch. "But if you give the locals good food and service in a sweet place, they'll be there."

"I've run the numbers," she said, as if I hadn't spoken. "It can't be done."

If you think it can or you think it can't—either way, you're right.

Half a wink after she left, the door flew open and in whirled a red-and-blue tornado, cape whipping danger-ously close to a display of Montana cherry wine. Behind him stood his mother, my sister, Chiara. (Say it with a hard C, and rhyme it with tiara.)

"Bring him back to the shop after lunch," she said and waved good-bye.

"Landon. My favorite nephew." I scooped up the five-year-old and planted a big wet smackaroonie on his cheek. He wiped it off, a sign of his advancing age, then wiped his hand on his blue tights.

"Your only nephew," he said, echoing his mother's stan-dard response. "Mom says the bakery has movie cookies and you can buy me one."

"As soon as Tracy gets back from lunch and her dog walk," I said. "Aren't you cold in that outfit?"

He scowled. "Auntie, I'm Superman."

A few minutes later, we popped next door into Le Panier. "A three-cheese panini. Panino. Whatever." I'm half Italian, but all American when it comes to messing up foreign words.

"And movie cookies," Landon said.

Wendy and her French-born husband, the Max of Chez Max, the delightful bistro adjacent to the bakery, have no children. But she always has a smile and a cookie for Landon.

She handed him a chocolate sandwich cookie with mint cream filling, wrapped in a waxed paper square that immediately drifted to the floor. I bent down to grab it. The door opened, the breeze blowing the paper under one of the café tables. I chased it around a corner, out of sight of the woman who stalked to the counter.

"How can anyone honestly believe," Sally said to Wendy, "that this town needs yet another festival?"

My fingers touched the waxed paper and I froze.

"You'd think those Murphys would have learned their lesson," she went on. "That Erin comes back and people start dropping like flies."

The yeasty, warm, cinnamon-scented air seemed to freeze.

"I'm a Murphy," Landon said, his voice as big as it could be through a mouthful of cookie. "Landon Thomas Murphy Phillips."

I backed my way out from under the café table and stood. "If you have a beef with me, Sally, bring it to me. Have the grace not to bad-mouth my family in front of a five-year-old."

Sally Grimes turned red. As red as Wendy's rubber clogs. As red as the red velvet cupcakes in the bakery case.

"I think the Film Festival's a great idea," Wendy said. "It's time we did something for ourselves instead of always for tourists."

"For fun," Landon said, gripping his cookie so tight the filling oozed out. The panini press buzzed, the aroma of toasted bread and cheese wafting over the chaos of conversation and conflict.

Sally glared at my nephew, at Wendy, and finally, at me. She'd hit a tender spot. Though everyone assured me over and over—everyone but Sally—that none of it was my fault, I did feel guilty when my first new festival, the Festa di Pasta di Jewel Bay, resulted in the murder of a good friend. And when more tragedy struck the Summer Art and Food Fair—Jewel Bay's longest-running festival, an event Fresca helped start when Nick was a baby. But Christine had been convinced that we could make a winter film festival fly, and when it comes to movies and food, I'm a sucker. As Wendy had said, it wasn't for the tourists. It was for the town. A little play, after all our hard work.

"You Murphys think you're the only ones around here with good ideas," she sputtered. I didn't point out that the Film Festival hadn't been my idea.

She left empty-handed, a cloud of fine white snow swirling in her wake.

"I think," Wendy said, "we all need another cookie."

"Good idea," Landon said, and I had to agree.

I delivered my nephew to his mother at her gallery, left the shop in Tracy's practiced hands, and took to the road.

Once across the one-lane bridge over the Jewel River, I pointed my sage green Subaru—the semi-official car of western Montana—east and followed the river along the narrow two-lane highway called Cutoff Road.

By early February, you can almost see the light growing stronger. These clear, sunny days are the coldest, but the light makes up for the lack of heat. New snow gleamed on the peaks of the Swan Range, and through a cut to the south, I caught a glimpse of the Mission Mountains, carved by the glacial hand of God.

Christine lived in a darling cottage, once a rectory, beside a decommissioned Catholic church. Iggy—aka Louise Ring—had bought the property on the corner of the highway and Mountain View Road decades ago, to save it from the wrecking ball when the parish built a new church north of town. After her husband died, Iggy moved in to the cottage and converted the church into an art studio and gallery. Friends and students had reclaimed the parking lot behind the church, planting an orchard and creating a community garden. Not content with tomatoes and beans, they also planted art: Fountains flow in giant clay pots, flowers blossom in tiled tire rims, and over it all reigns a horse welded from scrap metal.

Today, snow blanketed everything but the horse.

None of us had been surprised by Iggy's death last fall—she'd been ninety-seven, though she hadn't looked a day over eighty.

But we'd been astonished that she left the bulk of her estate, including the church and cottage and her art collection, to Christine. Who'd been more surprised than anyone.

I turned onto Mountain View and parked across from the church, painted white with forest green trim to match the cottage. Zayda had beat me here, the front wheel on the right side of her mother's old red Toyota perched awkwardly on a snow berm. I grabbed my blue leather tote bag—a remnant of my city wardrobe—and waded into the fresh white powder.

Last night's new snow lay undisturbed on the walkway to the cottage and its wide front steps. I headed for the well-trampled trail between the buildings, which forked left to the back door of the church and right to the side door of the cottage.

Where Zayda George huddled on the concrete steps, arms wrapped around her knees, the hood of her charcoal gray ski coat pulled over her head and face. She gave off an air of unhappiness far beyond being "too sensitive."

Careful, Erin. You're not her mother or teacher, or the Film Club advisor. You barely know her.

"Hey, there. You could have gone in. You didn't need to wait for me."

The hood slipped back. The brown eyes she'd gotten from the Greek side of her family were pained.

"What's wrong?" I said. No reply. My rib cage tightening with a nascent fear, I stepped around her and opened the screen. Knocked on the door.

No answer. No footsteps.

Behind the house, Christine's car stood under last night's thin blanket of snow. She hadn't gone anywhere.

I twisted the doorknob. Locked. "Did you try the studio? She must be waiting for us there."

Stricken. The only word for Zayda's expression.

At the back doors of the church, I tugged the big brass handle on first one dark red metal door, then the other. Rattled them. "Christine," I yelled.

No answer.

So I did what any veteran little sister would do. I called my big brother.

"The spare's underneath the Buddha behind the house," Nick said. "I'll be right there."

I upended three frosted Buddha statues before finding two keys on a thin wire ring. The faded yellow paper label read BACK. Church or house? I dashed to the red double doors, mentally rubbing the stars on my wrist. Keys and I don't always get along.

First key, no luck. I swore.

The second key fit and I turned it, but nothing happened. "The other way," I muttered, and the door creaked open.

"Christine?" I paused in the carpeted back entry, listening.

"Christine?" Nothing. I bounded up the half flight of

stairs to the sanctuary, a long straight nave with no transepts or alcoves. "Christine?" Light poured through the tall windows behind the altar. A marble statue on a pedestal gleamed, and a pair of bronzes gave off a subtle glow.

"Oh, God." She lay on the altar, facedown. Two long red braids trailed down her back, and a thin trickle of a deeper red crawled across the yellowed oak floor.

· *Four* ·

I did not want to see her. I did not want to touch her.

"Christine." I knelt, taking her wrist in my shaking fingers. Warm skin—a good sign. A faint throbbing. Her pulse, or mine?

"Uhhnnnh. Uhh-unh."

"Shush. It's Erin. Help is on the way." I lowered my face to hers, to hear and be heard. "Hang in there."

In response came a long, painful gurgling noise. Like a fish crying for water, she scrambled for air. Her shoulders heaved and bucked as she tried to raise her chest off the worn wood floor.

That's when I saw the pool of blood beneath her, the hole in her side.

Acid welled in my gut. "Hang on. Zayda's calling for help." An unmanned fire station stood kitty-corner across the highway, but the volunteer department could only be reached by calling county dispatch.

"Shop," she said, her speech obscured by the gasping, the gurgling, as blood filled her lungs. "Lrss."

"Shushhh. Don't try to talk."

"Shop," she repeated, her paint-stained fingers clawing and scraping.

"My shop is fine. Tracy's working today. Help is coming and you'll be fine. Hang in there." She would not be fine, and we both knew it.

I held her wrist, my other hand unsure where to land, finally settling lightly on her shoulder. Liz Pinsky had made me a feng shui convert last summer, demonstrating how a space holds energy. She would say that even after decommissioning, a church holds the prayers and intentions of the faithful who worshipped there.

I called on them now, and on the saints and angels, to not abandon this holy place because evil had violated it.

That is when we need all that is holy all the more.

In reply, sirens.

And then, "I'll take over now." An EMT—a mechanic by trade—touched my shoulder. I scooted back, making room for him and his bag. He reached for Christine's wrist, then her neck. On her other side, a second EMT saw the pool of blood. Hands in thin blue gloves, he raised her shirt to expose the wound and applied a pad. "Gotta stop this bleeding," he said, while the first man slid the business end of a stethoscope onto her bare back. Listened to her lungs. Raised his head and I saw the two men's eyes meet.

They did all they were supposed to do, but that brief glance confirmed that it would not be enough.

I sat on my heels. *Not again. Maybe Sally's right.*

"I'm Nick Murphy. My sister and my girlfriend are in there."

The strained voiced boomed from the rear of the sanctuary. Zayda had sunk against the back wall, beneath a black-and-gold Asian tapestry. She hugged her knees, her big coat enveloping her and her sadness. A deputy sheriff I did not know blocked Nick's way.

"I'm sorry, sir. This is a potential crime scene."

"Nick!" I ran down the altar steps and past Christine's easels and canvases, her worktable littered with tubes and knives and brushes. Past the display cabinets and the walls of paintings. "She's been shot. She's bleeding. I'm afraid . . ."

He pulled me into his arms, and through our coats, I felt my brother's heart pound, felt him tremble, felt him hold me tight, safe, and I tried to do the same for him.

"Where have you been?" I asked. Nick wore field gear: water-resistant pants, bright blue knee-high gaiters, boots, mittens that converted into fingerless gloves for note taking. Heavy-duty sun goggles peeked out of an upper pocket in his nylon shell.

"Up in the Jewel Basin, checking my packs." Wolf-breeding season. Nick tracked the packs by snowshoe or on skis, then watched for denning activity. "What happened?"

I told him what little I knew, and we stared, arms around each other, as the EMTs finished their work.

Sheriff's Detective Kim Caldwell and Undersheriff Ike Hoover arrived at the same time, Ike in full uniform, Kim in jeans, the belt that held her gun, radio, and other gear slung on her hip. Just looking at it gave me back pain. We'd become friendly again since my return to Jewel Bay, but nothing like the past. We'd been best buds from sixth grade, when her family moved back to help her grandparents run the Lodge, right up till February twenty-fourth our senior year. The night my father died, I lost my best friend, too.

When you get your badge, they give you extra eyes and a swivel in your neck. Both Kim and Ike scanned the old church quickly and thoroughly, seeming to take in everything. Kim spotted Zayda, knelt and said a few words, then stepped outside, phone in hand.

It hadn't occurred to me to call her parents. Some friend and mentor I was.

Ike pulled out a notebook. I perched on one of the leftover

pews, the dark wood polished by decades of backs and bottoms sliding across the grain, and repeated what little I knew. I nearly gagged at the part I didn't want Nick to hear—the part about the gurgling, the struggle to breathe, to speak. To live.

"She said *what*?" Ike said.

"Shop," I repeated. "She was asking about my shop. I don't know why. She was confused. She'd lost a lot of blood." Shivers overtook me.

Nick's eyes darkened and his gaze flicked across the room to the old barrister's bookcases that held Iggy's collection of bronzes and Western artifacts. Pain creased his brow. He ran a hand through his dark hair and trained his attention on Ike.

"Sheriff." The second EMT appeared at Ike's elbow. I recognized him from the lumberyard at Taylor's Building Supply. They stepped aside, and though we couldn't hear them, the meaning was clear.

Christine Vandeberg, of the red hair and colored glasses, my good friend, my partner in planning, the woman who might, not once but twice, have become my sister-in-law, was dead.

Outside, the sky had darkened. Leafless branches stood stark against the gray. The evergreens—fir, pine, blue spruce—leaned away from the cold front moving in.

We had not been inside long. But it doesn't take long for everything to change.

I tugged at my collar and hunched my shoulders against the biting wind, hard grains of snow pelting my face as we crossed Cutoff Road to the fire hall. Inside, our uniformed escort pointed to hard chairs set at long plastic tables. The concrete floor and white walls, plastered with huge section maps of the fire district, made the place seem colder.

A fireman strode in from the garage, shiny red engines visible behind him. He fiddled with a thermostat and started coffee. A deputy stood by each door, and while they did not bar the way or block us in, leaving did not feel like an option.

Nick and I huddled at one table, Zayda and her parents at the next. I tried to conjure warm thoughts, but that reminded me of Christine, her warm skin cooling, her warm heart stopping.

At least Nick was dressed for the weather. The Georges must have come straight from the Inn. Mimi had draped a coat over the black pants and blue blouse she wore to hostess, and Tony wore a faded baseball jacket over his grease-spattered chef's whites.

"Kim," Nick said, when she finally appeared. "It's freezing in here. Can't we talk somewhere else? Her cottage?"

"Still being searched," she said, and I felt a shock wave ripple through him. Nick had not been around last summer, when tragedy struck twice. Nick had not been around a lot these last few years, his field trips for work the reason Christine had given for breaking their engagement. It was finally hitting him that we were talking murder.

Kim extended her hand toward me. "Recognize this?"

In her palm lay a small plastic bag, a tiny silver horse-shoe shape inside. I squinted. "No."

Zayda's fingers flew to her left eyebrow. The silver ring she always wore was gone.

"Is it yours?" Mimi asked her daughter.

"Where did you find it?" Tony asked Kim.

"You're over sixteen," Kim told Zayda. "You can choose whether you want to have a parent present during your interview. Or whether you want to call a lawyer."

"I don't want to be interviewed," Zayda said, her voice high and thin.

"That's your right," Detective Kim Caldwell replied, "but you might want to think it over."

"She'll tell you anything she knows," Mimi said as Tony repeated, "Where did you find it?"

"Under the body."

Had it not been for the noisy wall heater, for the drip drip drip of the faucet onto the stainless steel sink, for the sighs and moans of the coffeemaker, you could have heard a pin drop. Or an eyebrow stud.

"I went in, but I didn't see her," Zayda said, "so I decided to wait outside." She wiped the back of her hand across her nose.

"Did you argue? Did you shoot her?"

At Nick's demands, Tony rose and took a step forward, chin high, nostrils flaring. "My daughter wouldn't hurt a flea. She doesn't even know how to shoot," Tony said. Mimi tugged at his sleeve, but she was clearly as upset as he.

Nick's brow furrowed and he glanced from father to daughter. I put a hand on his arm.

"How did you get in?" I asked the girl. "The back doors were locked. And there's a security system."

Her ponytail flapped. "No, it was off. And they were open. One of them, anyway. It must have locked automatically behind me."

"They don't lock automatically," Nick said. "You need to turn the bolt."

"We were supposed to meet Christine. That's why the alarm was off," I told Kim, then turned to Zayda. "But if the doors were open, why wait for me outside? Was someone else here? Did you hear a shot?"

Zayda sank into herself.

"Hey, that's enough." Kim held out her hands.

Tony George wrapped an arm protectively around his daughter. I could not imagine that anything in his years as a restaurateur or, before that, his career as a baseball player had prepared him for this.

"Deputy Oakland will keep you company while I speak with the Murphys," she told the Georges. "Please don't talk."

We followed her into the fire chief's office. Kim works

out of a satellite office the sheriff's department keeps at the fire hall in town, four or five miles away. Both that office and this one had been furnished from the same industrial supply room: a black vinyl chair behind a gray metal desk, two hard plastic chairs, a gray three-drawer file cabinet. Barely room for a wastebasket. More maps covered the walls.

"What the heck happened?" Nick barked the second Kim closed the door.

"I am so sorry." She sat behind the desk and gestured for us to sit. "How much do you know?"

Nick wriggled out of his coat, sweat beading behind his ear, above his navy wool turtleneck. "Nothing. I was up Noisy Creek when Erin called. I told her where to find the spare key and rushed here."

"All the doors were locked, but Christine's car was covered in snow, and it was obvious she hadn't gone anywhere," I said.

Kim held up a hand. "One at a time. Last night, we all left Red's about ten. You went to your cabin." She pointed at me. "With Adam, or alone?"

My blush was answer enough. She turned to Nick.

"I've been working early and late, checking my wolf packs. The rest of you were already at Red's when I came in."

She nodded. "And after?"

"I went back to the Orchard and Christine went home. Like I said, early call."

"Anybody see you?"

"I doubt it. No lights on at Mom's, so I didn't stop." Nick kept base camp, as he called it, in a haphazard cabin at the top of the Orchard, the homestead where we were raised. Where Fresca reigned. The precise history lost to time, we speculated that farmhands built the cabin during my great-grandparents' early years on the land. Wood heat, no insulation, but Nick always said he didn't mind, that it was a palace compared to field conditions.

Watching him alternately shiver and sweat worried me. "Kim, Nick's been out in the cold, sweating, then freezing. He needs to go home and warm up. Get into dry clothes."

"I'm fine," he said, though he did not sound fine.

"Why start so early? Jewel Basin's only ten miles from town."

His expression darkened. "I had a report of a wolf sighting to check. And I need to get into place before daybreak."

Wolf biologists walk a fine line in these politically charged times. They love and respect the animals, understand their ways and their need for habitat. For fresh food. They understand the conflicts that arise when wolves choose a young calf or lamb to sacrifice. But some folks harbor genuine hatred for wolves, shining it like they might polish their rifles or the family silver. Wolves didn't die out naturally in the 1930s; they were hunted to near extinction, bounties on their hides. Reintroduction came not from bleeding-heart tree huggers, but from wildlife managers who knew gray wolves were migrating into northwest Montana from Alberta and British Columbia. Controlled reintroduction in Yellowstone and in the central Idaho wilderness offered scientists an opportunity to study the carnivores' behavior more closely.

Nick was an unaffiliated scientist, not part of state or federal management teams, and no longer attached to a university. Grants and contracts funded his studies. His results were reported widely and debated heavily, but ultimately garnered respect. At least in the scientific community and among politicians and individuals genuinely interested in understanding our lupine neighbors.

But nothing can sway a dyed-in-the-sheep's-wool wolf hater.

"You carry a gun in the field?" Kim asked.

"Colt .45 semiauto. It's underneath the seat in my Jeep. Locked and loaded."

"When did you last carry it? When did you last fire it?"

"I always carry it in the woods. Haven't fired it since I last went to the range months ago."

"We'll need to see it."

They stared at each other. A moment later, Nick fished his keys out of his coat pocket and handed them to her. She opened the door and spoke to one of the deputies. "Bag it for ballistics."

Silent, Nick studied the corner of the desk. Reached out and probed a scratch.

"Did you talk to Christine after you left Red's?" Kim returned to the swivel chair. It squeaked.

"She called to let me know she was home, and say good night." His voice was soft, and sad.

"Did you call her this morning?"

He caught his bottom lip between his teeth and shook his head, eyes blank.

"Somebody must have been here, besides Zayda and me," I interjected. "Did you find tire tracks? Footprints?"

Kim ignored my interruption, her piercing blue eyes trained on Nick. "Anything bugging her lately?" Her eye flicked my way, including me in the question.

After a long moment, he raised his head and met her gaze. "Nothing you don't know about."

"She was focused on the Film Festival," I said. "Lots of details to manage, but no real problems."

"What time was your meeting?" she asked me. "Why didn't you and Zayda drive out together?"

"Never thought about it," I said. "The Georges live just up the hill. Straight shot from their house." No one seemed to notice my stupid choice of words. I didn't know whether Zayda had come from home or the Inn. "You know me. I run a shop, but I end up running all over."

Shop, Christine had said. Why had she asked about my shop? *Shock*, I decided.

Kim took me through my arrival, my conversation with

Zayda, and my movements. Nick blanched when I described finding Christine.

Finally, Kim stood. "My sympathies to you both. She had no family, right?"

"A cousin in Vermont," Nick said. He sat, not moving, then rubbed one hand across his eyebrow. "I—I can't believe any of this."

Before I could reach out, before I could touch him, he rose and left the office. I trailed behind in time to see him stride across the big room, not giving the Georges a glance. I stretched out a hand to Mimi and Zayda. I wanted to say, *It'll be all right. Detective Caldwell and Undersheriff Hoover will do everything. It will be all right.*

Ike had been a new detective when my father was killed. He had done everything he could. But he hadn't found the killer, and it hadn't been all right.

But even I can keep my mouth shut sometimes.

The wind was still swirling, the clouds still hovering, still spitting icy BBs at us. Across the highway, deputies had commandeered the snowy grounds of the former church. Industrial work lights on wheels illuminated the rapidly darkening scene. Light shone from the church windows.

Behind the cottage, near the wild horse sculpture, another work light blazed and two deputies consulted, heads together, one pointing at the ground.

Beyond them, a four-strand fence marked the property line. On the other side stood Jack Frost. Too far away, and the sky too dark and grim, to make out his expression, but his crossed arms and the body half-turned toward the deputies spoke a wary contempt. It did not speak grief for his departed neighbor.

We were nearly at our cars when Nick spoke. "Her cat."

"They'll find it." The cottage lights were on. *Still searching?* I'd lost all track of time.

"I'm not leaving it. Her." Nick strode toward the cottage, and I trotted behind. His foot hit the first step to the porch and a deputy appeared out of nowhere.

"If you can catch the thing, you're welcome to take her." The deputy grimaced and pushed back his sleeve. Three long red scratches.

Twenty minutes later, I drove away, the orange tabby yowling in a cardboard box in my backseat. I'd missed my chance to pick up fresh eggs and cheese, but there was no avoiding a stop for Band-Aids.

· Five ·

My mother punched off her phone and placed it carefully on her living room coffee table. "Bill says put calendula gel on the scratch, and take homeopathic ledum if it swells or starts to weep."

"I can't believe you took that devil cat home," Chiara said.

"I couldn't leave her. And Nick can't keep her." Wolf Man insisted on the rescue, but is conveniently allergic to all variety of cats, including DSH—domestic short hair. Although this one was clearly not domesticated.

"That's why they have shelters." My sister had tolerated Sparky the Border collie, our childhood family pet, much like she tolerated Mr. Sandburg, my cat, and Pepé, Mom's Scottie dog. My love of horses and Nick's career as a wildlife biologist baffle her. Pepé stared at the plate of truffles in her hand, pleading. "No. Chocolate's bad for dogs."

Chiara's husband, Jason, had taken Landon into Pondera for an early movie and pizza, leaving the Murphy girls to a long-planned evening of dinner and huckleberry martini and margarita tasting with a few girlfriends.

But with one of those friends dead, the others had stayed home. Heidi Hunter, the queen of Kitchenalia, and Kathy Jensen, owner of Dragonfly Dry Goods yarn and fabric shop and president of the Village Merchants' Association, had been as shocked as we were.

"How can you think about chocolate?" Fresca cast a disapproving eye at the plate and settled onto the couch, snugging her vintage silk kimono around her. This one featured Japanese fans scattered on a pale green background.

Unusual—and refreshing—to hear Fresca direct one of her food barbs at my sister instead of me.

After leaving Christine's, I'd stopped for Band-Aids and more cat litter. In my cabin, I tucked Pumpkin—aptly named—into my bedroom, then dug out Mr. Sandburg's carrying crate and left it open in the corner, in case she needed its security. Sandburg I left in charge of the main room. They could yell at each other—battle cries had begun the moment I hauled in the thumping cardboard box—through closed doors.

I'd showered, changed into black yoga pants and a long-sleeved purple fleece sweatshirt, and driven up to the Orchard. Though I haven't lived here in years, it will always be home.

Fresca had already taken refuge in her kimono, the minestrone she'd made earlier in the day giving the house a rich tomato-oregano aroma. Nick had stopped long enough to share the bad news, then retreated to his place.

"He shouldn't be up there alone," Fresca said now, reaching for one of the truffles she'd spurned.

"He's a grown man, Mom. Let him mourn in his own way." My sister's words seemed to take the bone out of Fresca's spine, and she sank into the upholstery, deflated. Pepé hopped up next to her, so attuned to changing moods that she ignored the truffle and rested her snout on my mother's thigh. Like any good dog or cat, she knows that to an animal lover, petting is as comforting to petter as to pettee.

"I brought all the ingredients—we might as well try the recipes." In the kitchen, I got out the blender and mixed a batch of huckleberry margaritas while my sister put together huckleberry martinis. People often mistake us for each other—we've got the same fair skin, dark eyes, and straight dark bobs, though mine's a little longer, and at five-five, I'm an inch taller. She's two years older and by far the freer spirit.

"Shaken or stirred?" she asked.

"Doesn't matter," I said. "Either way, we've put fruit in a martini. James Bond just had a heart attack and died. We've managed what Dr. No, Goldfinger, and Oddjob combined couldn't do."

Giggling, we carried the cocktail tray out to the living room. Pepé raised her head, saw that it was us, and went back to her nap.

"I can't imagine what you girls can find to laugh about at a time like this," Fresca said.

"Mom, it stinks. It really stinks." My voice got tight, my eyes watered, and my throat swelled—and not from the cat scratch on my neck. "But save it for the killer. Not us."

Chiara poured margaritas into thick glasses rimmed in cobalt blue, souvenirs from a trip to Puerto Vallarta. "Hard to believe Zayda George would kill anybody."

"At first, she said she waited outside for me, then she had to admit she'd gone inside. She swears nothing happened—the brow ring just fell out." I took a glass. "Doesn't make sense. Why go back outside? If she knew Christine was hurt, why not call for help? If she shot her, why stick around?"

Fresca accepted a margarita. "Doesn't seem like the girl we know."

The village merchants all see one another's children regularly. Older kids like Zayda, her brother, T.J., and

Dylan Washington work for their parents, the way we'd helped our grandfather when he ran the Merc. Landon and the other youngsters cut a wide swath, leaving smiles in their wake.

None of that means we really *know* any of the kids. But as president of the Film Club, Zayda had approached Christine and me about including the students' documentary in the Festival. She'd served as liaison between us—the food and organizational side—and her club and its advisor, Larry, on the technical side. She'd been capable and responsible.

Or so it seemed. But something had gone wrong today. And yesterday she'd been pestering Larry about some problem, though he'd waved off her worries.

"Good job, little sis," Chiara said, raising her margarita glass. "You make the huckleberry tequila?"

"Yep. Thanks. So why did Kim take Nick's gun? He was crawling around the woods, spying on wolves, when—well, when it happened." *It. Murder.*

"She's got to check everything, I guess. Did she ask you and Zayda about guns?"

"I don't own one. If she asked Zayda, it wasn't in front of us."

Fresca held her glass in one graceful hand. "She's always had her eye on your brother."

"Kim?" I dismissed it. "When we were kids, maybe. All my friends did."

"Mine, too. Ready for the next contestant?" Chiara positioned three martini glasses on the tray and raised the stainless steel shaker.

I nodded. "She's over it."

Fresca tilted her head. "I'm not so sure about that. Might have been hard for her, seeing him and Christine get back together."

I tried to picture Kim Friday night at Red's. Any jealous looks had escaped me. Since my return last May, she hadn't been involved with anyone, far as I knew. Last fall, on one of our semiregular Friday afternoon rides, I'd asked her about dating. "The gun gets in the way," was all she'd said. Her cousin Kyle was single, too, so it had been natural for them to pair up for pool league.

If they kept on beating the potato chips out of us, we might have to break them up.

"But you know who I wonder about. That Jack Frost character. He gives me the creeps." I took the handblown martini glass Chiara handed me, deep red swirls draped around the V-shaped bowl and down the stem. "And the other night—"

The glass shattered in my hand. "Criminy."

"What happened? Are you okay? I'll get a towel." Chiara jumped up and sprinted for the kitchen. Stunned, I stared at my hand, still holding part of the glass, the rest in pieces on my lap and on my mother's Persian rug. No blood—just wet, sticky, purple vodka.

"I can't believe it. Can't you kids leave one single pretty thing unbroken? One plate unchipped, one surface unscratched?" Fresca gathered her kimono around her and swept past my sister, standing in the doorway, kitchen towel in hand.

And as she left, even Pepé's mouth fell open in astonishment.

"Play nice," I told Mr. Sandburg. "Don't snarl at company."

Nobody, in any species, enjoys being displaced. Sandy had always had full run of the cabin, and most nights, slept on my feet or curled up behind my knees. I woke Sunday morning to find him occupying the ottoman in the living room, chin on his paws, staring out the French doors.

Bemoaning his exile, or lamenting Mr. Squirrel's absence?

Pumpkin had left the borrowed crate only to use the makeshift litter box I'd set up in the bathroom, sniff her food, and dip her tongue in the water. The deputy had shooed us away as soon as I coaxed her out from under Christine's bed, not letting me search for her toys or bed, but she seemed reassured by the crate's confines.

It's a universal thing. Consider the appeal of the log cabin. Even an upgraded one like this, with a gas fireplace and stainless steel appliances, is comforting in part because it's so compact.

After my talk with Sandy, I threw open the pine double doors between the main room—combined cooking, eating, and living space—and the luxurious bed-and-bath addition. Pumpkin would emerge when she was ready.

A pot of Cowboy Roast brewing, I cinched the belt on my fluffy white robe and got out flour, sugar, raisins, and buttermilk. Ground flaxseed. Zested an orange.

I slid the first tray of scones into the oven and closed the door, turning in time to see a giant orange butterball bound onto the black granite-topped island.

"No, you don't." I grabbed the cat in both hands and deposited her onto the pine plank floor quickly, avoiding those slashing claws. "House rules."

The cat sidled underneath a high-backed barstool, its wrought-iron legs a protective cage. Flicked her tail and wrapped it around herself.

Sandburg jumped on the back of the tweedy brown couch and glared at her, eyes narrowed, front paws together. His dark fur began to bristle as the energy built in his shoulders.

"Don't you dare," I said, in a warning tone. "No pouncing, and no hissy fits."

One hissy fit in the family had been enough. After Chiara and I had picked up the broken glass and sponged up the sticky mess, we'd polished off our drinks and debated what on earth had gotten into Fresca. Francesca Conti

Murphy was not given to flying off the handle, despite her Italian heritage. Strong-willed and capable of deep emotion, yes, but not a drama queen. With three kids in four years, she'd cleaned up plenty of childhood accidents, and Landon certainly caused his share. But her anger over the broken martini glass had been inexplicable.

"It's because of Christine," I'd said.

"Of course it is," Chiara had replied, but then we'd circled back, unable to understand why Fresca's grief had taken that particular form.

"I hope I don't lash out at Landon next time he spills his milk," she'd said. Then we'd hugged and gone home.

Now I crouched beside the terrified tabby. "You're confused, and you're mad, and I don't blame you. But you have to keep your claws to yourself. We all do." I resisted the urge to stroke her silky apricot fur.

"Talking to yourself? Who you got down there? Hello, Pumpkin."

I hadn't heard Adam come in. He crouched beside us and gave me the crooked smile that never failed to draw one from me.

We'd talked last night. He knew about Christine, and he knew not to touch the cat. His curled fingers rested lightly on the floor, as if they might hold a treat, and she sniffed in his direction before withdrawing into herself.

"Progress." We pushed ourselves up.

"All in good time," he said, and wrapped his arms around me. Our kiss was long and deep and everything I needed. Letting myself feel safe with him felt like a risk, weird as that might sound. In Seattle, every man I'd dated ultimately chose his career over me. I'd responded by focusing on my own career to the exclusion of almost everything else. Until I met a poetry-spouting retired English teacher named Roxy Turner on a walk around the reservoir in our Capitol Hill neighborhood. We quickly became good friends, and months later when she died, it had been natural to adopt her cat, Mr.

Sandburg. A cat my landlord hated. So when my mother needed help at the Merc, the timing was right to take my frustrated career ambitions, my frustrated personal ambitions, and my occasionally frustrating but mostly delightful cat and move home.

"I'm not keeping her," I said, stepping out of Adam's embrace. "Help me think of someone to pawn her off on."

"Did you just say 'paw her off'?"

"No, silly." I rattled a tin box of tuna-flavored treats. "Guests first," I told Sandy, and headed for the bathroom. By the time I'd sprinkled a few tidbits in her bowl and set it on the floor, Pumpkin had inched over the threshold. The moment I stepped back, she fell on those treats like Landon falls on cookies.

Back out front, I spilled out a few for Sandy. Adam poured coffee in two poppy red Reg Robbins mugs and we sat at the island, drinking in the scents of dark roast and baking scones.

"You okay? You're making quite a habit of this, you know."

Of finding bodies. I knew. "'Okay' is a relative thing. I'm not breaking dishes"—I'd told him last night about my mother and the martini glass—"and I'm not curled up in a ball in the corner. But I feel like a light's gone out."

"It has."

I love how he understands my metaphors. He doesn't always recognize the bits of poems and plays I draw from thin air and the deep recesses of memory, but he listens and responds thoughtfully.

What is that saying about stars being holes in the sky where the love of our lost ones shines down from heaven, to let us know they're happy and not to worry?

The timer buzzed and I slid the scones out of the oven. We carried our bounty to the couch, where Sandburg had reclaimed his position.

"Best couch-front view in town," Adam said. Jewel Bay

sits at the northeast end of Eagle Lake, the largest freshwater lake west of the Mississippi. Twenty-eight miles long, eleven miles wide near the south end. Named for the bay where the Jewel River meets the lake, the unincorporated town centers on the village—the original settlement, what some call downtown—but the community stretches for miles in all directions. Sparsely populated miles with stunning views.

Today, though, gray clouds hid the mountains and an ominous gloom shrouded the water.

"She was the force behind the Festival," I said, a warm buttered scone in hand. "I hope I can figure out what all needs to be done."

"Do you have to take over?" Adam said through a mouthful.

"Who else? Wendy's in charge of food, Mimi tickets, and Chiara publicity. All I have to do is wait for the movies to get here and make sure everyone does what they said they'd do."

"Just seems like you do a lot you don't get credit for."

His words hit home, and I didn't like it. "It's not about getting credit. And it's too late to recruit another volunteer. Easier to do it myself."

"Don't get mad. But this time, you can't say it's for the good of the town and the Merc. A midwinter festival is not going to boost business much, no matter how good the popcorn seasonings are."

"But it *is* for the good of the town. Building community. Having fun." In truth, I'd gotten tired of taking on tasks for the benefit of other merchants, who too often forgot to say thanks, or who griped at me when something went wrong. "Good-idea fairies" who piped up at the last minute with some harebrained notion they thought was wonderful and couldn't understand why it wouldn't work or was too late. "Besides, most of the work is done. And Larry and the kids can help."

Except that one of those kids might be under arrest, for all I knew.

"Mmm-hmm." Adam sipped coffee and changed the subject. "I've been thinking about that solar coffee roaster. It's got potential for a heckuva business." He reached for my hand.

I knew what he had in mind. A business we could build together. Combine my food and business savvy with his inventiveness and mechanical know-how. And our shared love of coffee.

Christine was dead, and I did not want to talk about our future.

"Need a refill?" I stood abruptly. I half wished the Merc weren't closed on Sunday, so I'd have somewhere to go.

Because for once, my own log cabin, my much adored, lovingly restored little cabin in the big woods, felt a touch uncomfortable.

· Six ·

My mother always says when you don't feel the way you want to, act as if you do, and before you know it, your mood will shift. Sounds crazy at first, but it works.

And this was the perfect time to act "as if."

"He's not answering," I told Adam, "and Mom hasn't seen him. You gotta leave Nick alone sometimes. He's always been that way."

Adam piled my cross-country gear in the back of his dirty black Xterra and shut the hatch. The gear of the season only leaves his car when he's using it. We'd separated the cats, leaving Pumpkin access to the crate if she felt the need. I wished, again, that the deputy had let me take a sweater or a T-shirt of Christine's so the cat could comfort herself with the scent. But, no. "Could be evidence, ma'am," he'd said. Heck, the cat could be evidence, but after she clawed him, he was all too thrilled to be rid of her.

"Let's stop at the Playhouse," I said as Adam pulled onto the highway. "Kim told me they'd give me Christine's three-ring binder with all the Festival details in a day or two, but I can't wait. I need a copy of the schedule she and Larry made. One should be posted somewhere."

"Sure." He reached for my hand and this time, I didn't pull away.

I had temporary custody of Playhouse keys and let myself in the front door. The lobby was dark, though sounds echoed somewhere in the building. A movie playing? More tests of the new equipment?

I found a schedule taped to the ticket office wall and peeled it off. It was an old one, still showing the documentary on Friday night, but it would have to do. While the copier warmed up, I stepped back into the lobby to scope it out with my "woman in charge" eyes.

The control room door stood ajar. A mix of voices, live and recorded, drifted out.

"You promised. You said if I—" Zayda George, her words obscured by the goose-like honk of an old-time car horn. Screening the documentary one more time?

A male replied. "But you didn't."

She interrupted. "I tried. It—"

It was impossible to hear, and anyway, Zayda's spat with her boyfriend had nothing to do with me.

Buffet tables along that wall. Drinks at the concession booth. Film Club display there. Most of Larry's posters would hang on the walls, where signs commemorating past years' productions now hung, but a few key pieces on easels would set the mood. *Where? Good visibility, but out of the way.* Pondering, pointing, talking to myself, I focused on the space.

And backed smack into Dylan Washington, coming out of the men's room.

"Oh, Erin. Hi." His cheeks pinked and he hurriedly finished zipping his fly.

Footsteps clomped across the lobby floor. "You won't believe—" Zayda broke off mid-rant.

So she hadn't been arguing with Dylan. Then who?

"How are you, Zayda? I hope Kim—Detective Caldwell—wasn't too hard on you yesterday."

A shadow crossed her face. "Everything I told her is the truth. I didn't have anything to do with—with what happened to Christine."

"It would be easier for her to believe you, if you'd told the truth from the start."

"I knew you wouldn't understand." She dashed past us and disappeared into the women's room, the door ka-thumping on its hinges.

Strange to be the adult now, part of the generation that doesn't understand.

Dylan watched her go, mouth open, his eyes hurt and confused. "I thought I understood her," he said, his voice catching, "but not anymore."

Twenty-eight degrees and four inches of new powder overnight. The Nordic trails had been freshly groomed, and we fairly flew down them.

I always say my favorite part about winter sports is the hot buttered rum by the fireplace afterward, and that's half-true. But the sensation of gliding through the frozen world is addictive. Whether it's for the endorphins, the muscle movement, or the opportunity to commune with the lesser-seen side of nature, I keep coming out here, winter after winter.

And when all your parts are moving in sync, keeping you warm and upright as you sail through the woods, it's hard to worry about everything that's wrong.

Cross-country skiing is a lot less work than traipsing up hill and over dale on snowshoes. No wonder Nick the Wolf Man is in such great shape.

I was behind Adam on our last loop through the woods, admiring his great shape, when he glanced over his shoulder to shoot me a goofy grin.

And caught a tip and bounded over his skis. His head

disappeared from view, poles flapping like the wings of a drunken bird, and he did a flying somersault. The air froze in my throat as he descended, dangerously close to the broad trunk of an old-growth ponderosa pine. I could not see him land, my vision obscured by a geyser of snow.

The air cleared. One ski had landed in the trail, facing the direction we'd come. The other stuck out of a drift, beside his maroon-and-gray knit hat. Our college colors.

"Adam!" I urged myself forward on the trail, then tugged off my skis and plowed toward him. One mitten appeared, then one sleeve, and another. A bellow broke the quiet hush, and two arms gathered me into the downy drift.

It is possible to make a double snow angel.

"You scared the bejeebers out of me when you flew off the trail," I said a few minutes later, tossing my ski boots in the back of his rig.

"Scared myself," he admitted. "Not ready to die crashing into a tree trunk."

We'd driven a mile or two from the trailhead when I said, "That retired newscaster and her husband have a house up here somewhere. They came to the Festa last summer, and their housekeeper shops at the Merc."

"That road. Go left, then back in a ways," he said. At my surprise, he explained. "I asked for a donation to the Wilderness Camp and they invited me out to hear more. Nice people, great house, big check. Your lighting director, Larry Abrams, lives down that way." He pointed to another road.

"You get around."

"A bit. Nice guy, generous. But, funny. Odd funny. Place is built of logs salvaged from old barns and cabins, and I swear, he knows where every wall came from. Hand-forged hardware—replicas that function with a modern security system. The place is huge, but I guess he needs all that space for his collections."

"What collections, besides the movie posters?"

"All kinds of stuff. I guess he's on museum boards all

over the state. Even I recognized some of the art. A giant Chatham over the fireplace. Amazing."

Russell Chatham, famous for multilayered lithos and oils that capture the changing moods of the Yellowstone River bottoms. "What else?"

"Horse paintings. Cowboys and Indians. And who's that guy—painted a lot of teepees? Your mother has a watercolor."

"Ace Powell. Wow. And here I thought he was just a quirky guy obsessed with reliving his childhood." But talking about Larry reminded me of Christine, and that dimmed the glow of the afternoon.

"His office is jammed—artifacts and old stuff everywhere. He's crazy for Russell." Adam turned down the Stage Road, taking the back way into the village.

Charles M. Russell, aka Charlie Russell or CMR. The most famous Montana artist, deeply admired for his chronicle of the Old West. Before homesteaders plowed up the cattle range and the horseless carriage chased the pinto and the paint into obscurity.

Adam started up the driveway of a buddy's house and a bevy of colored plastic sleds flew down the hill. "He's got this Chinese gong—"

"Is that Landon? What are we doing here?"

He parked behind my sister and brother-in-law's rig. "Don't you remember? Friday night? I said we'd stop by today if we came out this way."

What else had I forgotten, in the shock of yesterday's discovery?

Four couples, half a dozen kids, three dogs, and fresh powder: all the ingredients for delicious chaos.

"Froster time!" Adam's buddy, the homeowner, called, and chaos erupted. Jason helped Landon and the other kids make a snow castle in the yard, all wearing shorts or swim trunks and snow boots. The homeowner manned the snow-covered grill. Adam stripped to his shorts and boots, and struck a sunbathing pose in a lounge chair while Chiara did sun salutations on the deck in a borrowed bathing suit.

I kept my clothes on and snapped pictures. Someone had to record the insanity, even if it was temporary.

"Nothing cheers me up like making a total idiot of myself." Adam flashed me that lopsided grin that makes me melt, and we all dashed inside. Robes and blankets were found and cocoa poured, while chili bubbled on the stove.

Who can stay grouched up surrounded by silliness? Frosting, a trend that sweeps snowy regions every year or two, is the essence of acting "as if": acting as if the weather is so great, why wouldn't you be outside in next to nothing?

I sipped my cocoa and watched Landon. He'd grown so much the last few months. Not just taller, but even sweeter and more thoughtful.

The past year's sadness weighed heavily on me as the anniversary of my dad's death approached. Après–ski and frosting, I did feel lighter. But as I sank into the soft maroon leather couch in our friends' living room, my mood dipped, too. Did anyone here but me care that Christine was dead? Laughter felt a touch like betrayal.

Who had killed her? Surely not Zayda. Not anyone I knew.

Dangerous thinking, Erin. You know you never know.

Adam leaned over the back of the couch and whispered in my ear. "Relax. Let Ike and Kim do their job."

Across the room, my sister watched us. Her heart-shaped face so much like my own, her dark eyes framed in straight dark hair that brushed her collarbone, said the same thing.

But I wasn't sure my acting skills were up to it.

· Seven ·

M y family's big on tradition. On food, talk, and the Sunday gathering at the Orchard.

Call it the training ground for acting "as if."

"You don't have to go to your mother's house every Sunday, you know," Adam said as we pulled up next to my cabin.

"You know my mother."

"Maybe it's time she realizes she's not always going to be the center of your universe."

"It's not like that." Or was it? My mother and sister seemed to have reached an agreement: Chiara participated willingly in family traditions, and Fresca left her room to create her own. Nick's travels earned him a pass, but short of a crisis at the shop or a virus in the contagious stage, I felt an obligation to appear every Sunday. Close friends popped in when they were around. "Christine was practically a member of the family. I want to go to the Orchard tonight. But you don't have to come."

"If it's important to you, it's important to me. Besides,

it's my last chance to see you this week." Time for his recertification course in wilderness medicine. The field had grown far beyond splinting a broken arm with tree branches, and as camp director, he was responsible for training counselors as well as treating sick and injured kids.

Forty-five minutes later, we joined the gathering in my mother's living room. The Persian rug smelled of spot remover where Chiara and I had worked on the huckleberry spill, now a faint lavender.

"That's your favorite *soppressata* on the antipasto platter," Fresca told Adam as we hung up our coats and slipped off our boots. "Dig in. The lasagna's in the oven."

Beside me, Adam groaned. He adores Fresca's cooking. I'd never seriously imagined that he'd stay home tonight, if for no other reason.

Nick stood by the fireplace, nursing a glass of Chianti. It's impossible not to think of my father when I see my brother. The three of us mix and match our parents' genes. Other than our eyes—a blue-eyed boy and two brown-eyed girls—we're clearly peas in a pod, with Dad's fair Irish skin and Mom's straight hair, so dark brown it's nearly black. Nick puts Dad's height and athleticism to work in the wilderness, though, instead of in the orchard or with a ball.

The familiar blue eyes were downcast now, the strong shoulders sagging. A man in mourning, for a woman and possibilities.

Chiara sat on the couch, listening to Heidi's tales of the winter gift show in Las Vegas. I poured myself Chianti from the bottle on the side table, extra careful of the glass—a clear bowl above a stem of stacked colored marbles. Adam, who'd detoured to the kitchen for a beer, whispered in my ear. "Bill made Caesar salad and Chiara brought chocolate mousse."

Such a romantic.

From the back of the house came sounds of Landon and Jason rattling lightsabers.

My mother slid her arm around my waist and kissed my cheek. A sign that my transgression with the martini glass was forgiven?

"Nick, darling," she said. "We should plan a service for Christine."

"She hated funerals. She'd rather celebrate life."

"A party, then. To celebrate her life."

"What's happening to the Film Festival?" Heidi asked. "Her big deal, wasn't it?"

I smiled wryly and raised a hand.

My mother frowned. "You wanted to focus on the Merc this winter. And take time for yourself."

Nothing changes plans quite like murder.

"And the property?" Heidi continued.

We all looked at Nick. "Her cousin, I guess. Back in Vermont."

"Odd that Iggy left everything to Christine, instead of her own relatives." Heidi twirled her Prosecco, the diamonds wrapped around her left wrist sparkling. She is a Sunday regular at the Orchard, except when the boyfriend of the day has other plans. The last guy had taken off to sail the Caribbean the day after Thanksgiving and had not returned to Jewel Bay.

Fresca settled into a bentwood maple chair, her Chianti complementing the deep red florals in the upholstery. "Well, what would you do if Sally Grimes were your only living relative?"

"Sally? Is related to Iggy?" I said. Petite, stylish, ancient Iggy, oil painter, art collector, chocolate truffle connoisseur. And Sally, sour, peevish protester of progress.

"Iggy's late husband was Sally's first cousin, twice removed," Fresca said. Before I could ask what that removal stuff means, Chiara said, "That's Greek, Mom," and Bill, lawyer-turned-herbalist, explained. "It's not complicated," he said. "It simply means two generations further removed from the common ancestor. David Ring and Sally's grandmother were first cousins. Twice removed means Sally is two generations younger."

"Wouldn't that make them third cousins?" I asked.

"No. If David and Iggy had grandchildren, they would be Sally's third cousins. Same generation of descent, even if they weren't the same age."

"Wonder why they never had children," Chiara said.

"They had a son," Fresca said, and my sister and I stared in astonishment. "He was killed in Vietnam. David never got over it. He'd been a strong man, a forester. But he lost the will to live. He died a few years later."

"But she soldiered on," I said.

Fresca glanced at Nick, who was listening with sorrowful eyes. "You don't believe it yet, darling. But the world goes on."

I'd known Iggy Ring all my life, but had never given any thought to her family or her heartache. Nor, I realized, to Sally's. Shame on me.

"Wasn't Christine some kind of relative of Iggy's, too?" Chiara said.

"No," Nick said. "Iggy—Louise was her real name—and Christine's grandmother grew up together, back east. David was a Montana boy. They met when he went to forestry school at Yale. Christine's parents were killed when she was eight, and her grandmother raised her. She grew up hearing stories about Montana, so after college, she came out to work in Glacier for a summer. She and Iggy hit it off, and sort of adopted each other."

"What about Sally?" Time to make up for lost curiosity.

"She's local," Fresca said. "Married a man from Pondera. Sad case."

Nick interrupted, his words rushed, his tone raw. "They've got her place all roped off. They wouldn't let me in. I know it's a crime scene, but . . ."

Fresca's fingertips brushed his arm.

"Why would Zayda George shoot her?" Chiara said. "Bad blood?"

Nick swallowed hard, regaining composure. "More likely, it was Jack Frost. He hates progress. Foamed at the mouth over her talk about cleaning up the neighborhood."

"You'd think a guy who's got all those hubcaps and fenders lying around would love a neighbor who puts a welded horse sculpture in her backyard. He's sitting on an artist's gold mine." Trust Chiara, artist and art dealer, to think of that.

"Protecting his crops," Adam said. Heads turned and he spread his hands innocently. "Hey, I hear things."

Frost certainly hadn't liked seeing all those deputies yesterday afternoon. A cash crop would be one good reason.

"I got you, Auntie!" Landon leaped into view, brandishing a duct tape and cardboard tube lightsaber. I sank to my knees, clutching my chest with one hand, raising the wineglass above the fray. Chiara plucked it deftly from my fingers. "Noni, the Jedi win!"

"Jedi should wash their hands for dinner," my mother said, rising and leading her grandson out of the living room.

"Strangest thing last night," Chiara said as I reclaimed my wine. "We were testing martinis in those handblown glasses. I clinked too hard on the toast and Erin's glass broke. Mom flipped her lid. Did she and Dad buy those in Italy?"

Heidi shook her head. "We found them in a shop in Pondera. I was scouting the competition, and Fresca was my cover. They reminded her of her first date with your dad, and she had to have them."

I sat back on my heels and sipped. So the glasses were recent acquisitions, not souvenirs from her Grand Tour of Europe. The tour that ended in Florence where my California-born mother met my Montana-born father, then a student at Gonzaga University's Italian campus. That made her reaction all the more curious.

"Noni says time for dinner," Landon called from the doorway. "Uncle, you can sit by me. You'll feel better."

Nick scooped up Landon, who raised a hand to brush the ceiling. "I feel better already."

We wouldn't truly feel better until the killer was caught. *You're not investigating*, I told myself. *Not this time*. Tragic as it was, Christine's death had nothing to do with my shop. Too soon to tell if it might harm the reputation of our village, so dependent on showing tourists a good time.

But it gave me every reason to worry about my family.

Halfway into my lasagna, I hit on a solution to the problem nagging me. "Big brother, time to collect on my Christmas present. If the wolves will let you."

He squinted, obviously having forgotten his offer to work on the building.

"Loose ceiling tiles. Basement shelving to assemble. And the back hall hasn't been painted since Richard Nixon was president." My mother shot me a glance that said she grasped my dual purpose: Keep him busy, where we could keep an eye on him, while checking a few projects off the list.

"Yeah, sure," he said absently. "Whatever you need."

"Tomorrow morning, ten o'clock." My brother would be my handyman, and I would be his keeper.

· Eight ·

"You don't have to like each other," I told the cats Monday morning. "Just don't kill each other." They'd made a temporary peace overnight, Pumpkin cowering in the open crate, Sandburg supreme on the foot of my bed, one green eye vigilant.

My urban-chic wardrobe had included winter-in-Seattle necessities like a black umbrella, a red trench, and scarves to muffle the damp breeze that blows in off Puget Sound from September to May. It did not include winter-in-Montana necessities like long-sleeved tees and turtlenecks that look good layered or worn alone, wind-stopper pants that don't scream "ski slopes," and knee-high boots with nonskid soles.

I pulled on the black pants I'd been living in the last few weeks, a willow-green thermal top with a subtle burn-out, and a fleecy sweater sporting ribbed cuffs and collar. But while fleece wards off the winter chill in Seattle, it's a year-round fabric here.

A few village shops close after Christmas and reopen in

spring; others take a short sun break. I'm glad Wendy and Max are workaholics like me who never take a vacation.

"Hey, Wendy. The usual, please." Double tall skinny, and a *pain au chocolat*. Nonfat milk balances out the chocolate calories. I rubbed my hands both for heat and in anticipation, glancing into the backroom full of worktables and industrial ovens. Love a bakery that lets you watch your breads and treats spring to life, from scratch, by hand.

A hank of long brown hair had worked loose from Wendy's ponytail and she shoved it behind her ear. Wendy is not what you call warm and fuzzy. The problem isn't her plain features, but her moodiness. One look and you know how she feels.

In her hands, even the steamer sounded angry this morning.

"I don't know if I can do it, Erin." She set my latte on the counter and reached into the pastry case. "Pretend we're all friends having fun at the movies while a murder investigation is going on."

Wendy came from a theater family, but acting "as if" wasn't in her blood.

I took the white bag she held out and squeezed her hand. Some hurts even chocolate and caffeine can't heal.

We'd had to upgrade the Merc's furnace last fall, putting a sizable dent in the year's profits, but when I punched the thermostat and it roared to life, I thanked my lucky stars. Dumped my stuff on the front counter—the cash-wrap, in retail parlance—and grabbed the snow shovel. Once last night's dusting was gone, I found a bucket of salt mixed with sand and scattered a handful on an icy patch. Must keep the customers upright.

"Dang, it's cold." In the back hall, Tracy made a show of shivering. Her glass-bead earrings shook like chandeliers in an earthquake. She shrugged out of her coat—a decidedly un-chic powder blue imitation of a sleeping bag—and snared it on an iron hook original to the building. Vintage is not always tasteful. "Every time I say we're in for a slow day, something happens to prove me wrong."

"So say it," I said. "Work a little reverse psychology."

"You see the forecast? Snow every day this week. So much for a film festival." Her hand flew to her mouth. "Christine. Ohmygod. I can't believe it."

I slid off my stool and hugged her.

A few minutes later, the aroma of fresh-brewed coffee filled the shop and a bowl of Candy Divine's saltwater taffy sat on the stainless steel counter next to the coffeepot. *Bring 'em on!*

Fresca charged in, eyes blazing. "I can't believe you're taking on the Film Festival."

"Hey, you always say the object is to die with a full in-box." In other words, keep busy. "Christine cared about this, Mom. I want to see it through for her. Besides, it's too late to cancel. The Playhouse bought the gear, and the kids are premiering their documentary."

Although if Zayda was arrested, we'd lose our chief technical officer as well as our chief organizer. I perished the thought.

"Darling." Fresca cradled my face in angora-gloved hands, the same deep teal as her wool coat. "I don't know where you get your determination, but I'm glad for it."

Look in the mirror, Mom.

"I'm going across the street to give Sally my sympathies," she said. "If I'm not back in half an hour, send in the troops."

Typical Fresca. Sally and Christine were connected through Iggy, and the murder reopened the wound that was Iggy's loss. I couldn't bring myself to tag along.

Almost ten. Where was my brother?

The front door opened and a pink cloud swirled in. Not colored snow, but Candy Divine herself. "Oooh," she squealed. "I'm so cold I could eat an elephant."

She slipped off her black hooded cape, lined in pink

satin, to reveal an astonishing pink-and-white striped sweaterdress and sparkly pink Moon Boots. *Some ice cream shop has lost its awning.*

"I'm so sorry about Christine," she said, in the voice that always sounds like she swallowed helium. "It seems heartless to talk about candy—the treats, not me—after what happened, but . . ."

"Thanks. And no worries. Wendy's got the festival menu all planned, but Tracy and I thought it would be fun to offer handmade movie candy in the shop."

She spread a collection of recipes on the stainless steel counter for our perusal.

"Green tea truffles? Dark chocolate bark with candied mint and citrus peel?" I said. "Sounds yummy, but let's stick with the classics. Peppermint patties and snowcaps."

"Snowcaps? You mean oversized chocolate kisses covered in sprinkles?" Candy wrinkled her nose.

"I thought you love everything sweet and pink."

Tracy laughed. "Erin, you're the one who always says, 'Try new things. Get out of the food rut.'"

"There's a time for adventure, and a time for the tried-and-true." Unfortunately, the difference isn't always clear.

"Hey, little sister. Hi, Trace." Nick gave us each a hug, then extended his hand to Candy. I made introductions. A minute later, he headed downstairs.

"Oo-ooh." Candy's pitch rose to the roof. "He's dreamy."

"Christine's fiancé," I fudged, suppressing a twinge of guilt as the petal pink bow in her hair drooped.

I traipsed downstairs. Nick's cabin had never been intended for four-season living, let alone a home office, so rather than freeze—or half rebuild it—he'd taken over the basement workspace we'd created for Fresca. Plus, he gets free coffee and Wi-Fi.

He stood there now, staring at the piles of papers and books on his makeshift desk. "Wow," he said, looking up. "She's pink."

Good to laugh, if only for a moment.

We debated where to put the chrome shelf units I'd bought for the canning area. The producers who use our commercial kitchen would be able to cook, bottle, label, and store their products all in one location. I promised to pick out the hall paint this afternoon.

Back upstairs, Fresca had returned from her condolence call in one piece and started a batch of olive tapenade, a bestseller in all seasons. Its salty-tangy-garlicky aroma filled the air. My next snack.

All quiet on the shop floor, so I headed upstairs. Our POS—point of sale—inventory control system is a royal pain at times, and the crown jewel at others. Right now, the figures for Fresca's fresh pasta were off, but I spotted the problem, jiggered the software, and whipped them back in line.

As expected, sales had limped through January and stumbled into February. We'd changed our business model and product mix when I took over last May—tossing the gimmicky gift items and focusing on the local and regional, the whole and natural—so we had no basis for an annual comparison. But summer and fall had been strong enough to convince me that we'd found the right combo. Real food, sustainably grown, and a few ancillary items that mesh with our mission: Reg Robbins's earthenware, hand-sewn linens from Dragonfly Dry Goods, glasses crafted from recycled wine bottles paired with lovely vintages from Monte Verde.

Which reminded me of my mother's broken martini glass. I added finding a replacement to my to-do list.

The landline rang as I signed the last January commission check for our vendors. When Tracy didn't grab the phone by the third ring, I figured she was busy helping a customer.

"Glacier Mercantile. This is Erin Murphy."

The caller introduced himself, apologized for the interruption, and asked if I knew how to reach Nicholas

Murphy. "You're in luck. Would you prefer to hold, or have him call you back?"

He preferred to hold. I dashed down the stairs, wondering why one of Pondera's most prominent lawyers wanted my brother.

A few minutes later, when all was quiet, I snuck up the steps and peeked into my office. Nick sat in my chair, stunned. As if he'd been struck by one of his own darts—humane darts, used in tracking and collaring wolves. I pried the receiver from his hand, set it in the cradle, and waited.

After a long silence, he raised his eyes. "Her will names me her primary heir. The real estate, personal property, and cash and investments. Money I never imagined she had. There's a whatdoyoucallit? A bequest to the school district for the art program and another to the Art Center. A few other specific bequests."

"She never made any money. Her paintings were too affordable." The proof hung on the wall. "Did it come from Iggy?"

"Must have, but she never told me."

"Mom's here. You sit. I'll get lunch." I dashed next door and ordered Nick's favorite, the roast beef and Havarti on a baguette, and two Caprese panini.

In summer, there's a dip in traffic at noon, when shoppers with stomachs on standard time stop for a bite, and another at one o'clock when folks convinced the restaurants will be jammed at noon take their turn. On a snowy Monday in February, I can count the midday shoppers on one hand. So with Tracy gone for lunch and a dog walk, a trio of Murphys settled onto the red-topped stools and unwrapped our sandwiches. I ate and watched while Nick told Fresca about the unexpected inheritance.

Fresca laid her hand on his. "Oh, darling. You truly had no idea she meant for you to have all that?"

"Not a clue. Contingency planning, the lawyer called it. She was only thirty-four, but she knew what can happen." Losing a parent young—in her case, both parents and very young—was one of the things Nick and Christine had in common. "Why didn't I know? If she felt that strongly . . . I mean, we were getting back together. I was trying to figure out how to be home more, work closer to Jewel Bay. But . . ." He shook his head, mystified.

Fresca leaned closer. "You have nothing to feel guilty about, Nick. Nothing. The things unsaid . . ."

I knew she was thinking about her own loss. My father. Nick knew it, too. He turned his hand palm up and squeezed hers. My throat tightened. I reached for the unfinished sandwiches and began wrapping. "The worst part is—"

Our front door chimed and I stopped myself.

"Hello, Kimberly," Fresca said. "Just in time for lunch."

Thank goodness I'd held my tongue.

"I'm fine, thanks," Kim said. "Erin, Nick, I need formal statements about Saturday."

No hint of the romantic interest Fresca had speculated on in Kim's tone or her expression. But her left foot tapped the floor in a most peculiar way. She opened a black leather messenger-style purse and withdrew a cloth-wrapped bundle.

"We found the murder weapon, a .38 that matches the slug taken from the body. So, I brought your gun back." She opened the bundle to reveal Nick's .45.

"Where did you find it?" I asked. "The .38, I mean."

"I can't say. Not until the rest of the analysis—"

The chime clattered and clanged as the front door flew open, the century-old oak frame smacking the front counter. The vibration set the jelly jars quaking and I grabbed a pint of cherry preserves before it smashed onto the floor.

"He had motive and means." Sally jabbed her forefinger at Nick. "And if you've got the nerve to ask the right questions, I bet you'll find plenty of opportunity."

"Sally, what are you saying?" Fresca took her arm in a grip too firm to shake off. Sally wore no coat, and her thin brown tunic and tan suede loafers were no match for the weather.

"He had everything to gain, at my expense." She whipped her head toward Fresca. "Did you know that, when you came over this morning, acting all sympathetic?"

"Know what?" Kim said.

"Christine left him everything. Including what she stole from my family."

"Wait a minute." Kim extended her hands like a pair of stop signs. "Slowly, calmly, tell me what you're talking about."

"Iggy and I were family. Everyone thought Christine was her granddaughter, but she was a complete stranger who wormed her way into a lonely old lady's life." Sally spat out the words, ignoring Nick's sputtered protests. "That—that painter convinced Iggy to leave her everything. *Everything*. Cutting out her family, her rightful heirs."

Last summer, Sally had informed me that not everyone in the village approves of the emphasis on food. Apparently she didn't care for our reputation as a haven for artists, either.

"This one"—her mad eyes darted toward Nick—"made all lovey-dovey and got her to leave it all to him. And then—"

"I get the picture, Sally," Kim said.

Nick let out a long, ragged breath. "I won't pretend to know what two dead women—two kind, generous women—were thinking. But I loved Christine Vandeberg, and I had nothing to do with her death."

"How do you know any of this?" Kim asked Sally.

"Her lawyer called. He knew I'd been consulting about my rights to challenge Iggy's will. He wrote both wills— he'll be in deep doo-doo if I win. He said Christine added a codicil to her will, leaving me a few pieces of art. Trying to buy me off."

A buy-off? That made no sense. The heirs would inherit on Christine's death, and Sally had to be twenty years

older. In normal circumstances, Christine would have out-
lived her.

"I understand that Iggy's art collection was quite valuable," Kim said. "Christine may have been more generous
to you than you realize."

Sally waved a hand in dismissal, focusing instead on
Nick. "Where were you Saturday, Mr. Big Shot?"

"That is none of your business." I couldn't help myself.

"I don't mind telling you," Nick said, voice steady, blue
eyes unwavering. "Where I am most days, out tracking
wolves."

"I'll come over for a statement when I'm finished here."
Kim all but escorted Sally, still steaming, to the door.

Fresca barely waited till she was gone to share a piece
of her mind. "You know that is completely ridiculous. Sally
and her daughter may have been Iggy's only living relatives, but it was Christine who shopped for her, took her
to the doctor, and in the end, sat by her side for hours. They
were closer than blood."

Nothing like a mother in full protective mode.

But Sally had dared to talk about the elephant in the
room. What I'd been about to say when Kim arrived. No
matter what else happened, everyone would wonder about
Nick. Such is the power of a sizable inheritance. Especially
one out of the blue.

And small-town tongues love to wag.

The butcher's wife arrived toting a cooler full of sausage and fresh beef, giving me a reason to keep busy while
Kim interviewed Nick in my office. I heard his steps
descend, cross the hall, and head down to his basement
refuge. I steeled myself for the summons.

Kim sat in my chair and I tried not to fidget on the spare
seat, a creaky piano stool. Her open notebook and digital
recorder lay on my desk.

"Why were you meeting at the church?"

"Last-minute prep. Making sure we had all the details

in hand." Step by step, Kim led me from the moment I parked in front of the church to the gruesome discovery.

"Why call Nick?"

"All the doors were locked, and I needed to find her spare key."

"And where did he say he was?"

"Up in the Jewel Basin, checking his packs." What he'd said then, and what he'd repeated to Sally this morning. That's when I noticed an iPhone on the desk, in a slim silver case. Mine was in my blue leather tote bag. Kim kept hers in a sturdy black leather case, department issue.

That was Nick's phone.

"Reception's kind of iffy up there," she said, and my throat constricted. "You pick up on any tension between Christine and Zayda?"

"Zayda's a great kid. She admired Christine. She's moody, but what seventeen-year-old isn't?" I leaned forward, elbows on my knees. "Kim, she was alive when I found her. Zayda says she was fine. Was the killer lurking in the studio, waiting for us to leave?" If I'd gotten there two minutes earlier, Zayda and I would have been inside. Putting all three of us in danger. The thought gave me the pee-my-pants terrors.

"I'm not going to speculate," she said. "Not till we have all the evidence. ME should give us the manner and cause of death today."

A chill tore through me. "But you know the cause, don't you? Gunshot to the chest. And the manner—homicide, right? I mean, an accidental shooting is going to be to the hand or foot. And it didn't look like . . ." I couldn't say it. Not that I knew what suicide looks like.

The muscles in Kim's jaw tightened. "Don't get involved, Erin."

I sat back and held up my hands in a "who, me?" gesture.

She let out a knowing sigh. We've been friends a long time.

· *Nine* ·

I bundled up and grabbed our weekend deposit envelope. The piles of snow and a few unshoveled stretches of sidewalk made the trek to the bank treacherous, but driving would be worse.

Across Front Street, the Playhouse stood dark. Was it really such a good idea to go ahead with the Festival? Was I trying too hard to act as if nothing was wrong, and drag the whole town with me?

At the corner of Front and Hill, a bright red semi struggled in the heavy wet snow, sliding backward each time the driver downshifted. Instead of veering left onto Hill, I stayed out of the way, detouring across the intersection to an inviting log building.

Inside, above the cutting table, hung a quilted jewel of a dragonfly on a marbled green backdrop. Bolts of cloth racked the shelves, and skeins of yarn crammed cubbies and spilled out of oversized baskets. With all that wool and batting, how could Dragonfly Dry Goods be anything but warm and cozy?

The normally coolheaded leader of the Merchants' Association gripped the phone like a hand grenade with the pin pulled. "We pay Jack Frost to plow the village streets every night when it snows. Where the heck is he?"

"Stuck in a snowbank somewhere?"

"Well, if he doesn't get his backside down here and move some snow, he's going to be stuck with something a lot more painful."

Don't mess with a woman who sells knitting needles.

On my way back from the bank, I swung into Jewel Bay Print and Copy to pick up a few more Festival posters. "Snow everywhere out there," the owner said.

"Kathy Jensen's trying to round up Jack Frost, to plow."

"Good luck. He's an ornery old coot."

Ah, winter. Peace and quiet. Ice scrapers, snow shovels, tire chains, and balky heaters. Not to mention cranky neighbors. And dead friends.

Hot coffee beckoned. I climbed the steps to the Jewel Inn. In summer, it rocks all morning and well past lunch, but at the moment, it was me and the antelope head mounted above the hostess stand. A waitress pushed through the swinging kitchen doors, spotted me, and called over her shoulder, into the kitchen. A moment later, Mimi emerged. In the forty-eight hours since I'd last seen her, her perky blue eyes had sunk halfway to China and her highlighted hair had turned to moldy straw.

We took a booth in the corner and the waitress filled two heavy white mugs.

"She won't talk to us. She barely comes out of her room."

"School might be a buzzard today," I said.

"We let her stay home. Until we know whether Kim—Ike, the county attorney, whoever—is going to charge her . . . Oh, Erin. You know her. She couldn't possibly . . ."

I reached for her hand, small comfort that the gesture

was. "Saturday, did Zayda go straight from here to Christine's?"

"She wasn't working," Mimi said. "It's been slow and with all the Film Club meetings and run-throughs, learning to work the new equipment, she'd gotten behind on her schoolwork."

In other words, unless someone other than her parents and a café's worth of customers and cooks could vouch for her, Zayda had no alibi for the time of Christine's death.

"Kim asked the same question," Mimi continued. "She doubts my daughter, but she doesn't know her. You know better."

Did I? The more of this investigating stuff I do, the less I feel I know about my friends and neighbors.

And even my relatives.

Upstairs in the Merc, I punched on my computer and called up my old friend, the Spreadsheet of Suspicion. The empty columns mocked me, the facts too elusive to build a case.

The chair wobbled as I leaned back, arms folded, gripping my biceps through the thick fleece.

Though I'd been a business major, a course in logic had been one of my favorite classes and its clean simplicity appealed to me. "Never start with your conclusion," the professor intoned in my memory. "You cannot reach a true conclusion if you think you know it in advance."

But I did know: My brother did not kill Christine. No thesis or antithesis could ever make it so.

But Nick came first on my list because Sally wasn't the only person who would suspect him. Because I loved Christine and Iggy, and wanted their memories honored. And because the best way to do that was to prove what really happened.

Much as I hated to put Zayda on the list, I had to rule her in or out.

Sally, too. And no, that wasn't a move based in spite. She nursed a mighty grudge against Christine for having the chutzpah to inherit from Iggy. If she did challenge Iggy's will in court and it was overturned, would Sally inherit instead, as the next of kin?

Sally and her daughter, who'd left Jewel Bay ages ago. I made a note: "Ask Bill about the will."

Who else had a gripe about Christine? Jack Frost. Nick said the Junkman had spouted off, but hot air isn't evidence.

Onto the list he went. I could always delete him later. (Or clear the contents. In Excel, misuse of the delete key can be deadly.)

The Spreadsheet and I stared at each other for several long moments. I blinked first. Truth was, I didn't know much. Except that Christine was dead, there was a hole in my heart, and my brother was innocent. I hoped he wasn't taking out his own anger and frustration on my pricey new shelving.

For the next hour, I did my Monday thing: Paid bills. Called vendors to place orders and confirm time slots in the commercial kitchen. Returned a call from a baker in Spokane interested in our tea shop concept. She'd made an appointment to see the property and wanted to chat up a few village merchants during her visit.

Mid-afternoon, the UPS man delivered cases of canning jars for Fresca and a thick padded envelope for me. "Right on schedule," I said, and he grinned, then whisked his magic dolly away, a fresh jar of Fresca's tapenade in his wind-chapped hand.

I perched on a stool and pried up the tear strip on the back of the envelope. It broke off in my hand, giving me just enough room to poke a finger in and wriggle the thing open. Inside were five heavy-duty clear plastic cases, each holding one of the precious commercial-grade DVDs.

I smiled in satisfaction and texted Larry and Zayda: "Got the goods—the gig is on!"

Much as I love the shop, it's good to get away now and then. First stop, the paint counter at Taylor's Building Supply. Anything would be better than the scuffed white someone had slapped on to lighten up the hand-milled pine planking.

"Why not strip it back to original?" the Paint Yahoo said. (I swear, that's what his name tag says.) "Long as you're doing the work."

Long as Nick was doing the work. Easy peasy.

But did restoring an area customers rarely see matter? I'd persuaded Fresca to give me control over the building as well as the business, not anticipating all the decisions that would follow—or how minor decisions can become major headaches.

"Shame about Christine. She was a peach, that one," the Yahoo said as he brushed stain samples on a scrap of pine. "Scary times. Hope they catch the punk bas—sorry."

"It's okay. I've heard of punks before." I walked out carrying the damp pine scrap and half a dozen paint chips in shades of warm tan. Options, options, too many options.

Next stop: Gather the eggs and cheese I'd missed on Saturday.

The Creamery folks had left my order in a cooler inside the barn. I exchanged my empty for their full and drove another mile down the highway to Mountain View. Yellow crime scene tape still circled Christine's property.

"Just looking," I said to no one as I got out of my car. "Feeling the vibe."

A tall lilac hedge marked the south border, snow clinging to the bare limbs like snags of thick white cotton. I waded through deep powder, freeing snow-covered branches bent to the ground, careful not to dislodge the bird's nest huddled in one sturdy crook.

And realized, when I got to the end of the row, that I'd reached the property line Christine shared with Frost. My first clue? The sign reading HELL WITH DOG—BEWARE OF OWNER. Another, a few feet down the four-strand fence, read: PROTECTED BY SMITH & WESSON.

I peered through the woods, a mix of fir, spruce, and scrub pine, along with birch and red willow. The leafless trees and shrubs exposed a faded blue bus, its windshield shattered, and a dozen dead cars, their shapes and colors obscured by snow. Not for nothing was Jack Frost known as the Junkman.

No wonder Christine had wanted to clean up the neighborhood.

Freeing more branches as I went, I worked my way back to the road, a load of snow shivering down my neck as thanks.

I was still shaking it out of my hair when I reached my car. Two middle-aged women stood by the cluster of mailboxes, each clutching a stack of envelopes and catalogs.

"Sweet neighborhood," I said.

"Except for that one," the short, round woman said, glancing toward Frost's place.

"You're mad that his dog mistook your rosebush for a fire hydrant and killed it," the taller one said.

"My Mr. Lincoln tea rose," the first woman said. She turned to me, cheeks pink. "Christine invited the neighbors over last fall. For a potluck, to get to know one another. Shocked everybody that Frost and his wife came. When he heard Christine was thinking of starting an art school in the church basement, he blew a gasket, yelling about noise and traffic. From after-school art classes for kids, for Pete's sake. Probably thought she'd call the county and they'd make him clean up his property. Might find more than they bargained for, if you know what I mean."

Local legend tells of a lightning strike that started a fire on an old homestead out this way. Crews saved the house, but they all got high off the smoke from the burning pot. "How many acres does he own?"

"About twenty. From the pasture by the road, past the house and shop, into the woods." She gestured. Frost's land formed an L around Christine's much smaller acreage.

Her neighbor cocked her head. "Iggy fretted about his junk heap for years, but Christine had more oomph. I do recall seeing him out there one summer, shirtless. Walking through his pasture carrying a bottle of Roundup in one hand and a .22 in the other, shooting voles." She rolled her eyes.

"That's one way to clean up the neighborhood," I said. We waved good-bye, and I drove south on Mountain View, then turned on Rainbow Lake Road.

A little red hen scurried across the lane as I drove into Phyl and Jo's place. The garden beds lay dormant under a thick layer of straw mulch and a snowy white blanket.

"Gotchyer eggs," Phyl said. "Come in and warm up a bit. Talk about spring."

Rainbow Lake Garden is a bite of heaven, year-round. In summer, fruit and veg—as New Zealand–born Phyl calls it—sprout everywhere, accented by edible flowers and others grown for joy. Chickens, goats, and the occasional orphaned fawn grow here, too.

In the off season, human life revolves around yarn. Tall, blond, and Danish, Jo spins like a woman possessed, and Phyl, her freckles fading, dyes the skeins. Most of her colors draw on the garden or the surrounding woods: orange from onion skins, a golden-yellow from St. John's wort, lavender from elderberries. The customers at Dragonfly Dry Goods gobble them up.

"Seed orders," Phyl said. Catalogs and scribbled lists littered the round oak table. "Let me pour ya a cup of a blend we've been tinkering with."

"Erin." Jo rose from the table and embraced me, ponytail

swinging. She manages to look like sunshine all year round. Her hand-knit scarlet sweater bore a band of gold and orange flowers. "Such a loss, our Christine."

But even these earth mothers shied away from mournful talk. Much more pleasant to sit by the fire and chat about herbs over cups of a spritely mint, red clover, and lemon balm blend. To debate how much produce the Merc could sell next summer, how early they would have spinach and other hardy greens, and how many pounds of tomatoes Fresca would transform into her best-selling sauces.

Phyl tipped the last drops of tea into my mug. "Saw your brother drive by Saturday afternoon, heading north. Back toward town. We see him out this way quite a bit, though I suppose no more, not with Christine gone."

"Out here? On Rainbow Lake Road?" I squinted, tilting my head. "Saturday?"

She nodded. "I remember, 'cause you'd called for eggs, and I tried to wave him down, spare you the trip. But he was eyes on the road and moving fast."

Nick had lied, to me and to a deputy sheriff.

Why, Nick, why?

They say red clover tea settles the stomach. I downed the last swallow, hopeful, and studied the bits of leaves and twigs in the bottom of my mug, searching for an answer.

Eggs safely tucked into the Subaru, I crept north on icy Rainbow Lake Road, pondering Phyl's comment. When I'd called Nick, desperate to find the spare key, hadn't he'd said he was in the Jewel, checking his packs? Miles away, in the opposite direction.

I'd thought myself lucky to reach him, cell reception being iffy on the mountainside.

Had I misunderstood? Had he gone up early, come back down this direction, and returned to the Basin later?

No. He'd been adamant, repeating the lie to Kim: He'd

left the Orchard before daybreak and spent all day in the woods. He'd snowshoed into a blind he'd made of cut evergreens, then watched the wolves casing the area. On his way back to his Jeep, he'd noted a small elk herd and paused to assess their behavior.

Some folks in Montana are convinced that wolves have decimated the elk population and ruined hunting. They worry that elk calves are easy prey, fret over drops in elk and deer counts, and complain that families in need of meat can't compete with the far-ranging carnivores.

Others say wolves are a necessary part of the ecosystem, that without the pressure of their presence, elk stay in one place too long and browse too deeply, stunting tree growth and leading to a loss of habitat critical for everything from mountain bluebirds to grizzlies. The trophic cascade, Nick calls it. The loss of any one element—from wolves to aspen to sparrows—disrupts the entire chain of life.

"What about the hunters?" Nick is often asked. "They need to go where the elk go," he replies. "That's why it's called hunting."

I pulled over in front of Christine's cottage. I closed my eyes and tried to picture the scene when we'd emerged from the fire hall late Saturday afternoon.

Pewter gray clouds had moved in, darkening the sky. Swirling snow had whipped my cheeks. The ambulance had left. Zayda's parents had arrived. Sheriff's rigs had been scattered everywhere.

The Jeep had been right here, I realized, the red clover tea not enough, never enough, to settle the fear that followed. Pointing north. As though he had in fact driven north from Rainbow Lake, past Phyl and Jo's corner of paradise, turned onto Mountain View, and screeched to a halt in front of the cottage. Run to the church, seen me, seen Christine, told his lies.

Why, Nick? Why?

· *Ten* ·

Too many questions. I wanted answers, but the prospects terrified me.

Kim would have preliminary forensics and autopsy reports by now, and maybe ballistics analysis, but I hesitated to stop by her office. She has a sharp eye, and a keen nose for scenting trouble. And she knows me too well. If she sensed my fear and anxiety, it wouldn't be much of a leap to focus on Nick and question his alibi.

But I needed Christine's Festival notebook. Ticket sales counts, volunteer assignments, the draft program, the all-important list of donors to thank. How could I step into her Uggs without it?

Nothing wrong with giving in to one's inner chicken. Before pulling away from the cottage, I sent Kim a text. The nearly instant reply: "Waiting for fingerprints."

Great. I'll get it back covered in black powder that turns to ink when you touch it.

I forced myself to breathe calmly as I drove back to town. Lousy place to get distracted, especially in winter.

One wrong move at the wheel and a driver could plunge into the icy river.

I crossed the one-lane bridge into the village and drove up Front Street. In dragon-lady mode, Kathy had put the fear into Frost—a freshly plowed ribbon wove down our main street and side streets. I parked behind the Merc and unloaded the eggs and cheese. Waved to Tracy and headed for the Playhouse.

In front of the theater, flower beds slept under the snow, but the sidewalks—the square pavers engraved with names of donors and patrons—had been shoveled clean.

In the lobby, the kids sat on hand-painted benches and sprawled on the floor, eyes trained on Larry, who stood beside an easel holding a whiteboard, pointing at numbers and terms I couldn't decipher. Christine's sign hung overhead, a sparkling, poignant reminder of plans gone astray.

"Hey, there. Looks like you've got it all worked out."

Heads swiveled and voices called to me. "Hi, Erin."

Zayda and Dylan slouched on a bench against the far wall. You could have driven a Mack truck between them.

"So glad to see you all here. Christine's death"—the word stuck in my throat—"is inexplicable. A tragedy. It delighted her to see all of you working so hard on the Festival. She reveled in your energy and enthusiasm. Your love of movies and of Jewel Bay. Thanks to you, the show is going on." I clapped my hands together, my fingertips to my lips, momentarily overcome. Eager faces turned sad, eyes damp. A few feet away, on the floor in front of a pillar covered in a mosaic of iridescent glass tiles, Dana slid his arm around the red-haired girl and she sniffed back a sob.

"Gold in that there saddle bag," Larry said, nodding at my blue leather bag. I handed him the envelope.

"*Julie and Julia. Big Night. Tampopo*—a noodle Western. Love it. *Chocolat*. And *Ratatouille*. Perfect," Larry said, sliding out one case at a time. "Great choices. We'll run through them, make sure there's no problems. Let's get started." The kids pushed themselves up. A girl clapped and started a cheer: "MOO-vies. MOO-vies."

"Zayda," I called as she stood to follow Larry and the others out of the lobby. "Got a sec?"

Head bowed, eyes on the toe of one Doc Marten—back in style, thanks to Dr. Who—her jaw twitched but she didn't answer.

"Why did you go out there early?" I'd been right on time. To beat me there, go inside, struggle—or find Christine injured—and come back out to sit on the cottage steps would have taken a good ten minutes.

"I was just early, okay? No reason."

"How did you lose your eyebrow ring?"

She snorted. Frustrated with me? The situation? Finally, she met my gaze. "I didn't kill her, and nothing else I did is any of your business."

She stomped away. So much for thinking teenagers would talk to me because I'm younger than their parents. Or because I'm cool.

The sign Christine had labored over and been so proud of hung above me. "What happened?" I asked her spirit. "Who killed you?"

The fake jewels caught the light, and I swear, they winked.

Love love love the Merc's tin ceiling tiles. But over the years, a leaky roof had rusted one corner, and a few got bent by who knows what. I'd managed to take down the damaged tiles and repaint them, but reattaching them had defeated me. The tricky part is holding the panel, holding the hammer and nail, and leaving an edge to tuck the next one in, while standing on a ladder, arms lifted, neck bent.

Nick was obviously more talented than I. And taller.

"You're almost done."

"No sweat," he said, but it wasn't true. A thin bead crawled down the back of his neck. "Take this." He handed me the pneumatic nail gun. They look innocent enough, but feel like ninety tons of dynamite. A co-worker at SavClub nailed his foot to the floor of the West Seattle bungalow he was restoring and limped for ages. I set it down quickly.

"Looks great," I said. "Thanks."

"No sweat," he repeated, then folded the ladder and carted it out the back door.

I glanced at Tracy, who shrugged. Fresca had gone for the day, but the place still smelled like olives and garlic, and a whiff of sawdust. I got out a broom and swept up. A few minutes later, Nick's steps echoed in the back hallway and pounded down to the basement. Veteran little sister that I am, I trailed behind him.

"Hey, you got all the shelves together and put in place."

"Yep." He picked a small dark notebook off the tiny corner desk and slipped it into his pocket.

"The paint samples are in the hallway. Come take a look."

"Later," he said.

When we were kids and Nick didn't want to come inside for dinner, or leave his room, my mother often sent me to get him, and out he'd trot, as if no one else had asked. No such luck today. "Okay. Find out anything more about the will?"

A shadow crossed his eyes, and he sank into the chair, covering his face with his hands.

"Nick." I knelt beside him, a hand on his back. After a long moment, he buried his head in my shoulder. I held my big brother while his shoulders shook in waves of soundless sobs. He'd been away at school when my father died, and if he'd cried, it had been in private. By the time he got home a day later, he'd become the man of the family, shepherding the womenfolk, protecting us, eyes dry, face grim.

But who takes care of the shepherd when the wolf strikes?

"Nick," I said again. "It's not your fault. She knew you loved her."

"If I'd been there . . ." he said, straightening.

"Then you'd have been shot, too." Maybe. If Zayda had been the shooter, Nick could have overpowered her. Heck, Christine ought to have been able to overpower Zayda. They were about the same height, and Zayda was faster—track star—but Christine was stronger.

What the heck had happened in there?

Nick raised his head, not meeting my eyes. So many questions I wanted to ask. The most important one was the hardest. I angled my way in. "How are your wolves? Seen them since Saturday?"

He gave me a sideways glance. "Since when do you care about my wolves?"

Tell him the truth, Erin. "Since they became your alibi."

He turned to stone.

"Sally's gonna talk, big brother. And she's going to tell everyone in town that Christine pressured Iggy to leave her the money, and you killed Christine to get it. In Sally's version, she'll be the victim—the wronged relative deprived of what she deserved by the big bad Wolf Man."

"Erin, I appreciate you wanting to help. But I have already said I was in the Jewel Basin all day, until you called me, and nothing is going to change that." He pushed back his chair and stood. "Let me know when you're ready for me to paint."

And he was gone.

I slid into his still-warm chair. On the wall hung a short list of due dates for grant applications. On the desk—a countertop remnant I got cheap at the Building Supply—lay pens, copies of articles and scientific journals. His laptop. Nothing that told me where he'd really been last Saturday, and why he wouldn't tell me.

Think, Erin. Why would Nick lie?

Despite all Sally had said and would say, I never for a

nanosecond imagined he'd killed Christine. They'd been the best exes I'd ever seen—friends, never bad-mouthing, treating each other with love and respect. I believed him when he said they were working out their problems and getting back together.

And I believed him when he said he hadn't known about the will. Had she made it while they were engaged and simply never changed it, or written it after inheriting a sizable fortune?

But anybody who knew my brother—including Kim Caldwell and Ike Hoover—knew he didn't care about *things*. He only cared about his work.

Sally didn't know that. And she obviously hadn't known about Christine's will until the lawyer called.

But much as I dislike Sally and could readily believe her guilty of all variety of venal sins, from spreading malicious rumors to failing to shovel her sidewalk, it's a giant leap from gossip to murder. Besides, she'd been in her shop Saturday morning. I'd seen her myself.

I had bearded Wolf Man in his den and he had gotten away.

What was my brother up to?

· *Eleven* ·

"Here, Pumpkin. C'mon, kitty."

Mr. Sandburg greeted me at the door with his all-purpose yowl, the one that can mean anything from "You left me alone all day, witch" to "A new squirrel moved into the neighborhood and we're going to be great friends."

Pumpkin, on the other hand, did not show her face. She was not in her crate or under the bed. She was not behind my one potted plant, a ficus trimmed in tiny white lights, or hiding in the shower. Sandburg had never managed to open a fully closed cabinet or closet door, but I was beginning to think either I'd left one ajar or she had superpowers.

And then I spotted the wicker laundry basket in my bedroom, lid askew. "Ah, Pumpkin. Nice and soft in there, isn't?" I lifted her out, hoping I wouldn't regret it, but after wriggling for a moment, she relaxed against me. I took advantage of her shift in mood and perched on the chaise, cradling her in my arms. "I know. It's hard. I miss her, too."

Sandburg hopped onto the bed, watching in sympathy—

or jealousy. The three of us sat that way for several minutes, until the siren song of Cabernet lured me to the kitchen. Both cats followed and took up posts on opposite ends of the couch.

I'd picked up a few winter vegetables from Phyl and Jo's storage bin. The fennel would pair nicely with blood oranges snared from my mother's latest fruit-of-the-month delivery, from her brother's California orchard. I poured a glass of wine and popped a pan of hazelnuts in the oven to toast.

"Awful quiet in here," I told the cats. They had both fallen asleep. Adam usually takes charge of the music when he joins me for dinner. I plugged my iPod into its speakers and spun the dial. Bruno Mars? Too sweet. Adele? Too emotional. Neko Case? *Yes.*

I shaved fennel while Neko's voice filled the room, updating Perry Como by reminding us that you can catch a falling star, but then what? It will never be yours. Sang along as I peeled oranges, added shallots, olive oil, and the warm fragrant nuts. Snipped a few mint leaves off the plant in the window sill.

"What does it need?" I asked the nearest cat. "Ah. That's good. Thanks." A few chopped fennel fronds made the perfect garnish. And one of Wendy's ciabatta rolls for a taste of heaven.

When the weather turned, we'd hauled the café table and chairs in and settled them next to the French doors so I could pretend to eat outside without freezing my tush off. I sat there now. Sandburg took over my chocolate brown leather chair and Pumpkin stayed on the back of the couch, her eyes watching me.

"Tomorrow," I told her. "We'll find you a new home."

But despite the refreshing salad, the delectable wine, and the roll's crisp chewy crust and soft spongy inside, I could not stop thinking about Nick and Christine. My big brother was keeping a secret, and I feared it would cause big trouble.

Worse, it was clear that law enforcement considered him a viable suspect. And if he wasn't being truthful with me, I doubted he'd been more forthcoming with them.

Deception only deepens the danger.

I refilled my wineglass and started pacing. The secret wasn't his relationship with Christine. Didn't take long, after Nick came home from the field last fall, to realize they were hanging out. The pool games were their first public pairing. Understandable. Easier to take another run in private than under the double scrutiny of village and family.

And I had sensed no shade of guilt in his grief.

The will. Now that was strange. Obvious enough to name him her heir during their engagement, especially with her family history. But in those days, she'd been flat broke. And she'd broken things off. Why not change her will then? Inertia, or the lack of close relatives? Or hope for reconciliation?

Or had she'd rewritten her will recently? Iggy died in early September, a month or two before Nick's return. Made sense for Christine to make plans for the future, just in case.

But why Nick? And why not tell him?

I couldn't answer the first question, not for sure, but the answer to the second was plain enough: None of us expects *something* to happen. Even in a family already tainted by tragedy.

And maybe she hadn't wanted money to be a factor in his decision about their relationship. Which was ridiculous. But she might have wondered.

"Enough hypothesizing," I said. Why was I bothering? To stifle Sally's gossip?

Admit it, Erin. My doubts about Nick's whereabouts on Saturday had me questioning everything he'd said. I hated that.

A faint ringing pierced my thoughts. I scooped my

phone out of my bag, on the bench in the entry where I'd dropped it.

"Erin, Larry Abrams here. You won't believe this."

I caught my breath. Had Zayda been arrested?

"We got all the movies up and running, to check for glitches. Sorry to tell you, instead of *Chocolat*, we got this—thing. This kinda porn, trio of women fooling around with chocolate and, well, other things, and . . . I think there might be some parents upset with me, but I stopped it as soon as I realized what was going on."

"What? Back up. Instead of *Chocolat*, we got what?"

He explained again. "Somebody's idea of a joke, in some warehouse. Switching the labels on the disc. It's almost funny, but not really."

"No," I said. "Not really. I'll call the distributor in the morning and ask them to overnight us a new copy. *Chocolat* is scheduled for Saturday night. Valentine's Day."

"Make sure they check it first. We can always show four films instead of five if we have to."

"I'd hate to change the schedule again. If people show up for the wrong movie or miss one they wanted to see, they'll get cranky." We'd already changed the night of the student film, to avoid a conflict with a basketball tournament. The distributor factored how long we kept each movie into the charge, and had assured us we'd get them in ample time. Ha.

I loaded the dishwasher and put on jammies. Checked Pumpkin's bowl—she ate less than her figure suggested. Stress has the opposite effect on me.

On the couch with my laptop and wineglass, I pulled up the Spreadsheet, cells blank. Love spreadsheets. They give an illusion of tidy order to a messy world.

This one wasn't playing nice.

In a management class at SavClub, we'd learned a system of problem solving using circles and arrows. It reminded me of those cartoon ice cream cones with half a dozen scoops in different colors piled on top of one another. Tempting, and impossible to eat.

But when what you're doing isn't working, do something else. I scrounged up a notepad and colored pens, and drew two concentric circles. Labeled the doughnut hole "Christine." Around the edges, sprinkled everyone connected to her. Nick. Zayda, who'd arrived early, lost her eyebrow ring, and clammed up. Sally, ticked and now re-ticked over the inheritance.

Iggy. Gone, but not forgotten, and she might provide a valuable link. I drew a blue arrow between Iggy and Sally.

The neighbors had hinted at another beef. What had Frost said to Christine Friday night at Red's? I hadn't heard and fat chance Nick would tell me. If he knew. I made a note to quiz J.D.

Frost had also sparred with Iggy, though nothing that I knew linked him to the others. Zayda, too, seemed connected only to Christine.

Before long, I had a mess of arrows and interlocking circles—Venn diagrams, the most useful thing I learned in third grade, besides how to kick Bobby Hughes where it hurts.

It might be cheating to transfer the circle connections to my spreadsheet, but I did it anyway. My attitude improved instantly.

It improved even more after a bowl of vanilla ice cream—two scoops—drizzled with chocolate-Cabernet sauce.

Time to spy on my friends and family. I knew little about Frost, beyond what I'd heard in the last few days. In small towns, we think we know everything about everyone, but some folks fly under the radar. And sometimes what we think we know is wrong. Jack aka Jacob and Sherry—his wife?—owned twenty-two acres immediately east of the church, in a higgledy-piggledy pattern that, if I read the map on the property tax website right, included a house, outbuildings, and forested land.

His name appeared in the local paper once, when he protested the Rotary Club's plan to build a walking trail on the north side of the highway near his place, and in the *Pondera Post*, at a meeting to discuss the state's proposed wolf management plan. That article included a shot of Frost shaking his fist in the face of a state wildlife biologist.

Nick had never mentioned him. Had Frost gone after Christine to get to Nick? Had she given Frost a piece of her own mind on the carnivore conflict? Or did the changes she'd proposed to the neighborhood worry him that much? Change is rarely easy, but it makes some people downright nasty.

That appeared to be the end of Frost's short electronic trail.

Next up, Christine. "Look to your *veec-tum*," as Hercule Poirot put it. I hated this. It made my teeth hurt. But I'd waded in this far.

We were Facebook friends, so following her tracks there was easy. She didn't tweet, but kept up a lively blog and fabulous Pinterest boards, thick with images of her paintings and faves from other artists, many from around here. I got lost in her Etsy shop, enjoying pieces I'd always loved and others I'd never seen. I found myself smiling—a good thing when remembering a friend.

Not so good when you remember you're trying to track her killer.

Next, Google fed me a couple of arts websites, a Belgian woman of the same name, and another American who spelled their shared first name with a *K*. Yahoo! wanted to show me a pioneer graveyard in Oregon, and photos of a bodybuilder named Christopher Vandenberg, but I shuttered both attempts.

I dredged up the name of her Vermont hometown and narrowed the search. Found her high school graduating

class, and photos of her senior art show. Her parents' obitu-
aries, and a news account of the head-on collision on icy
roads that had killed them.

Ohmygod. I had never known she'd been in the car, too,
and spent a month in the hospital.

A shiver of sadness slipped through me. When I was a
teenager upset with a friend over a minor slight, my mother
had told me to always be kind, because you never know
what burdens people carry.

A spoon clattered against china. "You like ice cream?"
I asked Pumpkin. "Sorry I didn't leave you much, but it isn't
good for you. Let's find you a kitten treat." She let me scoop
her up, and I carried cat and bowl to the kitchen, then poured
her a few tuna tidbits. The sound of the treat tin summoned
Sandburg. "We should share, don't you think?"

I watched the cats eat, side by side. She shot him a few
nervous glances, but he behaved himself.

I took the opportunity to reclaim my chair and moved
to the next name on my list.

Do you need to do this? I asked myself. *Yes.* Kim or Ike
might well be running the same searches, right this minute.
My advantage was knowing the people and the community
in a way neither of them did. Kim lives here, too, but as
she'd observed about dating, the uniform and gun separate
her from the rest of us.

I reminded myself that I might not like what I found.

Better that than seeing my brother blamed for murder.

First obstacle: his name. I had to sort out Nick Murphy
the film director and Nick Murphy the Irish screenwriter,
Nick Murphy the ex–NFL punter, and two Nick Murphys
who had played professional soccer in England, twenty years
apart. Using *Nicholas* yielded another soccer player, several
dentists, and a gaggle of lawyers. I added *Montana* to the
search and up popped a picture of an astronomy professor
at U.M. and finally, my guy, posing with last year's field
assistants in an alpine meadow in Glacier National Park.

Google served up references to studies he'd participated in. Comments he'd made on proposed wolf management plans across the West. His role in tracking the legendary OR-7, a collared wolf who'd wandered hundreds of miles in Oregon, taking in the sights. His testimony against a Washington couple convicted of poaching and attempted pelt smuggling.

"What's this?" I skimmed the article titled "Grad Student Triggers Debate—Do Statistics Lie?" The piece triggered a vague memory of Nick snared in a controversy while working on his Ph.D. I jumped back to the top and began reading slowly. He'd been lead author on a study of wolf migration and predation—attacks on livestock—that enraged the anti-wolf lobby. Several U.S. congressmen challenged his university and its research funding because the conclusions were unpopular in their districts.

Nick doesn't rant or rave much—unlike the female side of the family—but one sure way to get him rolling is to interject politics into science.

He always says he chooses to work independently so he can stay out of the classroom and in the field. But I had to wonder whether this episode had left scars.

Next up, an interview at the height of the controversy. "The study results are sound," Nick had told a national newspaper. "We used reliable methods of fieldwork and statistical analysis. Nothing that hasn't been done dozens of times. But rumors get repeated until they gain traction. People believe what they want to believe, and make me out to be some rogue tree hugger. A team of a dozen scientists did this work, but I won, or lost, the coin toss to be named first and handle the P.R. Ultimately, the extra attention is giving us the chance to show other scientists what we're seeing and let them reach their own conclusions.

"I understand politicians have to make decisions and that's fine, but if they choose to ignore the science, they need to accept that responsibility. And don't attack the scientists."

I stood and paced between the couch and kitchen island. An academic and political dustup ten years ago may have influenced Nick's choice of career path, but what possible connection could his work have had to Christine's murder?

My phone rang again as Google spit up the goods on Sally Grimes.

"Hey, there. So the cats haven't clawed you to death yet?" Adam asked.

"They've actually spent most of the evening in the same room." I set my laptop aside. "Turns out Pumpkin adores ice cream. How's the class?"

He gave me the rundown. "Every time I think, *I already know this stuff*, we learn a new technique, or hear about a tragedy avoided. So, I hate being away, but it's good."

I filled him in on the film snafu and he laughed and assured me I'd work it out. Then I told him what I'd uncovered about Nick not being where he'd said he was on Saturday, and Adam did not laugh. He did not respond. I felt my throat tighten and my hackles—whatever hackles are—rise. I'd ended one relationship before it got rolling when a guy tried to keep me from investigating. Maybe I had overreacted, but when Chiara had said Mr. Right might not like my habit of sticking my nose in other people's business, I'd told her if that's what he thinks, he isn't Mr. Right.

And I still feel that way. I want to call my own shots. But even more, I want a partner who supports my choices. Who trusts that I'm not going to jump off the deep end just because it's there, that I look before I leap, and land on my feet more times than I fall. Who will help me, with love and respect, to work my way through life's challenges and come out stronger, and expect me to do the same for him.

High hopes. But not impossible ones.

"So why would Nick lie?" Adam said after a long silence, and tension I hadn't realized was gripping me drained out of every cell.

"That's what I can't figure," I said, the words rushing

out. "It may not have anything to do with what happened to Christine, but . . . I thought you were going to tell me to stop asking questions."

"Would you?"

Truth or dare. "No."

"Right. So, why bother?" Though he was a hundred miles away, I pictured his crooked smile. "Hey, I wish we were having this conversation in person. I won't pretend not to worry. You're trying to expose a secret that somebody killed to protect."

For a microsecond, I stopped breathing. Blunt way to put it, but true.

"But that's one of the things I love about you," he continued. "You follow your heart. You may jump when you see a mouse, but when it comes to the people you care about, you have more courage than anyone I've ever met. Why would I want to interfere with that?"

"That class better be a good one," I said, and the warmth in his laughter carried me all the way to sleepy time.

Good night, Adam. Good night, Mr. Maybe Right.

· Twelve ·

I slept like a rock.
   Like a rock tossed by waves on the shore, or kicked by giants who'd lost their soccer ball. Like a rock tumbling down an avalanche chute.

Alas, I was a stone gathering moss in the morning, stumbling around my cabin bleary-eyed and foul of mood. Even an extra-strong dose of Cowboy Roast barely boosted me out of low gear.

And that was before Pumpkin decided to sit on the chocolate leather chair and Sandberg decided she was an interloping Ferengi to be chased under the bed.

"Truce, you two." I waded through the snarling, hauled Sandburg back to the living room, and shut the bedroom door. Pumpkin hopped onto the chaise and buried her head in her paws, less from embarrassment than irritation at having her fight broken up. My interpretation, anyway. I may not be fluent in cat, but I get by, with a strong human accent.

Tuesday had dawned bright and clear, which meant too

cold and too dry to snow. Dressing as if it were spring wouldn't make it so, so I pulled on my favorite black pants, then pulled them off and grabbed black fleece-lined tights and a purple corduroy skirt. A long-sleeved T-shirt in a red-and-orange print similar to Jo's Nordic knits, and a fleecy plum vest whose texture reminded me of my grandmother's Persian lamb coat.

And because winter's ice keeps my red cowboy boots tucked away for special occasions, comfy black boots that fit like a sweater but don't make my feet sweat in the shop.

I studied myself in the mirror. The eyes gave it away. "Desperate nights call for desperate measures," I said, and reached for the makeup.

The problem, I realized on the drive into the village, was that helping my big brother meant taking him off his pedestal. The one where I'd put him to keep him safe.

In the Merc's back hall, I flicked on the heat and lights. Paused to study the paint chips taped to the wall and realign them in order of this morning's preference. Started coffee. Grabbed a banana from the fruit bowl on the counter—seventy-five-cent bananas are a big hit among shoppers and my downtown neighbors.

Lacking Christine's magic notebook with our customer ID info, I slogged my way through the film distributor's multiple-choice voice mail system till a human answered.

A human who had not had enough coffee.

"Yes, that's the code number on the box and the disc," I told the customer service rep, struggling to keep my tone snark-free. "But that's not what you sent."

She repeated, as if to a preschooler, that they'd sent us a disc with the code number of the film we'd ordered and that was all they were obligated to do.

"Listen, I don't give a fig about your code numbers. We didn't order a code number. We ordered a copy of *Chocolat*, and that's not what we got."

Round and round she went, until I asked for a supervisor.

Two and a half, maybe three seconds later, I had the promise of a new disc, and profuse apologies.

"I'll watch the first few minutes myself to make sure it's right," she assured me. "We'll expedite it, at our expense, and we won't charge you for this film. We're delighted to be part of a new festival, and so sorry about the mix-up."

That's how customer service ought to work. But I'd fret until I had the right film in hand.

Nick walked in as I refilled my coffee mug. "Smells good."

My chance to demand he let me help him. But what if he wouldn't talk? What if he kept stonewalling? What if I couldn't persuade him to tell me the truth, that if he didn't, he risked being caught in a web of lies that made him look guilty. And if people think you're guilty of something, it's not hard for them to make the leap and believe you guilty of something worse. "Ceiling looks great," I said. "Shelves, too."

He reached for the coffeepot.

"I'll get paint this week," I continued. The courage Adam had praised vaporized like profit in February.

"No rush. I'll be around till April or so. Only fair that I do my share. Got plenty of my own work, though. Stats to collate, grants to write. Field assistants to recruit."

"And a will to probate, property to manage, and decisions to make."

His fingers twitched as he dropped two sugar cubes into his cup.

"When you're ready, I'll help you clean out Christine's cottage, and the studio. So will Chiara and Mom." I hadn't asked, but knew they'd agree. Of course, it was turning out that I didn't know my family quite as well as I thought. "But Nick, you have to talk to us. You have to tell me . . ."

He stared at his coffee, jaw muscles working. Then, as if he hadn't surprised me enough already this week, he leaned down and kissed my cheek before striding off to the basement.

I was still staring after him when Tracy chugged in, Diet Coke in one hand, a paper bag in the other. Bagel and cream cheese, or a maple bar? She looked as bedraggled as I felt.

"Erin, I need the afternoon off. Bozo's sick. His vet's in Hawaii, and I don't want to cart him all the way to a new vet in Pondera, but . . ."

"Trace, of course. Poor guy." Minor brainstorm. "Talk to Bill. He treated Pepé when she got that tick bite last spring. She recovered beautifully—no problems."

Tracy pursed her lips and tilted her head, her black-and-white puppy dog earrings wagging.

"Talk to Bill about what?" Fresca said, slipping out of her coat. She kissed me on the cheek, and I left Tracy to explain. On my way upstairs, I heard my mother say, "I'll call him right now."

Time to focus on our drink line. I called the winners of our chai contest and made plans to carry both blends. Then I pulled up price quotes for metal tea canisters and my sales projections, and started working up cost estimates. The landline rang. Figuring Fresca and Tracy were preoccupied with canine care, I picked it up myself.

Moments later, I walked down to the basement slowly, the caller's message burning in my gut.

Nick frowned at the interruption, then shifted to a hard smile of expectation. I was ten again, sent to summon him, dinner cooling on the table, my father waiting. Little sister invading big brother's den.

But this was as much my den as his. And the message I relayed far more serious, the consequences of obeying and disobeying equally harsh.

Like the wolves he studies, Nick is strong and sure of himself. But for a moment, for a flash of an instant, he was neither. And then, like the wolf, master of its domain, so swift that the animal seems like a figment of an overwrought imagination, the fear vanished.

"A few questions, she said. I'm sure it's no big deal." My attempt at reassurance fooled neither of us.

He thanked me and picked up his coat by the collar, flinging it over one shoulder. I surveyed the transformation that signaled a new life for this old sandstone edifice. Both building and business were part of our family legacy. I'd come home and taken over to preserve it, to rebuild it, to keep the Merc and the Murphys a vital part of Jewel Bay.

It was the Murphys—one in particular—who mattered more to me right now than the Merc. But I'd done all I could. It was up to Nick to decide what to tell Undersheriff Hoover and Detective Caldwell.

"What was that about?" my mother said when I reached the main floor.

But I didn't have the heart to tell her Nick had been summoned for more questioning. "Just somebody trying to reach him. Cops still have his cell."

I forced myself to focus on the numbers for the drink line, figuring and refiguring. Finally occurred to me to skip the pricy tea and coffee suppliers and call the company that provides the jars and labels for our bottling machine. *Bingo*, as Old Ned would say. Yes, they carried what we needed, and they'd send samples out today. Plus a tin and label order would push us to the next level of discounts for all our orders.

Nothing like the sound of discounts on the horizon.

We were getting closer to a new product line. Closer to making the Merc a player in the regional foods market, beyond the doors of our little shop.

Big dreams can bring big headaches, but we'd be ready. *Bring it on*.

Recruiting a tea shop to town had not been my idea, but with Mimi focused on Zayda and the chamber president under the weather, chatting up the next prospect fell to me.

I'd begun to sense a theme.

About my age and likewise bundled in boots, tights, and layers, Kendra Cox bubbled about the food biz. Ray Ramirez of Ray's Bayside Grill, aka the Grillie, ushered us into a booth, along with the real estate agent who'd showed Kendra spaces suitable for a fun and funky tea shop. What a kick it would be to bring another energetic, creative young business owner to town. She'd worked in a SavClub deli for a year, giving her experience in mid-level production and packaged foods—and us something else in common.

But while she loved baking in a casual-chic French bakery and café in Spokane, she had an urge to run her own shop, and the food and atmosphere we had in mind suited her.

The three of us chatted about decor, marketing ideas, and food, food, food.

"Can I ask you a personal question?" she said when the real estate agent headed to the restroom. "What do you do for fun here? The population seems to skew older, with all the retirees, and that's good for business. They have more disposable income, and eat out more. But what about having a life?"

I'd never thought of Jewel Bay that way. "There's plenty of young people here, single and with families. My brother and sister. Tracy, whom you met. Heck, even Ray's young by some standards."

Ray cackled as he set our Reubens with beer-soaked sauerkraut and fries on the table, the tail of his scorpion tattoo peeking out from the open collar of his chef's jacket. The agent slid in beside me, and talk turned back to food and business.

"I'm not convinced I can do enough business to make it through the winter," Kendra said.

"It's a challenge," I admitted, "to figure out how to scale up for summer and down for winter, while treating your staff fairly. Things change every day. But that's true in any business, anywhere. Hey, Ray, got a minute?"

Ray pulled up a chair and answered Kendra's questions. His cooks handle breakfast and lunch, while he takes charge of the stove for dinner. Today, he was filling in for the front-of-house manager—demonstrating the flexibility required in running your own op.

But his flashing dark eyes and wide smile didn't sway her. I stifled my disappointment in losing a potential kindred spirit.

It takes a certain kind of risk-taker to make it in a seasonal town.

Even a jewel like this one.

· *Thirteen* ·

We said our good-byes and I'll-get-back-to-yous, but it was clear as the cloudless, cerulean sky above the drowsy village that we were seeing the last of Kendra Cox.

If she didn't feel the vibe, nothing we could do.

As I climbed over the snow berm, a shiny white Cadillac SUV parked in front of Puddle Jumpers and the driver hopped out, his fleece-topped rubber boots smashing through the snow.

"Hey, Larry!" I caught him as he opened the shop door. He stepped aside, giving me no choice but to go in.

Into a grandmother's heaven and a new mother's dream. From the red satin hearts hanging in the zebra-striped doorframe to the piles of red and pink baby caps, heart-splashed onesies, and more Valentine's Day decor than you could shake a heart-print pencil at, Puddle Jumpers was ready for the big day. All year round, Sally stocks the cutest children's clothing and toys in western Montana. Or so I'm told, having no reason to study such things. Yet. But I had kept my promise to buy Landon one of the stick horses with a stuffed calico head and a Crayola-bright yarn mane, as penance for my part in the chaos that occurred last summer when an imposter chef tried to make a getaway by leading sheriff's deputies on a chase through Sally's shop.

The frost in her pale blue eyes said she hadn't forgiven me.

"The distributor is expediting a new copy of the DVD. They promise delivery tomorrow," I told Larry.

"Meaning you'll be lucky to get it by Thursday. If they can manage to send the right one this time." Sally crossed her arms, the V-neck of her navy knit tunic revealing a white lace-trimmed top beneath. She'd obviously heard about the snafu.

I forced a pleasant expression, remembering Fresca's caution.

Some people make it hard to be nice.

"Thanks, Erin. I'm sure they'll make it right." Larry turned to Sally. "You look great today."

The polar ice melted. Larry was obviously a better person than I.

I angled across the street to Red's, hoping to jog J.D.'s memory about Friday night. A long shot, that a bartender might remember what one patron said to another days ago.

Behind the bar, Old Ned polished glasses, a clean white apron around his middle. His spark had brightened since his grandson came to town, right after Christmas. On one giant TV screen, race cars screamed around a track. On the other, women in bikinis played beach volleyball. The sole customer nursed a whiskey-colored drink, gaze darting between the two screens.

"Hey, girlie." Ned's customary greeting. "How's tricks?"

I slid onto a barstool, its unripped upholstery another sign of the building's new ownership, though the business itself still belonged to the Redaways. Impossible to think of this ancient watering hole in anyone else's hands.

"Good. J.D. around? Got a question for him."

"He'll be in later. He had to meet a guy out at—at his cabin." Ned unscrewed the cap on a bottle of Pellegrino and poured me a glass, a sure sign he wanted to talk. "You left a good thing in the city to come back to the family business. How'd you know that was what you wanted to do?"

The bubbles tickled my nose and throat. "I didn't, at first. Fresca had been dropping hints for a while, but I loved my job and I loved Seattle. But bit by bit, the stars lined up and pointed home."

The logjam above me on the corporate ladder. The guys who chose their careers over me. The friend who died and left me her cat. The landlord who threatened eviction over the lease prohibiting pets. One too many dark gray days.

He grunted. "Boy's got something on his mind he ain't telling me."

I reached across the bar and touched Ned's beefy paw. "You're worried that J.D.'s having second thoughts about the move. I don't think you need to be concerned. But I'll talk to him, if you want."

He reached for a clean towel, an excuse to hide his damp eyes. "I always say, you Murphy girls make this town what it is."

If there hadn't been a bar between us, I'd have kissed him.

Nick walked in the Merc's rear door as I walked in the front, and we met by the coat hooks in the back hall.

"From Kim." He bit off the words and thrust the white Festival notebook at me.

Old Ned had cheered me out of my bad mood. What would fix Nick's?

Nick disappeared into the basement. I headed next door.

Wendy angled a pan of cookies to give me a better view. Cookies shaped like Oscars and painted with scenes from movies. "For the contest at Cookie Con."

"Wow. You are a shoo-in."

She beamed and took my order.

Loot in hand, I trod down to Nick's lair. He sprawled in his chair, legs outstretched, arms and ankles crossed, his boots dripping melted snow on the rag rug.

His posture said, "Leave me alone," but I pushed my little-sister advantage. "Milk, sugar, and caffeine. The trifecta of comfort food."

He grunted and warmed his hands on the paper cup.

"Kim and Ike leaning on you?"

After a long moment and a tentative sip, he spoke. "They wanted to know more about the will, and whether I knew about it. I didn't. But there's no way I can prove that."

"Don't blame Kim. She takes her job seriously."

He jerked his head up and glared at me. "So do I and I don't care to have my commitment to it questioned."

I leaned against the labeling machine. "Nick, I know you weren't in the Jewel Saturday. Sounds like Kim knows it, too. They're talking to everyone who might have seen you, to Christine's neighbors, anyone who—"

He stood abruptly, cup in hand. "I need to check a report of an elk kill by Lake Kokanee." He reached back and snatched up the bag of cookies.

We're not kids anymore, Nick, I thought, watching him bound up the steps two at a time. *You can't hide in the woods until dinner and hope your mother's spaghetti makes all the bad things disappear.*

"Thanks, Kathy. Back before five, promise."

I tugged my stocking cap low, fired up Kathy Jensen's silver Honda, and followed Nick's green Jeep Cherokee out of the village. He did not turn north on the highway toward Lake Kokanee.

No. He drove south to Cutoff, then east. Toward Christine's. *Why, Nick, why?*

The unfamiliar car sped up too easily and I took my foot off the accelerator, swallowing the burst of fire in my chest. My knee struck the steering wheel and I winced, groping for the lever that would slide the seat back. Kept my eyes steeled on the road.

And why can't you tell me?

Mid-aft, mid-Feb, our highways don't get much traffic. I fell back, terrified that he'd recognize the borrowed car.

"Criminy." I'd left too much distance—he'd vanished. The road looked bare and dry, but where it winds above the river, mist can form black ice, even midday. I mentally rubbed my lucky stars and eased the Honda forward.

As I rounded the big curve by the Old Steel Bridge, I spotted taillights. Prayed Nick was too focused on his own plans to recognize me in his rearview mirror. Hoped the car ahead was Nick's.

Yes.

I kept that distance, my breath short and shallow, for another mile. The Jeep slowed as we neared Mountain View Road, in front of the church. "What are you up to?" I said out loud. If he turned, and I followed, he'd see me for sure.

He turned. I slowed, debating. An oncoming red Chevy pickup turned in front of me without signaling—a stupid driving trick that normally gets me boiling. Not this time.

Our unholy caravan, the unsuspecting truck driver my hero and shield, paraded past the church and cottage. The truck was hard to see around from my low seat. I leaned forward, peering through the fine mist of snow. The silver dragonfly pendant looped over the rearview mirror thwacked my forehead.

"Oww." I slowed involuntarily, hand to my hairline. Glanced in the mirror. No blood. Glanced back at the road. The truck had zoomed way ahead and I hoped hoped hoped that in my split-second distraction, I hadn't lost Nick. I edged across the center line—or my estimate of it, buried beneath hard-packed snow, and sighed in relief. The Jeep still led the way.

After another mile, the truck turned off. "Son of a buzzard." I dropped back and hunched low in the seat.

The road grew narrower, the ruts deeper. My shoulders tensed. I blasted the heater on full but my fingers still felt like frozen sausages. And if my jaw hadn't been clenched, my teeth would have rattled like a snake.

The dark green Jeep blended in with the trees as we wound past a dozen icy, rutted roads. No other traffic met us. Not even the mail carrier ventures out this way, the roads officially private, me officially trespassing. If I got too close, he'd spot me. But if I lost him, I'd never find him.

Not sure which was worse.

The rear wheels slipped as we rounded the corner near Phyl and Jo's. Maybe he'd think that's where I was going. If he even noticed the car behind him.

Not far beyond their place, the road forks. I muttered, peering over the dash to spot the freshest tire tracks.

The left fork. The end of the road for me—I didn't dare follow. Not in a borrowed car with front-wheel drive and without studded tires. I pulled into the wide spot at the end of the road, where swimmers and kayakers park. Rainbow Lake is small, just up from a pond. Shallow and warm in the summer, it rarely freezes over. But this was a rare winter.

I climbed out and picked my way over icy ruts to the water's edge. Along the shoreline, frozen cattails stood like wary sentinels.

Could I follow Nick on foot? I stretched one boot forward, testing the ice. It felt solid. But I suspected he'd taken an old logging road to the far side of the lake, where a few cabins stood on land leased from the state. Too far for me to go on foot, on ice.

A creaky branch broke the silence. I shielded my eyes, peering across the frozen water. A raven made slow, swooping circles above the far shore.

Why, Nick? Why?

I wrapped my arms around myself, finding no comfort.

Back in the Honda, I fed the engine gas. The rear wheels spun and went nowhere. I closed my eyes, conjuring up lessons from driver's ed. It had nearly been that long since I'd driven a front-wheel car in snow. *Backward, forward, rock it, slowly—sloooowly.*

Nothing.

Again. Twice more. Finally, the tires started to catch. I tossed a prayer to the goddesses who watch over snoopy little sisters and depressed the accelerator.

Whoosh. With a spit and sputter of frozen mud and snow loud enough to hear with the windows shut tight, the car rose and fell and shot out of its ruts, bouncing with a heavy metal thud. I braked quickly but carefully, to avoid the big spruce behind me.

And got the heck out of there.

I drove north, breathing deeply, shaking my head to clear the mental fog from my close call. Slowed at the sight of a woman crossing the road on foot. A stocky woman about my height in a bulky black coat and a green-and-orange knit hat, a multicolored pom-pom on top.

Phyl, cradling a critter that did not want to be held. I crept closer. A bony claw-foot poked out between her arms, and half a dozen reddish-brown feathers floated up and drifted off.

I rolled down the passenger-side window. The chicken's head popped up, her eyes dark and angry, and she let out a string of clucks.

"*Fowl*-mouthed thing," I said.

"She tried to cross the road," Phyl replied, and we both half died from laughing. Phyl hopped in the car. At the garden gate, she released the hen to the company of her friends and we clomped inside.

"What brings you out this way?" Jo put a plate of Scottish shortbread cookies on the table.

I warmed my hands on a cup of wild herb tea. No cover story in my pocket, and none sprouted to mind. We'd been so busy laughing on the short drive in that I hadn't thought to invent one.

But apparently the color on my cheeks wasn't all from the cold, and revealed me. An old boss of mine at SavClub had taken EST training in the early 1980s and often spoke of "enrolling" others to get them to help you solve a problem.

I made a quick decision. "You don't get into town much in the winter—"

"Or in summer," Jo said. "We let town come to us."

"But there's talk. Unpleasant talk. Iggy left almost everything to Christine, who left most of it to Nick. And there are people—some carrying badges—who think that smells funny. They—Nick and Christine—were engaged a while back, until she broke it off. But they were giving it another go."

Phyl and Jo watched me in silence, expressions somber.

"It makes no sense to think he killed her. He loved her. He didn't know about the money, and he wouldn't have cared anyway. And he just wouldn't do that." A giant balloon of anxiety seemed to fill my chest and choke off my oxygen supply. The women's faces gave away nothing. "What worries me is . . . when I realized something was wrong at Christine's, I called him to find out where she kept her spare key. He said he was in the Jewel, checking on wolves. There's no way to confirm that—it was snowing like crazy and his tracks would have filled in before nightfall. But you saw him down here Saturday morning. Miles from the Jewel."

I paused, my breath ragged. "And he's down here again today, out at Rainbow Lake. Which is not where he said he was going when he left the shop."

"So you followed him," Phyl said. "Wondered why you had Kathy's car."

"It's one thing to not tell me the truth. But it's another

to lie to law enforcement. How can he not know the trouble that could cause?" Phyl and Jo make a habit of respecting privacy. If you've got a secret you really need to keep, but you really want to get it off your chest, tell one of them. They might tell each other, but beyond that, only the goats and chickens would ever catch wind.

And here I was asking them to tell me my brother's business. Beneath the table, I swiped my thumb across my wrist.

In a distant room, a cuckoo clock rang the hour. In the garden, a hen clucked and another responded. Outside, fat snowflakes filled the sky.

"We've been seeing Nick drive by for a few weeks," Phyl finally said. "Early, when we go out to feed the animals and gather eggs."

"But we don't know where he's going," Jo said. "Or why."

What else did I need to know? "So he heads out before dawn," I said, hooking my thumb toward the lake. "And when does he come back, toward town?"

"Early afternoon," Phyl said. "Like on Saturday. 'Course, now we know, Saturday, he was going to Christine's, 'cause you called."

Jo cocked her head. "First time we saw him was that morning after we heard the ruckus in the chicken coop. We were in and out all night, didn't sleep a wink."

"No sign of the usual foxes, and the grizzlies are hibernating. I could swear I heard a wolf howl."

"Half past six, we saw lights on the road. Southbound, remember?" Jo continued. "We thought it was odd."

Odd, yes. And a wolf? "When Kim came by, making her rounds, I expect you told her you saw Nick on Saturday?"

They nodded. The implications were clear. She knew he'd lied. She had his phone. If they got his phone records, could they pinpoint where he'd been when he got my call?

And what else could they figure out? Could they tell

whether he'd doubled back to the church, killed Christine, then snuck out to the woods? If I left my phone on and lost it, I could ping it and dig it out of the laundry basket or trace it to a shelf in the Merc where I'd set it down while showing off jam flavors or restocking the coffee display.

I tucked my worries away while I navigated the twists and turns of the road home. It felt like driving inside a giant snow globe shaken by an unseen hand. You'd think wildlife would stay home curled in front of their own fires during a snowstorm, but no. Like Phyl and Jo's wayward chicken, deer often roam during unsettled weather, making narrow, slippery roads even more treacherous.

A squirrel darted in front of me and I slowed to let him cross safely. That reminded me of Sandburg and Pumpkin, relegated to separate quarters. With Bozo ill and aging, Tracy would not want to take on a new cat, and Phyl and Jo had a full complement of house and barn cats. Kathy had a sweet Siamese who was probably no more interested in adopting a sibling than Sandburg was. Who else? I knew better than to ask Chiara, and Heidi had acted like I'd lost my marbles.

Near Cutoff and the church property, the sky darkened and the snow became harder, sleetier, pelting the windshield. I flicked the wipers to high.

And cursed when the right blade flew off the car and vaulted over the borrow pit into a snowy field. If I could find it, maybe I could reattach it—driving all the way back to the village without it would be nearly impossible.

Take it from me, it ain't easy to find an eighteen-inch-long slice of black rubber in a snowbank, an occasional fencepost warning me of barbed wire. I spotted the blade poking up between two piles left by a plow and was staggering toward them when a raspy voice stopped me.

"Not one more step."

Off-balance in the deep snow, I turned my head slowly. Jack Frost, in brown Carhartts and a ball cap, stood in a narrow lane, freshly plowed, holding a shotgun.

A minor blessing: It wasn't pointed at me. But his face said one wrong move, one wrong word, and it would be.

"Sign says NO TRESPASSING. Don't you read?"

Disoriented by the snow and flat light, I'd wandered into the back lane leading to his place. I raised my gloved hands. "Jack. So sorry. Wiper blade flew off and in this storm, gotta have it." I pointed to the blade, jutting out of a snow pile beyond my reach.

Frost jerked the blade free and flung it toward me. It dropped between us like a broken boomerang, and I squinted, afraid to move, while snow stabbed my cheeks. He lurched forward, grabbed the thing, and thrust it at me.

"Next time, I won't be so nice."

The threat in his words barely registered. I was too focused on his cap and its logo: a circle of red on a white background, a slash across the outline of a wolf's head.

· Fourteen ·

The wheel rattled—from the rutted ice or my shaking hands—as I turned onto the highway, speeding away from Jack Frost.

My eyes blinked in astonishment. The snowstorm had stopped. The wind that had stung my eyes had torn open the clouds and light streamed onto the forested hillsides and danced on the mountain peaks. The horizon shimmered, a patchwork quilt of dappled greens, rippling blues, and silky browns, stitched in gold and silver.

My mother had drilled into me the credo that you never return anything in worse condition than when you borrowed it, so I pulled into the gas station. Yanked the hose over the back of the car and jammed the nozzle in—the tank is always on the wrong side on other people's cars—and waved at the UPS driver. Walked inside, clutching the busted wiper blade.

And ran smack into Ike Hoover. The hot coffee he held splashed onto his bare hand and down his brown wool shirt.

"No problem," he said, tugging a napkin from a nearby dispenser and sponging up the mess. I might have come back later if I'd seen the sheriff's rig but the UPS van had blocked my view. Ike nodded toward the broken blade. "Need a hand?"

Kim emerged from between the aisles carrying a Coke, the station owner puffing up behind her.

"Hot on the trail, investigating that poor girl's murder? Sure hope you nail the SOB. Sally says—" The owner's ears reddened, leaving little doubt she'd been about to regurgitate nasty rumors about Nick.

The wiper blade emergency had forced me into the hornet's nest of Gossip Central, its owner the undeclared queen of the faction that regularly rails against village shopkeepers for our snootiness, putting on festivals that bring people downtown, and ignoring the highway merchants.

Nobody ever threw a party for unleaded gas and expected presents.

"This one oughta fit." Ike held up a yellow box and headed out to my car. Kathy's car. I trotted after him. As undersheriff, Ike oversaw all felony investigations. He had a much-lauded solve rate, but I knew one unsolved case haunted him: The death of my father in a hit-and-run on the bridge, where Jewel Bay flows into Eagle Lake. Two weeks from today, it would be fifteen years.

Whether out of guilt or inherent kindness, Ike often shows unexpected tenderness toward me and my mother. My brother and sister had rushed home from college, but after those first anguished days, it had been our grief-stained faces searching his for answers when he came to the Orchard to report on the investigation. And my grandfather's. A vibrant man in his late seventies then, losing his oldest son took more out of him than the cancer death of his wife a few years earlier.

If only that sense of guilt prompted Ike to think twice—or thrice—before accusing Nick of murder.

"Fits. There you go." Ike slapped the box into my palm. "Now, away from prying ears, tell me why you look like the hounds are on your tail."

"Oh, uh, just a little run-in with Jack Frost. Not exactly a threat, in so many words, but . . ."

"In exactly what words, and don't leave any out." Ike leaned against Kathy's car, not seeming to care about the muck rubbing off onto his uniform. Notebook in hand, Kim listened intently.

Fear had imprinted the details, though Frost's words sounded less threatening now than they had at the time. "You're going to tell me it's nothing, he's harmless."

"I wouldn't go that far," Ike said. "No crime in what you've reported, but watch your step."

"Is he a suspect? You talked to the neighbors—you know he was livid over Christine's plans for the property."

"Can't tell you that," he said. Which was as good as saying yes.

I swirled spit inside my dry mouth, hoping they wouldn't ask why I'd gone out that way. Or guess that I was trying to confirm Nick's faulty alibi.

I gestured toward the convenience store. "What rumors is the Gossip Queen spreading now? Trash talk from Sally Grimes?"

"You can guess," Ike said. "What's the story between your family and hers?"

"Sally's? There is no story. She resents Nick's inheritance, and Christine's before that. She feels hurt and she's lashing out at Nick. The last thing my brother cares about is money."

Ike's steady gaze unnerved me. So did his words. "Is that true, Erin? He doesn't get university funding. He relies on grants. That inheritance would pay for a lot of research."

"How can you—? You don't think—?" Jolted, I turned from Ike to Kim, who'd known Nick as long as she'd known me. She fought visibly to relax her frozen features, to act as if Ike's words hadn't shocked her, too.

I wanted to jump in the car and speed away. I wanted to puke. "Haven't you learned yet, Ike? I know things about this town you'll never know. You need me." I brandished the wiper blade box and stalked away.

Inside, I dug in my pockets for cash. Threw it on the counter and ignored the two cents change the silent woman laid on the scratched laminate. I glanced outside furtively. Kim's hand chopped the air, her back to me as she lectured Ike.

I took refuge in the women's room.

When I raised my wet face from the sink, Kim handed me a paper towel. Our eyes met in the mirror. "You know better, Kim. Can't you set him straight?"

"*You* know better, Erin. You know we have to look at everyone. Follow the evidence."

I spun halfway, facing her. "So the ravings of a bitter, jealous woman are evidence? Sally always says she never makes any money. She wants to challenge Iggy's will. Suppose she confronted Christine and shot her?"

But Sally had been at her shop Saturday morning. I'd seen her myself. Seen her making googly eyes at Larry in her doorway.

Then the thing I should have said to Ike occurred to me. "Wait a sec. Everybody knows a killer can't inherit from his victim. If there's no other motive, then money doesn't make sense."

"Motive isn't evidence, Erin."

I stared at her. "You have evidence you're not telling me about. Besides . . ."

"Besides what?"

But I couldn't say it. I couldn't help Nick further the lie that he'd spent the day tracking wolves. Because I no longer believed it. "Motive may not be evidence, but evidence can be misinterpreted. Evidence doesn't explain why." I reached past her to stuff the damp towels in the overflowing wastebasket.

"Always asking why. Murder never means anything, Erin. That's for books and philosophers, and Pollyannas who try to see a lesson in every bad thing. Don't go all Pollyanna. It doesn't suit you."

"How do you know what suits me? When my father was killed, you dropped me like a hot rock. Ever since I came back, you can hardly stand to be around me. We go riding, but half the time you drum up some excuse to skip out. You play pool with the rest of us, but you stand apart, acting superior because you're a deputy sheriff or a Caldwell or whatever you think you are." I ripped the words out of my throat, hot and sharp, knowing I might regret them later and not caring.

The cool blonde in front of me, in her navy blue pantsuit and her stylish boots and her expensive wool coat, turned to ice. "You. Don't. Know."

Then she was gone and I sank back against the sink, drained. Why bad stuff happens to good people, the eternal question. Fifteen years later and I still felt wounded by Kim's desertion, the night of our senior year when I lost my father and my best friend. I'd thought the two were connected, but it turned out only time linked them. The real explanation had been teenage jealousy, that a lucky streak on the back of a horse had given me the rodeo crown she'd coveted. Then I left for college in Missoula and later moved to Seattle, and a chink that might have mended with time and proximity became a chasm.

I've thought a lot, over the years, about crime and meaning. My father's death may have been an accident, but it was also a crime—and every member of my family its victim.

It didn't happen to teach me a lesson. It didn't happen to make me more grateful for being his kid, or to teach me to love my family, or any of the other Hallmark sayings people fall back on. It didn't happen to make us more careful drivers, or prompt us to "live life to the fullest."

It happened because some creephole had gone too fast on the icy bridge, striking my dad's car and sending it spinning until it smashed into the guardrail so hard the impact killed him.

Kim had it wrong. I wasn't looking for meaning. I was looking for an explanation. For someone to take responsibility.

Not the same thing.

And I wasn't going to stop. Someone out there knew what had happened to Christine. I couldn't pretend Nick wasn't acting oddly, but while Kim and Ike were busy pinning murder on him, I would suss out the real explanation.

Because it's the people who believe in us, who believe in justice, who give life and all that happens meaning.

The voices in my mind nattered on as I drove into the village. They harangued me as I parked Kathy's car and trudged my way to Dragonfly. They did not shut up as I plopped her keys onto her cutting counter.

I told the voices to stuff it and put on my retail face. Kathy wasn't fooled—she rarely is—but she said nothing, her eyes flickering to the open classroom at the front of the shop. Six or eight women chatted while twisting crochet hooks around what appeared to be plastic bags. A woman who taught needlework moved around the circle, giving pointers.

"Upcycling," Kathy said. "Tell me about the tea shop prospect."

"You know, I started to think maybe these people are right, maybe Jewel Bay *is* too small for one more restaurant, one more food lovers' shop, but if those women can crochet plastic bags, anything's possible."

The instructor called for her students' attention and demonstrated a finishing technique. I recognized her as one of the women-about-town who make a part-time career out of retail. A woman who might work Tuesdays at the kitchen shop and fill in on Thursdays at the quilt shop, help out at a gallery one summer, and pitch in for the antique dealer next. Cheery and chatty, they work as much for fun and to keep busy as for income.

I might need one of them soon myself, if the Merc kept growing. Especially if Tracy left to start her own shop—a prospect so distressing it gave me night sweats in midday.

"Crochet teacher working for you this summer?" No poaching, an unwritten rule. At least not from a friend.

"I asked, but she's already committed to work for Sally. She rescheduled this group from last Saturday, to fill in there. Your sister's been taking the class, but she's working today."

What? Two surprises. I'd been in the children's shop last Saturday. Had seen Sally.

Had she hired help and snuck out to the church?

Was she a serious suspect after all?

"Kath, you're on the Art Center board, right? You and Larry and I don't know who else."

She murmured agreement, her capable hands rewinding scarlet yarn into a skein.

"The board was talking with Christine about a donation." Christine had told me so, but I wanted corroboration. Ike insinuated motive for murder in his belief that Nick needed money.

Kathy's fingers and wrists bent this way and that. "We were. It's a great collection. Right up our alley—art and artifacts from western Montana, mainly early twentieth century. A few came from the Ring family."

"So where did things stand when Christine died?"

She tucked in a tail of yarn and dropped the skein into a basket on the counter. "We were searching for funding to beef up our security system. Theft is a chronic problem for small museums and it's getting worse. She was supposed to finish the inventory Iggy started, but it was a daunting task. We couldn't get an appraisal until then."

She raised her eyes to mine, not saying what we were both thinking. *If Nick got to decide what happened to her money . . . If Nick hadn't killed her.*

"Thanks for lending me the car. I replaced your wiper blades—don't ask." I waved farewell as she raised her eyebrows and reached for another pile of yarn.

Outside, the sunshine had disappeared. I shivered, my skin raw from the strain of investigating, of putting on a brave face, of acting as if everything was okay when it absolutely, one-hundred percent was not okay.

Get over it, Erin. You can't sell soap and salami, let alone pasta and pickles, if you let the sourness seep into you, too. And you can't sell the village to prospective merchants and restaurateurs if you don't truly believe.

Worse, how could I keep living here myself, if Jewel Bay no longer felt like everything I wanted it to be?

· *Fifteen* ·

I dashed back to the Merc and found my mother and Candy Divine unpacking bags of handmade cinnamon gummy hearts, marshmallows, and heart-shaped lollipops. Candy's sweaterdress-and-leggings combo contrasted with my mother's red Keds and veggie-print apron. Pink fluff and practical chic.

"Let's display the candy next to the cherry wine and chocolates," Fresca said. "Not-so-subtle suggestions for Valentine's Day."

"Mom. Sorry." I paused to catch my breath. So much for thinking myself organized, efficient, and considerate. "Emergency. I meant to get back here before Tracy left for the vet, but I got caught up and completely forgot."

"That's all right, darling." She continued arranging bags and bottles, her tight lips indicating the displeasure she would not voice in front of someone not part of the family. *Lucky me.*

"Nick here? I need to talk to him."

Fresca opened her mouth, then closed it, exhaling

loudly. "Candy, dear, make a little tower of those marsh-mallow blocks of yours." She grabbed my arm and jerked me into the kitchen, out of earshot.

"I don't know what you're up to, you or your brother. You've both been treating this shop like a train station, stomping in and out and dashing off without a word. You wanted to run this business without my interference and I gave you my blessing, but if you don't start remembering that you have a shop to run and people counting on you, I'll—"

"Auntie! Noni!" The front door chimed and little snow boots pounded across the weathered plank floor.

Saved by a five-year-old.

I kissed Fresca's cheek. "You're right. I promise I'll do better. Landon!" I scooped him up. "What are you wearing?"

"I'm a teenager," he said. "From my mom's gallery."

I squinted, then laughed. If you say "teenage ninja turtle" too fast, it does sound like "teenager." A red band around his emerald green crocheted cap led to two red tails, tied in back in a warrior's knot. Best of all: the eye holes, giant red frames that came halfway down his cheeks.

"That is brilliant." I set him down. Ninja turtles get heavy. "Is she making them?"

"You'd know that if you were paying more attention to your family instead of running around doing heaven knows what."

"Point made, Mom. Truce?"

A quick nod. "It's almost closing time. I'll finish up down here. You probably have phone calls and Twitter-Face. Oh, that's right. No one calls anymore. They text."

Which reminded me. "Fingers crossed for a confirmation that the movie shipped."

"*Chocolat*? I have a copy. You can use mine."

"Won't do. It's got to be HD, super-duper, I don't know what all. Not your basic home DVD. But thanks, Mom. Thanks, Candy. Landon, how about a marshmallow heart?" He picked a white marshmallow square, a red heart stenciled on top. I offered the bag to Fresca, who chose a pink heart, then headed up to my office.

Mom's right about texting, but sometimes only the phone will do.

"Hey, Jason. Got a moment? I've got questions." A computer geek brother-in-law is a great asset to any small-business manager, especially a snoopy one.

"You're partly right," he said after listening to my half-formed questions. "They use the pings off the towers, then triangulate to identify the general location."

"How general?" I dropped math for drama senior year, but it didn't take an in-depth knowledge of calculus to add up big trouble. "And what about that app or whatever it is that says—well, I turned it off because it got annoying, but if you post on Facebook from your phone, it says you were at Caffe Dolce in Missoula and you ordered the mozzarella and tomato panino with artichoke spread and a double latte. Or if you lose your phone, or it gets stolen, you can track it down."

"Two different technologies," he said. "And there are other factors to consider." Jason has a gift for explaining complicated matters simply, but in seconds, I was as lost as the hypothetical phone—SIM cards, raw radio data, real-time only, blah blah blah. My brain was too busy worrying whether Nick was in more trouble than I'd thought, or less.

"Bottom line is," he said, "with the records, they can tell where you were from the calls you made and received. My guess is, it's pretty accurate in the city, where there are more towers, but it gets tricky in the mountains. But they can't track your movements without a special device. I gotta run, but I think for the sake of my marriage that I will completely forget we had this call."

"We haven't talked since Sunday," I said. "And thanks."

I stared at the wall. Fired up the laptop. Swiveled my second-hand chair, thinking. Stopped, as my eye fell on the piece I'd bought from Christine at the Art Fair last summer, lime green and purple letters stenciled on a background spattered in yellow, orange, red, purple, and green:

DREAM
CREATE
SNICKER
DOODLE

I whipped back to the desk and opened the Spreadsheet. Now I knew that Nick had not been in the Jewel Basin when Christine was attacked, but at Rainbow Lake. Kim and Ike knew it, too—no doubt the phone records confirmed what the witnesses had said.

Zayda had been at home, a mile or two north, and on the scene minutes before Christine's death. And she'd lied about it, until forced to admit that was her eyebrow stud found under Christine's body.

Labels above the columns read MOTIVE, MEANS, OPPORTUNITY, and WHEREABOUTS. Or, in my computer shorthand: WHABOUTS. I added one: SECRETS. In Zayda's row, I wrote, "Hiding??? What??? Who???"

In Nick's Whabouts, I struck out Jewel Basin and added Rainbow Lake. In the Secrets column, "Why lie?" Under Motive, "Money?"

Jack Frost. Motive? To stop Christine, but from what? The neighborhood cleanup? The art school? I made a note to ask Nick more about Christine's plans for the property. Means? A guy who put up signs bragging about his guns and confronts an accidental trespasser with one—yeah, a meanie with means.

Not to mention opportunity. He lived next door. He'd been leaning on a fencepost when Nick and I came out of the fire hall. Where had he been when the attack occurred?

Secrets? If he grew pot, wouldn't he be extra careful not to bring the sheriff calling? Had he feared Christine's plans would somehow lead to his discovery?

Reason to kill? Maybe.

Next, Sally Grimes. Sally Sourpuss. What did a smart, successful, civic-oriented man like Larry Abrams see in her?

"Oh, what a gift the giftee give us, to see ourselves as others see us." Robbie Burns's words could be spun the other way as well: A good investigator needs to see people as they see themselves.

Or, as one of my management professors used to say, no one is a jerk in his own mind.

Ike had quizzed me about the history between Sally and my family, and I'd been certain that there wasn't one. Was that true? I'd never bothered to wonder what motivated her. What she cared about. I hadn't looked past her whining and complaining and petty jealousies to consider the woman herself.

How to summarize all that on a spreadsheet? Under Motive, I wrote, "Resentment, will, money." But no opportunity—not until I knew for sure where Sally had been last Saturday.

Means. Much as I disliked Sally, it was nearly impossible to imagine her shooting someone.

Which for no obvious reason reminded me of the White Queen telling Alice she'd believed in as many as six impossible things before breakfast.

But a bigger question lurked. Why had Iggy left Sally out of her will?

I'd been wondering whether Sally's anger stemmed from need, or a sense of being cast aside. Or worse: treated as she deserved?

There is the family you're born into and the family you choose. Some people aren't as lucky as I am.

Adam's call last night had interrupted my online research into my brother's professional pursuits and squabbles. I glanced at the time and headed downstairs.

Fresca had just locked the front door.

"Thanks for stepping in, Mom. Did you hear from Tracy, about Bozo?"

"You're welcome, darling. Half an hour with Candy Divine is more than enough to make me appreciate how much you've done here." She smiled weakly. Candy gave me a sugar headache, too, but her confections had proven unexpectedly popular. "Tracy called. Bill's remedies are easing the pain. I told her not to worry, do what she needs to do to take care of her baby."

"Perfect."

Fresca left. Back upstairs, I returned to my chair, my questions, and my research. First, property tax records. Turned out Sally owned the building housing Puddle Jumpers, the florist next door, and a trio of second-floor offices. My eyes widened at the assessed property value. It backs up to Jewel Bay, but a greenbelt easement created years ago means hefty taxes with no option for developing the waterfront. But the rentals should make the expenses affordable.

According to the records, she also owned a good-sized house on half an acre in a subdivision south of town, again with a healthy property value. I'd always assumed her money gripes were exaggerated—what my grandfather called poor-mouthing—but based on reality. Retail isn't easy. Now I didn't know what to think.

Especially when I scrolled further. Unless another Sarah Marler Grimes was also a local land baron, Sally held title to two parcels on Main Street in Pondera. Primo downtown property.

I expanded my search across western Montana. She owned half a city block in Libby, and parcels in Thompson Falls, Plains, and Superior.

In Missoula, she owned one downtown building and property in a popular residential neighborhood called the Rattlesnake. College friends of mine had lived on the same street. I found the house on Google Earth. The block had improved considerably since my student days. I searched the address to find the occupants' names: N. and S. Flynn. Her daughter and family?

Dang. Sally's daughter had been a couple of years behind me in high school. *What is her name?*

I clicked a few more keys. Sally was not on Facebook. Puddle Jumpers had a page that said little beyond the location and hours. I clicked on the photos.

Bingo, to quote my buddy Ned. Several pictures showed Sally beside a young woman who shared her features and held a beautifully dressed baby girl. I clicked and found the tags: Mom, me, Olivia. So, Sally's daughter had posted the pics. I'd never seen her and baby Olivia around.

The picture—uploaded more than a year ago—was the last update.

What had happened?

Dumbfounded, I crossed my arms and leaned back. How had Sally gotten all that real estate? Not by selling onesies and stick horses. Inheritance?

Was that how she knew about challenging wills? Plenty of folks are land rich and cash poor, but from the locations, I guessed most of these were prime commercial rentals.

I peered at the photos more closely. Sally's features, softer than I had ever seen, radiated pure love.

That, I realized, *is what Sally would kill for.*

Had I stumbled onto the reason for her anger at being left out of Iggy's will? The loss of the chance to pass Iggy's assets—family assets, in a spiderwebby way—to her daughter and granddaughter?

It didn't seem possible.

I scrolled back through my spreadsheet. None of it seemed possible.

Time for a lesson from the White Queen.

· Sixteen ·

"We have to talk. Now."

"Can't." One arm in his coat sleeve, Nick tossed the word over his shoulder. "Gotta grab a bite, then get back to work. Galley proofs due on a critical habitat study jammed with stats."

"Then you've got company for dinner."

Five minutes later, we sat nursing beers and waiting on burgers and fries at Red's. Nick had started to grab a seat at the bar, but I led him to the Greenhouse, Ned's name for a glassed-in nook off the main seating area. Midwinter, the occasional chilly draft keeps the nook's tall tables and stools private.

And as Jason says, when a Murphy girl wants to talk, nothing short of a dentist's drill will stop her.

"Look, I know you feel guilty about this inheritance," I said. Nick's chin rose and his hands squeezed the glass of Eagle Lake Stout. "I also know you've never taken town gossip seriously." He shifted uncomfortably on the stool, staring into the dark, bitter beer.

"Listen, Nick. This time is different. It's life and death. Literally." I leaned forward, forcing him to look at me. "They're saying the money gives you motive—"

"But I didn't know." He spoke through clenched teeth, his voice low, urgent.

"We can't prove that. And you walking around with your head sunk into your shoulders, staring at the ground when old friends offer sympathy, makes it worse. Acting guilty raises people's suspicions." The line between grief and guilt is a faint shadow.

"People?" His tone was dismissive. "You mean Sally Grimes."

"And others. I'm hearing the talk all over town. So is Mom. And Ike Hoover is listening."

Mouth open, he exhaled heavily and ran a hand through his shaggy hair.

"Here's my plan. Got any big grants you're ready to make public, to show you don't need her money for your research?"

"I wish."

"Then the best way to prove yourself a man of goodwill— and make your case for innocence, without saying a word to dignify ridiculous accusations—is charity." Nick tilted his head, not understanding. I forged on. "Christine planned to give most of Iggy's collection to the Art Center, right? The Russell and Remington statues. The Ace Powell paintings."

"And the Winold Reiss portraits." A German artist best known in these parts for his paintings of Glacier National Park and the Blackfeet Indians, commissioned by the Great Northern Railway for its advertising calendars. Intact calendars are as valuable as the original paintings— or more.

"Perfect. The Art Center's mission includes showcasing the art of the Park. So you go talk to the board. Say you'll carry out her intentions. Tell them you want the news to go public now, to reassure the community that the pieces will stay here. Oh, I know!" My hands flew up in excitement and I nearly smacked a burger basket out of J.D.'s grasp. "The Merc and the Murphy family will sponsor the opening exhibit and a public reception. And in a corner, we set up a display explaining your work."

Nick leaned back, eyes gleaming, as J.D. gauged the zone of safety. "Little sister, that is brilliant."

I beamed, glancing from my dark-haired brother to our redheaded bartender.

"Hey, J.D. Got a sec?" I said.

He set our burgers and fries on the table and wiped his big hands on his apron. "Gramps said you were asking for me."

"Last Friday, when we were shooting pool, Jack Frost was sitting at the bar. Christine came out of the women's room and Frost said something to her. A sharp exchange, if I read it right."

"You think he killed her? Gramps said you—well, he said you have a knack for asking the right questions." He flushed. He hadn't been here for last summer's tragedies, and if I read his face right, he'd been momentarily excited at the prospect of being involved in an investigation, until he remembered what we were investigating.

"Thanks. Just trying to piece together her last twenty-four hours. Anything you remember could be helpful."

"It was weird. He comes in regularly, and he's mouthy, but . . ."

"What did he say?"

J.D. scrunched up his face. "He started it, but he had his back to me, so I didn't hear. And Friday nights are noisy. I think she said something like 'out of my hands.' If that makes any sense. Pissed him off royally. Downed his drink and stomped out the back door."

To avoid Christine? Frost had come in the front. Though Nick had grown incredibly still, I saw wheels spinning behind his eyes. "Thanks, J.D. Hey, I hope you're happy in Jewel Bay. Not having any second thoughts."

Behind his stubbly beard, the six-foot redhead turned pensive. "It's—been interesting." He glanced at Nick. "A few surprises, but no, no second thoughts."

Surprises? That involved Nick? Before I could ask, my brother spoke. "I'll take another beer." J.D. gave a mock salute and spun away.

"Frost," he said the moment J.D. left. "Now I'm convinced. Had to be him."

I squirted mustard next to my fries. "Seriously? Over art classes?"

"Her vision had evolved way beyond that. She was planning to build cabins in the woods and expand the kitchen in the church basement, so she could offer year-round retreats and summer camps for adults. Like the Jazz Festival and Workshop, but for painters and potters."

Another festival that Sally, the gas station owner, and their ilk had contended we didn't need—until they discovered that amateur musicians and concertgoers spend hundreds of thousands of dollars on food, gas, and other goods and services.

I took a long sip of my beer, letting the slightly bitter taste roll around my mouth. "Does—did—she have enough land for that? Was she trying to buy some of his? He's pretty protective of that property." I described my encounter with Frost, leaving out the part about trailing Nick to Rainbow Lake. Had that been just this afternoon?

A fry midway to his mouth, Nick looked at me as if deciding what to say.

I beat him to it. "Don't say it. I'll be careful. And don't you go confronting him, either. Back to the Art Center donation. I've been working with Larry Abrams on the Film Festival, and he's on the board, plus boards of half a dozen other museums. Kathy said he was working on finding an appraiser. Let me talk to him."

Nick reached for the ketchup. "That might be jumping the gun. I promise, I'll talk to Bill."

"You talking to him about the will and Sally's threats to challenge it?" Nice to have a lawyer in the clan, even if he only practices on us.

His hand stopped midair. The bottle burped and spit all over his plate. "Murphy's Law," he muttered, then swiped a fry through a pool of ketchup that had settled on a pickle.

"Hey, you Murphys." Kyle Caldwell kissed my cheek and held out a hand to Nick, who waved messy red fingers. Kyle grinned. "You guys won't believe this. You remember Danny Davis, the other night? I told him about my GTO being in the kids' documentary. He called it a piece of junk. Scrap. On the way out, he said I should sell it and get a real car. Now he's called me up. Offered me twenty grand."

"Holy cow. Is it worth that much?" To Nick, cars were transportation, nothing more.

"Maybe he wants to use it to advertise his rental biz." That was how we had met, or remet, last summer, over a scratched fender.

"Way more than that, if I get it running smooth again. Even without the original paint. I told Kim—she 'bout popped an eyeball. She can't fathom me doing anything right." A dark-haired woman rapped on the other side of the glass and held up a pool cue. "My turn. See you guys later."

We ate in silence, Nick using half the napkins in the holder and washing down the excess ketchup with his stout. But I didn't grow up in the same house as a sensitive artist and a brooding biologist without developing a decent sense of intuition.

"Okay. Out with it," I said. He flashed me the face of a kid caught stealing cookies ten minutes before dinner. "What else is on your mind?"

He swallowed before answering. "Umm, well, yeah. The lawyer said I could start cleaning out the cottage and church. So, meet me there in the morning? I have to check my packs first, but we can clean out the fridge, sort the papers—bank statements, mail. And go through her clothes. Take whatever you want, donate the rest."

"Her stuff will fit Chiara better than me, but sure. I'll help. Ten thirty? After we get the Merc open."

"Good. She can sort the art supplies."

"Settled, then." But not in my mind. A guy who wears the same pants six and a half days a week—seven, if he isn't going to his mother's for Sunday dinner—anxious to clean out his dead girlfriend's closets?

Something's rotten in the state of Denmark, as Hamlet's buddy said when the dead king's ghost beckoned.

Something besides Nick's socks.

"**Y**ou text, I deliver. Hey, boy." I couldn't see around the giant box of chocolate in my arms, but the click of dog nails on the tile in Tracy's entry told me Bozo was up and at 'em.

"Hooray! Did you imagine how many extra orders we'd get for Valentine's Day? Not to mention the movie candy."

The aroma of warm, sweet chocolate drew me to the kitchen. Notes of vanilla and ginger, and a sharp-but-fruity hint of chili. "I hate to say this, but you need to work in a certified kitchen."

"I know." Her fingers wiggled beneath her chestnut ponytail and massaged the base of her skull. Today's earrings: silver and turquoise feathers. "Just this once, so I can keep an eye on him." Two chairs blocked the entry to her cramped kitchen. Bozo curled up against the makeshift barrier, his giant black-and-white head on his paws.

I set the box on the counter. "How's he doing?"

"Better. For now." Her forehead rose in soft wrinkles and she rubbed her left eyebrow. "But I think we're talking Rainbow Bridge before long."

"Oh, sweetie. I'm sorry."

She bit her lip and nodded quickly, then reached for a knife to slit the box open. Chocolate, the ultimate distraction. I peered inside, mouth watering. Pounds and pounds of rich Belgian chocolate. *Couverture*—both milk and dark—for dipping and coating. Chocolate for ganache, the rich dense filling I adore. White chocolate for accents and cocoa powder for dusting. And bags of nibs. Tracy sliced one open, spilled a quarter cup into a small bowl, and set it on the counter between us.

"Mmm." A few bits of the fermented, dried, and roasted cacao beans were plenty. No sugar meant they were almost bitter. Crunchy and complex, with notes of dark cherry. "What are you doing with the nibs?"

"Wendy's using them as garnish on the chocolate torte at Chez Max, and on her amazing dried cherry brownies. I've started mixing them into ganache for a super chocolaty filling. These truffles—" she gestured toward a covered tray on her dining room table—"are garnished with a combination of crystallized ginger and candied nibs."

"Are nibs what Kyle uses in his steak gravy?" The secret ingredient that fools everyone.

"Yep. I'm also using them in this great recipe for cocoa. You make it in a French press. Rick loves it." She blushed sweetly, swinging from impending loss to new love. "Want a cup?"

I sat at the counter while Tracy chopped nibs, heated milk, and readied the press. Loaded trays covered every surface, protected from dog hair and other detritus by plastic wrap. "Truffles always remind me of Iggy."

Nice going, Murphy, I told myself as Tracy swallowed back tears. I snaked a finger under a bit of plastic and snared one dusted in yellow—ginger? I bit in. "Chocolate and lavender, but what else? Weird, but good."

"Lavender and chamomile rolled in bee pollen. I got the idea from your tea blends. Bill gave me the pollen when he treated the dog."

"Sage. That's Sally Grimes's daughter's name. You know her?"

Tracy swished hot water in two mugs and set them on the counter. "No. But last summer, when Iggy was still dropping by for truffles, she said Sally was going to lose her daughter if she didn't watch out. Apparently, Sally didn't approve of the husband and would only see Sage and the baby without him. So Sage stopped coming up and refused to let Sally visit them in Missoula."

Where they lived in a house Sally owned, if I'd guessed right. "Let's hope Larry can talk sense into her. He's good with the high school kids. I mean, Sally may be right about the husband, but you can't try to control a grown kid like that." Not that plenty of parents don't try.

Tracy strained the hot nib-milk mixture into the French press, then gave the hot cocoa a quick stir, licked the spoon, and tossed it into the white porcelain sink where it clattered. "Maybe. Iggy didn't think much of him. Larry, I mean."

"Why? They both loved Western art."

"I dunno." She slowly pumped the plunger. Thick, choco-laty bubbles filled the glass pot. "Something about pieces he thought she should sell but she wasn't sure. That's all I know."

We carried our mugs of frothy cocoa into the living room, Bozo trailing behind. Tracy had kept the house when her former husband moved on, and I knew the payments were a stretch. Handmade truffles and dog biscuits might be just the ticket to a little financial freedom. Her cheap-chic shopping habits extended to the decor as well, and I settled into a wing-back chair she'd rescued from the dump and re-covered with burlap coffee sacks. Surprisingly not scratchy, their aroma sent me to the jungle—in my mind.

"Ahhh." The first sip went down sweet and smooth. Liquid heaven. "Rick has good taste."

Tracy colored. Her first serious relationship since her divorce.

"Don't be embarrassed," I said. "I saw it coming. You two are much better suited than he and I."

She bent to scratch behind Bozo's floppy black ear. "He's coming over this weekend for the Film Festival."

"Great. Trace, you may not have thought this far ahead—" *Fat chance. Every woman thinks this far ahead.* "And I don't mean to put you on the spot, but I'm thinking about the shop and summer and . . ." My turn to go red.

"Oh, no," she said, her voice firm. "Don't you worry. I moved three times when Mitch got itchy feet, always thinking the grass was greener and the fish bigger someplace else. I'm never moving for a man again." She cradled the mug close to her face. "But I won't have·to. If it works out, Rick can work from Jewel Bay as easily as from the farm."

True enough. Modern technology had expanded the range of work-from-home jobs, a huge boost for Montana's economy. And for those who'd rather not wear shoes on the job.

"Good. I've also been wondering if—well, if you're going to want to start your own chocolate shop. I mean, if it's what you want, great. Go for it. Don't let me or anybody hold you back. I've always hoped the Merc could be a business incubator, and I'd be thrilled to see you succeed, but—well, we'd be kinda lost without you."

Her expression said I'd hit the target this time. Before she could reply, the old dog lumbered to his feet, barked once, and limped purposefully toward the back door.

"Potty time," she said. I carried our mugs to the kitchen, where she put a goldfish box into my hands. Another bark. "I've been experimenting. You pooh-poohed the green tea truffles, but try 'em. Hang on, Boze. I'm coming."

Treasure box in hand, I let myself out. The snow had started up again and the temperature had fallen. The day's sunshine had warmed the roads in Tracy's hilltop subdivision just enough to leave a thin sheet of ice. Like driving behind a Zamboni.

Down the hill I crept till I reached the highway, surprised to discover I'd been holding my breath. In Seattle, an inch of snow stops the city. Newcomers from the Rockies or the Midwest laugh at the natives, until they try to drive the city's hills in wet slush. Nobody can do it. When the first snow fell here shortly after Halloween, it had taken me a week or two to feel comfortable on the roads.

As I drove south along the lake, my headlights glinting off roadside reflectors, competing thoughts struggled for mental airtime. The Merc needed Tracy and her truffles. Few customers can resist the lure of locally made chocolates. They come in for one, buy a box, and load up on pasta, cheese, and sauces. Then they come back. My vendors count on that ripple effect.

On the other hand, I understood the desire to build your own business. To be your own boss. Enormously satisfying, but never easy. Would she want to take on that kind of commitment? Her chocolate combined with Rick's business acumen could be a killer recipe.

A flash of light caught my eye and I glanced in the rearview mirror. An SUV with its brights on swerved around me, tucking back into our lane as a semi approached, its giant wheels throwing a cascade of half-melted snow and ice my way. I flicked on the wipers a moment too late: Thick, gray-brown mush caked my windshield and began to freeze.

I muttered and crept toward the shoulder, pulling into the next driveway. Flicked the defroster to full blast. Groped on the floor for my snow brush and scraper. Did my best to clear the windshield and wiper blades, then remembered the headlights.

Filthy. I scooped up a handful of clean snow and scrubbed first one light, then the other. Not perfect, but clean enough to get me home.

I tossed the scraper into the backseat and reached for my door handle. A whooshing sound filled my ears and a jolt of adrenaline filled my veins. Slush from passing wheels hit the back of my legs and knocked me against my car.

I am dead.

Not dead. Just soaked and freezing, standing on the narrow shoulder of a narrow highway. The truck zoomed on by, its driver heedless. I brushed myself off. Climbed in and let my forehead fall onto the steering wheel.

The goldfish box sang to me. One more truffle wouldn't hurt, would it? As a reward for surviving my own stupidity?

Eyes on the road and hands on the wheel, Erin. People, and cats, are counting on you.

· *Seventeen* ·

Two roads diverged in a wood, and I took the road not plowed.

Again.

The next morning, I stood outside Christine's cottage for the second time in less than a week, sniffing out trouble.

Six inches of fluffy white powder covered the walk and steps, punctuated by the hooves of a young doe who'd cut across the yard to nibble the tender tips of an evergreen.

So, carrying a latte in each hand and a bag of pastries, I detoured to the side door. I'd trudged a few steps down the unshoveled path between the two buildings when I realized no Jeep. No tire tracks.

But someone had been here. The screen door swung loose on its hinges like a warning in a late-night horror movie. The main door stood ajar, shards of glass scattered across the threshold.

I pushed it open with the toe of one boot and peered in. Clumps of snow and mud tracked across the kitchen and out of sight.

Get out. Go in. Someone could be inside. Someone could be hurt.

I froze, warring thoughts racing through my brain. I steadied my breath and studied the snowy back step and passageway between cottage and church.

The tracks went in and the tracks came out.

I swallowed the urge to follow. Instead, I explained it all to the 911 dispatcher—thinking, *Here we go again*, warning her that approaching officers needed to avoid trampling the footsteps, that they should follow the tracks away from the cottage to find the culprit. Who was probably long gone. I didn't think the church had been broken into—no footsteps. And unlike the cottage, it had a security system.

"No," I assured her, "the house is empty. Or should be." But while my father had taught us to recognize the signs of our woodland neighbors—whitetail, mule deer, elk, fox, hares, coyote, and the wild cats—tracking the far more dangerous human animal was outside my expertise.

So glad we'd rescued Pumpkin last weekend. After losing her human, the trauma of a break-in might have been too much for her—not to mention Sandburg and me.

I waded through the snow back to the front porch—unmarred by the intruder—and sat. Cupped my still-warm latte in my gloved hands. My shaking hands.

Two patrol cars arrived, both officers heeding my warning about the footprints. They were inside when Deputy Kim Caldwell turned onto Mountain View, pulled a U-ey, and parked in front of the cottage, engine running, overhead lights ablaze.

Why? The danger is over. Announcing her presence to the neighborhood? Marking her territory?

Much of what she does in the name of law enforcement baffles me.

"Figured I'd find you here," she said. A patrol deputy rounded the corner, saving me from a response.

"'Morning, Detective." He'd been here Saturday, too. "Cottage is trashed. Someone searching for something."

A car door slammed. "Erin!" Feet thudded through the snow. "Erin!"

Nick stopped halfway up the walk, his eyes darting from Kim to me and back. "You okay? What happened now?"

"No one's hurt. But someone's broken into the cottage." Kim turned to the deputy. "See where those tracks lead. But don't go off the property until backup arrives."

I heard her, but I wasn't really listening. I was too busy noticing that my brother had driven in from the south—from the direction of Rainbow Lake. Not from the north, the road he would have taken from the Jewel. And Kim had noticed, too.

"You check your packs?" I asked, afraid of the answer. Afraid of another lie.

"What?" he said, distracted. "Yeah. What happened? You sure you're okay? Dammit, Erin. Why does it seem like everywhere you go, something goes wrong?"

A flush of anger crawled up my throat. I handed Kim the latte I'd brought for Nick.

"Thanks," she said, assessing the current between my brother and me. "You two come inside. The deputies have cleared the space and photographed the wet footprints. But we haven't taken other photos or prints yet, so don't touch anything. Just tell me what might be missing. What the burglar might have been after."

Not that I would know. I'd only been in the cottage a time or two, including Saturday afternoon when my focus had been on subduing a feisty ball of fur long enough to get her to safety. Which reminded me, I still needed to find her a home. Kim?

Yeah, right. But, maybe.

You never know how people live. As I'd discovered last summer, women who organize their business lives to a T can create complete chaos in their living space and never blink. People whose kitchens would give Martha Stewart pantry envy don't know what a car wash is. My cabin stays picked up most of the time, but my closet won't win any ribbons.

But I'd seen enough during my cat hunt to know that while Christine's closets were no better than mine, her cottage had not looked like this. In the kitchen, a box of Special K lay dumped on the counter, and hand-thrown pottery canisters had come to rest on mounds of the flour and sugar they'd once held.

We passed into the dining area, separated from the living room by the front door. An oversized red willow basket of gloves and hats lay upside down, its contents a wooly, fleecy heap.

From there, we followed Kim through an arch into a windowless hall. Ahead lay the bathroom; to the left, a guest room and stairs to the attic, to the right, Christine's bed-room. Socks spilled out of half-opened dresser drawers, the laundry basket empty on the bed, the mattress partway off the frame.

Nick's wind-chapped cheeks had gone pale, and I didn't feel too hot, either. "Who would do this?"

"And why in such a hurry?" Kim scanned the mess. "If you'd scared them off, I'd expect a more methodical search, ending abruptly. But this is almost random."

"Or desperate."

Nick moved silently through the cottage, expressionless—except for his eyes. They saw everything, and I guessed, understood nothing. He turned back to the living room while Kim and I went upstairs. More of the same. On a second tour through the main floor, I followed his gaze as he focused on the walls and shelves. Christine's own playful work brightened the kitchen and bathroom. An acrylic painting of an old black rotary phone occupied an arched phone nook in the back hall.

In the living room, a huge framed dye-on-silk portrait

of a psychedelic moose sat on the shelf above the fireplace. No need to read the signature to recognize Nancy Cawdrey's work. Hand-built pottery occupied the windowsills on either side of the fireplace, above the glass-front bookshelves. I did not need to turn them over to identify the potters. Like many artists, Christine had built an impressive collection of work she admired.

A Dan Doak lidded tureen lay shattered on the oak floor. But I spotted no empty hooks on the walls, no gaps in displays, no telltale rings of dust. Most of these pieces had not been touched.

"Anything missing, Nick?" Kim asked.

He squinted. "Hard to tell, but I don't think so." He crossed the room to an antique secretary in the corner, a lovely walnut piece, and ran his hand over the drop-down writing surface. "She kept her papers here. The valuable artwork was all in the church."

I closed my eyes and pulled up a mental slide of the Spreadsheet of Suspicion. If the break-in was related to the murder, was the suspect already on my list? Break-ins during funerals are common enough that neighbors often sit on the front porch while the family's away holding a service. Was this another despicable trend, looting a murder victim's home? A ripe target—if the victim lived alone, who would know?

Tricky timing. You'd have to wait until the sheriff stopped watching the place, but strike before the family started cleaning out.

I gripped the back of a chair to steady myself.

This was no random burglary. The intruder had been searching for something of less obvious value. Christine's jewelry box stood open but tidy. Her grandmother's pearls lay on top of her dresser, in a velvet-lined clamshell. A carved wooden hand held her rings in its palm: a pearl in a gold setting, an amethyst I knew had been her mother's, the diamond solitaire she'd tried to give back but that Nick had insisted she keep.

The ring they wouldn't be using after all.

I followed my brother outside, Kim behind us. She signaled us to hang tight while she spoke to two officers waiting to complete the investigation inside. A uniformed officer finished photographing the footprints in the snow, and set up a frame for casting impressions. The flat light and lack of wind would help, though it couldn't be comfortable working in twenty degrees.

It could have been worse.

A cluster of reserve deputies stood nearby, comparing notes. The crew leader broke away and trotted over.

"We followed the footprints north." He pointed to the heavily wooded properties across the highway. "I'm bettin' he hid his rig in the driveway of a house closed up for winter. We photographed the tire tracks and took impressions. State lab can identify the tread, but we'll need the vehicle to make a match."

Kim clenched her jaw. "Thanks. Finish the perimeter search and let me know what else you find."

Sounds from near the garden drew our attention. "You got no right to go snooping around my property," Jack Frost shouted at a uniformed deputy.

"Sir, we did not—"

"What's going on?" Kim broke in, and Frost flung his anger at her. "Your deputies trespassed on my private property, is what's going on."

"The tracks go right along the fence line, then veer north through the woods and over the highway," the deputy told Kim. "I don't think we crossed over, but . . ."

"Sir," she told Frost, "this is an active investigation into criminal trespass and felony burglary, and possible felony theft, related to an ongoing murder investigation. Deputies in active pursuit of a suspect may follow that suspect, or his tracks, wherever they lead, private property or not. My deputy was only doing his job. Now, if he caused any damage . . ."

"No, he din't. What's happened now?"

"I was hoping you could help us figure that out. In fact, I was on my way over to interview you and your wife."

"Sherry ain't home. She's been in Spokane all week, babysitting our grandkids. She heard about this murder, she wanted me to come over, too, till he's caught. Thinks it's ain't safe here. But I'm not being scared out of my home, no sirree. No, ma'am." A shock of steel gray hair flopped over one eye.

His boots. Kim noticed them, too. "No match," her deputy mouthed.

"You didn't get along with Ms. Vandeberg," Kim said, and at his look of confusion, clarified. "The victim. Or with Mrs. Ring, who lived here for decades."

"Hey, I didn't like the old bag, or the redhead, but I didn't kill nobody. Check out that guy what drives the fancy car. Or Wolf Man." He sneered in Nick's direction. "He inherits the whole shebang, right?"

I couldn't stop myself. "That's ridiculous. Nick had no reason to break in to his own house and trash it. He's got a key. And he knew I'd be here." Kim had seen for herself that he'd been genuinely shocked by the wreckage inside.

Nick put a warning hand on my arm. But I wasn't finished. "Doesn't this break-in prove Nick had nothing to do with Christine's death? The two are obviously connected."

"Nothing's obvious," Kim said, her eyes trained on Frost.

But while he makes a lot of people mad and is easy to blame, the break-in pretty much eliminated Frost, too. Far as we knew, his conflict with Christine had nothing to do with her possessions. It centered on her plans for the future.

What's more, he had no reason to flee north or hide a truck in the woods. His own woods offered plenty of close cover.

I pictured my list of suspects. Zayda? If her parents had kept her out of school another day, they'd be at the restaurant, not home keeping an eye on her. But why would she break in? Nothing hinted at a conflict between her and Christine.

Sally? She might break in and take what she thought rightfully hers. But a ransacking? Impossible. If the murder and break-in were related, Sally was an unlikely culprit.

"Mr. Frost, may we talk inside somewhere? At your home, or the fire station?" Kim gestured across the highway. "I'll meet you and the deputy in a moment and you can tell me what you know."

Frost nodded and he and the deputy started walking. Kim turned back to us. "Why were you here, anyway?"

"Nick wanted to start cleaning and sorting," I said. "Oh, criminy. Now we've got a major mess. The fridge is gonna start stinking pretty soon."

"We should be finished in a few hours. I'll let you know."

Nick and I walked to our cars in silence.

"I almost forgot. I brought breakfast." I tossed Nick the bag of squished croissants. As he reached out to grab it, his unzipped coat flew open and I saw the gun on his hip.

Though I've never had a reason to own a gun, they don't scare me. But seeing my brother packin' heat at the scene of his girlfriend's murder was alarming. "Nick, the gun. You don't think you're in danger, too?"

"I always carry when I go out to check the packs," he said.

"Your packs are up north. I watched you drive up. From the south."

He stared at me, wheels churning. Deciding. "Leave it alone, Erin. It has nothing to do with you."

"You're making things worse, Nick. Kim and Ike know you weren't in the Jewel last Saturday. If they think you had role in Christine's death—"

Shooting me one last long frosty look, Nick climbed in his Jeep and started the ignition. Left me standing there watching him drive away, my throat cramping, tears hot in my eyes.

Nobody can hurt you like the ones you love.

· Eighteen ·

"Hey, Bozo. How you doin', boy?" The Great Dane raised his big head and I rubbed behind one ear. Contentment filled his dark eyes, and I wished every male was so easy to read—and to please.

"Thanks for letting me bring him to work," Tracy said from the door between the shop floor and the hall.

"Long as he stays back here, we'll be fine." I tugged off my gloves and shucked my coat. If the health inspector dropped in unannounced, I'd take my lumps. Worth it to keep a good employee happy.

"I didn't expect you for hours," Tracy said. I followed her into the shop and poured a cup of strong coffee. Explained what we'd found. She clapped a hand to her mouth. "His footprints were still melting? What was he after? Thank God you didn't get there earlier."

I grimaced and headed to my office.

Outside the church and cottage, Nick had sped off without a backward glance, and when he reached the highway, drove east. Away. Maybe he did have a pack in the Jewel.

I wasn't sure I cared. His refusal to talk—to let me help him—spiked my Jell-O.

But I knew myself. If Kim wasn't convinced that Nick had nothing to do with the murder or the break-in, then I couldn't stop searching for the killer.

Though it was harder and harder to justify pointing a finger at Frost. Easy targets aren't always the right ones.

Tracy had asked the right question: What did he want? But was that the right pronoun, I wondered, toeing off my boots. Mine leave a distinctly female footprint, but Kim had worn a pair of slip-on snow boots as bulky as Frost's and her deputies' boots. As big as Nick's.

Zayda's clunky Doc Martens popped into my mind's eye. A lot of kids wear oversized boots these days. I closed my eyes and tried to remember whether she'd worn a pair last Saturday. No luck. I replayed finding Christine's bloody body every night in my sleep, but when I rolled the mental tape now, I couldn't see Zayda's feet.

No doubt the footwear examiner at the state crime lab would use the casts and photos to identify brand, model, and shoe size from the measurements and tread patterns. No doubt it would take a day or two, at least—unlike *CSI* on TV. And no doubt they wouldn't tell me.

But how could they track down the owner, especially now that so many people shop online? I had visions of deputies setting up watch outside the grocery store and post office, or the Building Supply, scouting for a one-hundred-and-sixty-pound man with a slight left limp and a pronated heel, wearing a size-twelve Sorel, rubber shell, leather upper, and a fleecy frost cuff, sold in brown with a red stripe or black with a yellow stripe.

No. Sherlock Holmes and Lieutenant Columbo may pick up on all those clues, but they're fictional.

Back to real life. Back to Zayda. Her behavior baffled me: Nothing suspicious about her going inside the church as soon as she arrived, but why leave and wait outside?

And why lie, until the found eyebrow ring proved her presence?

If she'd shot Christine, would she have stayed? Again, why? And if she had been the intruder this morning, what was she searching for?

The impasse made my insides hurt. That kind of post-adrenaline-surge hangover that tightens your chest and makes you feel like the blood and oxygen aren't circulating the way they ought to.

Coffee. I took a big gulp and forced myself to attend to business. I returned a few e-mails and texts. But still no tracking info for *Chocolat*.

I'd told Larry we couldn't adjust the film schedule, but it's always good to have a backup plan.

When we cleaned up the basement, we'd moved Fresca's cookbooks and magazines downstairs, leaving a few of my favorites on the office shelves. They gave me an idea. What about a staged reading of foodie fiction and essays? I caught the high school speech and drama coach between classes and pitched my idea. "If you think the kids can do this, let's schedule it as a special performance between movies on Saturday. If the second movie doesn't arrive, then the kids can wrap up the evening. Give them a chance to show off their talents to the community."

"Oh, that's *per*fect. The state tournament's over, so this will be a fun new challenge." She had a naturally infectious voice, the kind that makes you think she thinks you're brilliant. A great quality in a teacher. "Any pieces to suggest?"

"Yeah. A juicy poem about pie, if I can find it."

"This will be a treat. Thanks for thinking of us."

Oh, no, thank YOU.

I trotted down to the shop in time to help Luci the Splash Artist, one of my favorite vendors, haul in new stock. The platinum-haired pixie sported another vintage apron, this one bib style, knee length, in a black-and-white

Greek key print with a solid black sash, worn over black pants and a black turtleneck.

We unpacked soaps and lotions and Tracy rearranged the displays. Luci's products had quickly garnered repeat customers, always a positive sign. Plus she is cheery and easy to work with.

Most of the time.

"Erin, can we talk?" Her dark blue eyes were serious, and her dimples had disappeared. I gestured to the red-topped stools.

She set a basket on the counter. "Samples. A new soap—olive oil castile. Super pure and natural. Nontoxic, eco-friendly. It's even biodegradable—for people with septic tanks."

Tracy sniffed a small square. "Mmm. Olive oil soap is great for dry skin."

"Thanks," I said. "What's on your mind?"

"Well, it's . . ." She sighed heavily. "It's winter, and sales . . . aren't so great."

"Your products sold beautifully over the holidays. Some of the highest sales per square foot in the store." After truffles. "We're featuring your rose-scented soap and lotion for Valentine's Day. Listen, this is a tough time of year. But you're growing sales. And you're working on new products, which is crucial."

We'd talked about this last summer, when Luci decided to turn her hobby into a business. But sometimes reality bites.

"What about goat's milk soap?" Tracy said. "Or baby shampoo."

"You could create a line of cleaning supplies. Try soap in shapes, besides rectangles. The state of Montana." My left hand cupped an imaginary bar, fingers gripping the Canadian line, my thumb poking up through Idaho.

"I like those ideas," Luci said, her tone hesitant.

But they would take time to develop, and cash for

supplies. *Think fast, Erin.* As Project Tea Shop was proving, the challenge in seasonal retail is bringing in enough summer income to carry the business through the off-season. Without a ski area close by, winter traffic would never close the gap. And a rainy June or a smoky August can be fatal. That, as the Againsters could never grasp, is why I love special events. Festival fatigue is a danger, but not if we mix it up and stay creative. The stakes are too high.

As the somber face of the normally perky young blonde in front of me demonstrated.

A customer arrived and Tracy went off to greet her.

"We may need part-time help this summer," I said. But Luci's face made clear that might be too late.

Another possibility waved from the recesses of my mind. We did a decent mail-order business, mainly tourists and snowbirds who got home to Georgia or Arizona and realized no spinach fettuccine holds a tomato to Fresca's, and they honestly did feel friskier all day after a nice cuppa Cowboy Roast in the a.m. But I'd been reluctant to pursue web sales whole-hog, at least until we had more products under our own label. Adding that expense on top of the sixty percent of each sale that goes to the vendor made my head swim.

And I kinda like keeping things small and manageable. Of course, my sister says I have control issues.

But in business, you gotta grow, you gotta change, to stay alive.

I made up the plan as I talked. "So you'd work for Jason, setting up an e-commerce site. Take pictures, write copy, input product details. Say, twenty hours a week during the design and construction phase, and five or ten after it gets going, adding new products, taking down old ones. You'd have plenty of time for soap making, and to develop new items for summer."

The sun came out. Crocuses bloomed under the snow. Kittens were cute again and ice cream tasted sweet once more. "Oh, Erin! That's so perfect. I worked on websites in art school, and I know I can do exactly what you need. Thank you, thank you, thank you."

She grabbed my shoulders and hugged me, her black mascara forming a tiny teardrop at the outer corner of her left eye.

Perfect ideas twice in one morning. A girl can get used to that.

Luci threw on her Mexican poncho and grabbed her basket. "I'll go see Jason right now. Erin, thank you so much."

Which gave me two minutes to call Jason and confess. He'd been after me to ramp up the web biz for a while, but even so, he would appreciate the warning.

I waved good-bye, smiling. And caught Tracy eying me thoughtfully.

"What?" I said.

"Nothing." Her hammered silver hoops swayed.

Upstairs, I called Jason and we agreed on a plan. "Don't work her too hard. Just enough to keep her afloat, but leave her plenty of time to play with soap."

I grabbed my jacket and stepped around the corner to Bill's clinic for a consult about Christine's will. But the Wizard of Wild Medicine had a full waiting room. Later, darn it.

Back at the Merc, I handled the shop while Tracy took the dog for a quick walk and ate lunch. A foursome of sixty-ish women popped in for snacks to take to their weekly bridge game. Outside, a man studied the Valentine's Day window, then came inside for a basket of wine, cheese, crackers, salami, and artichoke pesto—all locally grown or made. I offered a sample truffle and he bought four mix-and-match boxes.

At twelve thirty, Ginny Washington from Food for Thought, the local bookstore, arrived and we headed downstairs to sort the cookbooks I'd been given last summer by the family of a much-admired chef. I'd plucked out some promising titles, but hadn't had time to go through every box. After an hour, we called it quits, leaving more than half the boxes unopened. I'd set aside a few books to keep or give to friends—clearly, Tracy needed *The Art of the Chocolatier*, and a few volumes on baking might interest Wendy. After school, Ginny's son, Dylan, would cart the boxed rejects across the street to the bookstore for resale.

Back upstairs, I presented the book to Tracy, who was immediately entranced. The door chime rang and Kathy arrived, toting a plastic crate of quilted table runners, place mats, and napkins, all sewn by local women using Dragonfly fabrics. Our pairing is a natural fit—the linens soften our displays and add color, and I'd rather promote a neighboring business than sell cheap imported goods.

"We've been sorting Drew Baker's cookbooks," I said, gesturing to my dusty apron. "Hundreds. Thousands. No exaggeration."

"International, modern, baking," Ginny added. "He shopped with me regularly, but I had no idea he'd built such a collection. Some quite old, even rare."

"So, why search out, buy, hold on to more of whatever it is than you'll ever use?" I asked. "More art than you have walls. More books than you can read or cook from—some of these look like they'd never been opened."

"Stamp collecting," Tracy said. "What's the point?"

"Earrings," I said.

"They're useful. I wear them."

"The thrill of the hunt," Kathy suggested. "Searching high and low for the missing piece. Putting together a complete set, the best examples."

"My mother-in-law collects dolls." Ginny sipped a cool Pellegrino. "She grew up poor, and played with a corn husk doll. A classmate had a doll with a porcelain head and real human hair. When my mother-in-law started working after high school, she bought one for herself. And another, and another. Unfortunately, she has three sons and six grandsons. What we'll do with them when she goes, I have no idea."

"She has an emotional connection to them. Another woman might have turned that connection into a career as a dollmaker." Like Larry Abrams's early passion for movies had led him to a career he loved.

"And they're pretty. She's very feminine, and loves the hair and clothing—all that silk and lace." Ginny wrinkled her nose. "Although some of the faces are almost creepy."

"Growing up, my best friend's mom was a hoarder," Tracy said. "She never let anyone come to their house, except me. A few years ago, her mom tripped over a mess of empty boxes and broke her hip, so while she was in the hospital, we helped her dad clean out. Rented a Dumpster. It took days." Her face turned grave. "They saw a counselor and my friend hired a cleaning service. Occasionally, her mom decides she needs to save empty pill bottles or wrapping paper tubes and a pile builds up, but it's manageable now."

Kathy laid a runner on a display table while Tracy tucked matching napkins and jars of jam in coffee mugs.

"But hoarding isn't collecting, is it?" I said. "It's more random and indiscriminate."

"Collecting can serve an emotional purpose without being obsessive," Kathy said. "Like the dolls. And some people just love the stuff. God bless the customers who buy far more yarn and fabric than they'll ever need."

Ah. A simple explanation for my mother's love of hand-blown martini glasses? They remind her of that magical year traveling in Italy—when she met my dad—but she also loves the colors and shapes.

The broken glass shattered not only her memories, but the comfort they'd given her.

Ginny left, and Tracy helped a customer needing fresh eggs and jam.

"Speaking of collecting," Kathy said as we unpacked the last place mats and napkins. "I don't want to pester Nick, but the sooner he decides whether to follow through with Christine's plan to donate Iggy's collection to the Art Center, the better."

"I'm working on him. Love this pattern. What's it called?" I held up a place mat. Four groups of triangles in red, gold, and brown prints on a creamy backdrop, each pointing toward a corner.

"Bear paw."

Talk about obvious. "Apparently someone tried to buy a piece that Iggy wanted the Art Center to have, but we don't know what it was. Nick wants to find out, to make sure we honor her intentions."

She slipped on her coat and picked up the empty tote. "I'll ask the board if anyone knows. Larry might—he had quite a few conversations with her."

A Brooklyn boy who made his fortune in Hollywood, but yearned for Montana.

Plenty of room for all kinds under the Big Sky. Which is a good thing, because there are all kinds.

· *Nineteen* ·

First stop: Taylor's Building Supply. Five minutes with the Paint Yahoo and I had a gallon of Squirrel Tail—a goofy name for a totally delish paint the color of a mocha latte—and all the associated doodah.

"Guess that shooting's got us all worried," the cashier said as I approached. Took me a second to realize she was speaking to a man picking out signs from a spinning rack.

Neon green on black, reading NO TRESPASSING.

"Hey, Jack," I said, and set my shopping basket on the counter. It's rude to not acknowledge someone. Even if they've recently pointed a gun in your general vicinity.

I chose to interpret his grunt as "Hey."

Though I'd all but ruled Frost out as Christine's killer, I wondered what he was protecting. What had him worried. He wore his usual grubby coverall, and a cap advertising a car parts dealer.

That, and his crack this morning about guys with fancy cars, reminded me of the kids and their documentary, Kyle

Caldwell and his muscle car, and Danny Davis's offer to buy the GTO after calling it a piece of junk.

Humans. Sometimes there's no explaining us.

Jack didn't drive a fancy car. I knew which truck in the lot was his by the cherry red plow on the front and the bumper sticker on the rear: The silhouette of a wolf and the slogan SMOKE A PACK A DAY.

Whether by chance or choice, Nick had found himself in a dangerous line of work.

J ack Frost aside, I sing the praises of snowplow drivers. I sing them in squalls and blizzards, whiteouts and flurries, in slip, slide, and slush. I sing them too in wet and powder, in blinding pellets, in soft snow drifting from the sky like petals from an apple tree. High above the road the plow drivers sit, in lumbering orange mastodons with chains on their tires and engines that could turn the earth on its axis. Mastodons with blades for tusks, capable of moving mountains, sand and gravel in their bellies. Neither snow nor rain nor gloom of night can stop them, though they pause to refill the gas tank and coffee cup. They march across dale and thunder over hill, cleaning up the messes Mother Nature makes to remind us that she is in charge, not we—we human few who dare cut paths through the wilderness and pave paradise.

I sing the praises of snowplow drivers, even as they hog the roads, ice and sand spitting out from under their massive wheels. Brave men and women who keep the roads clear and all us idiots safe.

Creeping the twenty-two miles into Pondera behind a plow gave me plenty of time to think. About Christine's house and someone's search for—what? Had she been killed for this missing item, that none of us, not even Nick, knew existed?

Obviously Iggy, her inventory incomplete, was not a

compulsive collector—unlike a stamp dealer with his lists or my mother's friend the former DJ who'd cataloged his thousands of albums and forty-fives on three-by-five cards.

I passed a driveway marked by a row of birdhouses, each a different style and color. By our collections, you shall know us. If clothing counts, my eight denim jackets. And my heart-shaped objects—rocks, shells, pins, cookie cutters. The entire collection fits on the bathroom window-sill where it brightens the morning. The latest addition: a pink agate heart Adam gave me at Christmas.

But while I love them—and wear my jackets often—they don't make my heart race. If you'll pardon the pun. If I come across one that catches my eye, great, but I've never spent an afternoon scouting for hearts, or wandering consignment and thrift shops for the jacket to complete my life list. Or whatever.

I'd rather spend that time perfecting a scone or a stew.

We all have our passions.

While the line between enthusiasm and obsession might be fine, there's no question which side murder falls on.

Finally, we reached a four-lane stretch and I scooted past the plow, waving my thanks.

Like the village, downtown Pondera is long on charm and short on parking. I squeezed the Subaru into a space on a side street and headed for the Main Street gallery and gift shop where Heidi recalled Fresca buying the martini glasses.

The Honeysuckle Glass Gallery building dates from the same era as the Merc. Metal stock tanks flanked the entry, live evergreens poking out of the snow. Inside, exposed brick walls, maple floors, and painted tin tiles set off luminous handblown hanging lights.

I'd met the owner, Trish Flynn, at a state tourism office event on promoting the arts. Her stained glass workshop fills the back of the shop, but she also carries glasswork by artists from across the Northwest.

Soft sax-y jazz drifted around me. Amid the floor lamps, table lamps, night-lights, chandeliers, windows, bowls, plates, jewelry—anything that could be made of glass—would I find what I was searching for?

"You look like you're on the hunt." Trish emerged from her office, running a chapped hand through short, dark curls. "We've met—remind me your name."

"Erin Murphy. From the Merc in Jewel Bay. What a magical place." I pulled Chiara's sketch out of my blue tote. "I'm hoping to find a glass like this."

"Mmm, yeah." She led me to a corner where goblets and martini glasses sparkled in the gallery's medley of light. "Each one is different. Part of the beauty of handmade."

I fingered them. Raised one as if to drink—a light but solid feel. "The colors are so clean and pure. And the swirls of color around the bowl and stem. They look like they're— dancing."

Like potato chips, it was impossible to pick just one. So I chose three, telling myself they were future gifts. Or I could keep two for myself, replacements for the plain glass jobbies I'd found in a liquor store for two dollars apiece during a martini emergency. With any luck, my mother would see in this gift a shimmer of my love and admiration.

Trish wrapped them carefully in heavy paper. "Every medium has its appeal, but when I started working in glass, I found my soul work. Glass combines all the elements: earth, fire, water, metal, and air. You're never completely in control of the outcome, no matter how hard you work."

"Sounds disheartening."

"It can be," she admitted. "When a piece you've sweated over for hours, sometimes days, breaks. Teaches us detachment. I love the element of surprise, of co-creating with the Divine."

She'd lost me, but not by the explanation of her artistic process. My eyes were riveted on the corkboard behind her. "Community Baby Shower," a poster read. "Give young mothers and their babies a warm, fuzzy start. Bring new, unwrapped clothes and baby items, and stay for an afternoon of games, gifts, and baby-whispering."

The date: Last Saturday, here in Pondera. "Contact: Sally," followed by a Jewel Bay phone number. I whipped out my phone and checked the number. Puddle Jumpers.

"Forgot to take that down." Trish tore it off the board and was about to toss it in the recycling when I held out my hand.

"The contact person. Sally Grimes?" I tucked the poster in my bag. "Part of the crew?"

"Worked as hard as the rest of us," Trish said. "From midmorning coffee and setup to teardown. The mothers arrived at noon for lunch—fifteen of them. Part of a special program the school district runs for girls who've decided to keep their babies, to help them stay in school. They left at three p.m. We finished around five."

A mental slide of the property tax records dropped into view. "Sally's your landlady."

Trish nodded, snapping open a sturdy brown paper shopping bag. "She donated a diaper bag for every mother. A few had already had their babies, and she made sure each little one got a plush toy. And I gave the mothers a glass keepsake."

"How did you two get involved?"

"Because of Sage. We're related, through my son, Nathan." The glow on her face had nothing to do with all the lamps shining around us. "And my granddaughter, Princess Olivia. Enjoy your glassware."

Next door, in another building Sally owns, is a bakery almost as sweet as Le Panier, so I popped in for a latte and a chunky peanut butter cookie. *Research*, I told myself, silencing the voice of my mother commenting on calories. The potential sources of mother-daughter tension are endless, but at least ours are benign—unlike the struggles between Sally and Sage.

"Because of Sage," Trish had said. I puzzled over that as I picked my way back to my car, careful of my fragile bounty and the icy sidewalks. Sage had to be thirty, and Sally over fifty. No teenage mothers there, unless I had misjudged Sally's age along with everything else.

The Google search for the house in Missoula had identified the residents as N. and S. Flynn. Suspicions confirmed: Nathan and Sage lived in the house her mother owned.

My horn beeped and the lights flickered as I clicked the lock open. Very useful in a valley where every fourth vehicle is a Subaru.

Through no fault of my own, I'd established Sally's alibi for the shooting. Witnesses galore could swear to Sally's whabouts—witnesses with gifts attesting to her presence and generosity. In the process of buying my mother a gift, I had unintentionally proven the woman I liked least in town innocent of murder. The woman convinced of my own brother's guilt.

Talk about the law of unintended consequences.

Accompanied by a lesson in mistaken assumptions. The skin on my face warmed with shame. I had wanted to believe Sally guilty, no matter how unlikely it seemed. When it came to planning—for the village, anyway—she prefers whining to action, and murder is the ultimate action.

I had let my own feelings override my logic. Exactly as I'd accused her of doing when it came to Nick.

The drive home took half the time of my trip to Pondera, thanks to the freshly plowed roads. Winter days here can be gloomy, but not this one. Fresh snow sparkled on the mountains that ring the valley. A little ditty we'd memorized in second or third grade floated into mind: "I'm glad the sky is painted blue, the earth is painted green, with such a lot of nice fresh air all sandwiched in between."

Substitute white for green, put on your shades, and be glad.

Back in Jewel Bay, I turned off the highway and drove

down Hill Street into the village, the frozen bay on my right. Jack Frost had done his work, scraping the streets smooth. They wouldn't be bare and dry for weeks, but at least they were safe to walk and drive.

I passed the public dock and boat launch—a launch to nowhere, this time of year—then reached the narrow alley that separates the Front Street buildings from the greenbelt surrounding the bay. A whitebelt, today.

A heavyset man in a blue parka puffed up the alley behind the Playhouse, headed my way. Danny Davis?

No time for a closer look, or to stop and chat, as a delivery truck churned up the slope behind me. Ahead, a teal blue van with front-wheel drive and bad tires lost its grip on the road and slid sideways toward me.

Another day in a paradise of tranquility.

· *Twenty* ·

I parked behind the Merc, breathing quickly after my near miss with the van.

It probably speaks ill of me to say I felt greater relief at finding a replacement glass for Fresca's collection than at proving Sally's innocence. Not that I'm shallow and petty—or not *just* that. Proving her innocence left me one less suspect, and dozens of new questions.

The Merc smelled heavenly. Like coffee, but our bags of fresh-roasted beans are delivered on Fridays.

Like pie. Pumpkin pie.

"Mom? What are you doing here? This isn't your day in the kitchen." Wednesday mornings, a woman treks in from the edge of the wilderness to stir up soup and salad dressing mixes, but the afternoon slot is open. Add filling that to my list.

"This morning over coffee, I remembered that blend you sent me when you lived in Seattle. From Fancy Jim's, or whatever it's called. Thought I'd try making my own."

"Trader Joe's Pumpkin Spice Coffee," I said. "You hated it."

"No. Well, maybe at first." She slid a mug across the counter. "Try this."

I sniffed, then sipped. "Cinnamon, ginger, nutmeg, and cloves." All the pie spices and none of the overly sweet pseudo-pumpkin flavors often added to coffee drinks. "And a dash of cardamom."

She beamed. "I knew I raised you right. We can add it to your new drink line."

Customers would love the blend. Adam would hate it. He could eat pizza every night—and often did, before he started hanging out with me. But when it comes to coffee, he is a purist. Cream and sugar he acknowledges as acceptable additions—but none for him, thank you. Add even a hint of vanilla or chocolate, and he rolls his eyes. "Spoils the fun."

Or so he says. I can never tell when he's teasing me about my foodie ways.

I perched on a red-topped stool and warmed my hands on the heavy china mug. "So what prompted the kitchen session?"

She picked up her own coffee. "I needed a distraction from all this . . . gossip about your brother. It's hard enough to see him grieving. On top of that, the finger-pointing, the questions—I remember it all too well."

The front door chimed and I heard Tracy greet the mail carrier.

"I'm torn between wishing you'd stay out of it and praying you'll identify the killer before something else happens."

My hands froze, mug halfway to my mouth. My mother had refused to acknowledge my unofficial investigations over the last few months, let alone encourage them.

"Erin, there's mail for Nick, but he's out." Tracy said.

"Thanks. I'll take it." I glanced at my mother, but she'd

returned to her spices and bowls, and the yellow pad where she'd scribbled measurements.

I hung up my coat and set my bag on the loft stairs. Nick had used the Merc as a mail drop for years. I scooped up the delivery and trotted downstairs.

For a guy who claims to love fieldwork and hate academia, his winter den is as chaotic as any professor's office I've ever seen. Stacks of books and journals covered the desk, the floor, the chair. I scooted a pile of scientific journals aside to clear a space for the mail.

And there, underneath *The Journal of Wildlife Management* lay a stone chop. I reached out, tentatively, and picked it up. About the size of a granola bar—a flat slab, a carved lion's head on top, Chinese characters carved along one flat side, and more characters carved on the narrow bottom. Heavy, but it fit in the hand beautifully, as it was meant to do, so the owner could stamp his signature on a document or drawing.

Was the basement always this cold?

One hand out, I groped for Nick's chair, shoving the stack of papers back and perching on the edge.

Oh, Nick. You knew—and you never said. The "shop," she'd told me with her dying breath. Or so I'd thought.

Had he told Ike and Kim what Christine meant? Had he taken this from the church studio, or from her house?

Images raced through my brain, a PowerPoint presentation on fast-forward. Christine on the altar, eyes wide, skin pale, the color seeming to leak out of her red hair as I watched. The trickle of blood. Zayda, crumpled against the wall. The shock and anger mingled on Nick's dear face.

Was this chop what the killer—and the burglar—was searching for?

What was it doing here?

Above me, the floorboards in the back hall creaked. The brass doorknob rattled in its fittings and the hinge on the heavy basement door squeaked.

My fingers gripped the chop.

"What are you doing, messing with my things?"

"Why do you have this, Nick? The last thing a dying woman thought about?"

"Stay out of it, Erin."

Nick reached for the chop, but I jerked it away. "I'm already in it, Nick. Neck deep. And if the killer suspects you have this, we're all in it."

I had never seen my brother afraid. I've seen him elated, angry, grieving, worried. Nervous. Hopeful. Anxious. Annoyed.

But never frightened.

"Erin, I don't know what's going on. I don't know who killed Christine, or what that old Chinese relic has to do with it." He gestured with a trembling hand. His voice shook.

I stood. "Where were you Saturday, Nick? That's got to be part of this."

"What are you talking about? That has nothing to do with the—with Christine."

"Then tell me where you were." There were connections, somewhere.

"Erin. I can't. I've made promises."

I slammed the chop down on the desk. The stack of journals slid onto the floor. "Fine. Keep your secrets. Get arrested and charged with murder and who knows what else. You're so determined to do things yourself, you get out of jail yourself."

And then I did what I, Erin Margaret Murphy, would have sworn mere minutes ago that I would never, ever do. I walked out on family.

My boots crunched on the cold dry snow of the Nature Trail, aka the River Road. Hard to imagine now that this dirt path, eight feet at its widest, was once the loggers' and homesteaders' wagon trail into town. Replaced eons ago by the state highway on the south side of the Jewel River—the Cutoff Road—it had been an overgrown tangle when my grandfather Murphy and his sons led the volunteer effort to establish an easement and reclaim it for the community.

Hard to imagine Jewel Bay without it.

When my mother needs to work out her emotions, she cooks. My sister paints. Kathy quilts, and thanks her lucky stars that other women find their refuge in knitting and sewing.

I drive. Or walk.

In summer, the calm waters of the Jewel River slip over the concrete dam built more than a century ago, then rush over rocks and fallen logs, through twists and turns and underwater cliffs, creating Class IV rapids that summon whitewater maniacs from all across the West to try their luck and test their pluck on the Wild Mile.

In summer, baby osprey watch the crazy humans from their nests, from platforms built by the power company to keep them alive and off the lines. They learn to fly over the river and to chirp and shriek and whistle.

In summer, children race bikes down the trail, laughing and shouting. Parents push cooing babies in sturdy strollers. Old friends chit and chat and call hello to neighbors they haven't seen since last winter, or yesterday. Black Labs and Golden Retrievers splash in the shallows, bark at unsuspecting geese, and spray river water on their people. Bill Schmidt leads folks on herb walks. Birders raise their binoculars and tourists hope to spot a bear and wonder what will happen if they do.

But in winter, the River Road falls nearly silent. At the top of the first rise, a gray squirrel dashed across the trail, then perched on an algae-stained rock warmed by the sun, chattering like an old pal. Seeking company, or warning me off his cone stash?

A little farther on, a tree branch creaked under the

weight of ice and snow, and the grinding of a semi shifting gears on the highway echoed across the river canyon.

But mainly, it was me, my footfalls, and the committee inside my head. Lively debate is healthy, good for the soul. It clarifies one's thinking. It's good to hear to all points of view, consider all the possibilities.

It was driving me nuts. What if I didn't do what I said I'd do, what everyone expected? Save the Festival, track down the missing movie, plan an alternate program, make sure this got done and that showed up and this person was where they needed to be and this and that and that and this.

If just this once, I kept my mouth shut and my hand in my pocket, would the village, and the Merc, and my family fall apart?

I stomped down the trail, swinging my arms, hoping the increased blood flow would go to my brain.

Other employers might draw the line when a salesclerk needs time off for her sick dog. They might not create a job for a young vendor desperate for cash.

What if I didn't stick my neck out, put my head on the line, put my right foot in and left foot out? What if I weren't always trying to be the perfect sister and the perfect daughter, boss, building manager, volunteer coordinator, blah blah blah?

What if I did what I wanted to do, and the heck with everybody else?

A shadow flew across the white trail and I raised my face, shielding my eyes from the sun. A raven, wings four feet across, circled slowly overhead. "What do you want, Grandfather?" I said, using the Indian title my own grandfather had taught us when the majestic scavengers cruised the orchard.

The bird perched high on a snag, not moving a feather.

"Okay, you're right." I pulled off my glove and wiped my runny nose on the back of my hand. "Truth is, I want to help people. But it gets to be too much sometimes, you know? Things were settling down nicely, and then Iggy died. I got used to that, and then Christine gets killed. And now the anniversary is coming up. After fifteen years, I thought I was okay with it, but every time somebody else dies, it's like my skin gets ripped open, you know?

"And Adam's not here, and I don't know if I could tell him all this anyway. He'd probably think I'm a blubbering idiot.

"I can't solve everybody's problems," I told the empty trail. "I can recommend jam and cheese, and suggest the perfect hostess gift. I can help a husband pick out scented lotion or wine and chocolates for Valentine's Day, but I can't fill every void in the village. I can't even find a home for the darned cat."

Grandfather Raven remained silent. Only I could answer my own questions.

And, I realized as I headed back toward town, only the individuals involved could solve their problems. It wasn't up to me to take on their grief, their guilt, their fears and anxieties. I could listen, make suggestions, offer to help. But I had to let Nick, Tracy, and Luci decide what to do.

That didn't mean turning my back on them. It just meant remembering their problems were theirs. I always want things to go smoothly, thinking that if I dive in, if everyone does what I say, all will be peaches and cream.

I could almost hear my mother saying, *Darling, don't be so sensitive.*

Or in my sister's words, *Don't be such a bossy pants.*

The raven circled three times, let out a single caw, and flew down the canyon, wings wide, riding the currents of air.

"Next festival," I said to a particularly attentive Douglas fir, scarlet mahonia leaves peeking out of the snow at its roots. "I'm saying the Merc will contribute food or cash, but I'm busy. Call someone else."

My little buddy sat in the road, holding a cone in his tiny pink hands. Bright brown eyes stared up at me.

"As squirrel is my witness."

· Twenty-one ·

A mini run hit the Merc mid-afternoon.

"Storm coming?" I asked Tracy, both of us nearly breathless after a surge of customers wiped us out of eggs, cheese, and meat. Not to mention we'd gotten requests for twice as many freshly butchered chickens as our poultry supplier had delivered.

She rolled her eyes and blew out a breath. "They're saying another six inches of snow tonight, blustery winds, gusts up to forty miles an hour. Ten below."

I thanked my stars for good insulation and a gas fireplace. Most days, being caretaker requires little of me, but I'd have to check the Pinskys' house tonight. "The winter that won't quit."

But the late afternoon trade we owed to Valentine's Day. Some poor woman out there hoping for a diamond bracelet might be disappointed with a pasta sampler or a pound of organic Montana popcorn and a trio of seasonings. Not my fault. I tried mightily to steer all the men toward wine and chocolates, or suggest adding wild rose bath gel to their purchases, but even my persuasive powers have their limits.

"Erin, a moment?"

Nick watched me intently, the skin around his eyes dark and pinched. Look up *anguish* and *grief* in the dictionary and you'd see my brother's face at that moment.

"Go. I got this." Voice low, Tracy angled her head toward the sole customer, a woman browsing the pastas and sauces.

In the back hall, Nick handed me a compact notebook with a black binding and thick, dark green cardboard covers. It felt like the weight of a life.

"Go on," he said. "I'll wait." He sank onto my office steps, one knee bent, one long leg outstretched.

Silently, I carried his logbook upstairs. Did I really want to know Nick's secrets?

I steadied myself and opened the field notes. On the upper left of each page, he'd written "N. Murphy" and the year in clear block printing. Saturday's entry, dates and times noted in the left margin, began with the location, underlined: "Three-eighths mile west of Rainbow Lake Road and Redaway Lane, Timberlake County, Montana." I heard myself gasp.

"Presence of young adult male and female gray wolf confirmed by tracking and visual observation. Digital photos taken, images 00204—224. Pre-denning activity observed. Will attempt to locate tracks safely away from suspected den site for possible impressions, and obtain sign for further analysis." Sign, aka poop. The notes gave GPS coordinates and a detailed description of each wolf, including estimated size, and its travels.

I flipped back to earlier entries. For ten days, he'd been tracking, observing, searching for the den site. Two entries stood out: "Informant/observer reports howling potentially indicative of mating, midnight to two a.m. Advised him to record." And the next: "Listened to informant's recording; copied to my phone. Confirmed as suspected."

Biologist speak, but I knew what it meant. Following a tip from a resident, Nick had discovered a previously unknown wolf pair near Rainbow Lake, hot for each other and setting up house. New in the neighborhood, after leaving an established pack. Critical as it is to confirm and document all packs, it's equally critical to not alarm the public or announce a discovery prematurely. While most people have a healthy respect for the majestic carnivore, Jack Frost was not alone in his venom, and the wolves' presence so close by could trigger itchy fingers.

Over and over, I had asked myself why my brother would lie. Now I knew.

Nick always insists that humans have little to fear from wolves, but they do attack livestock and wild game. I wasn't sure whether hunting and trapping were in season, but no matter: Poachers driven by irrational fears could wipe out a pack before it became established. Or kill a pregnant female, or orphan helpless pups.

I pored back over the notes. The informant/observer was not named or otherwise identified. No contact information. Nick was protecting someone.

And I knew who. Ned Redaway lives along the river close to town, but he owns a large parcel out that direction—forty acres and a homestead-era cabin. Perfect for a grandson in his mid-twenties, who wouldn't mind the isolation. Might even appreciate it, after all the hub and bub of tending bar.

That isolation explained why the young wolves' appearance hadn't sparked rumors—and might protect them. But wasn't Nick required to report the sightings at some point?

The notes went on to say "Confirmed informant has no domestic animals or livestock, and advised on avoiding contact. Nearest year-round residence roughly one mile from suspected den site."

I closed the logbook and held it in my lap. Had Nick contacted the informant in person on Saturday, he would have a human witness. But the notes didn't indicate any conversation—I imagined J.D. had worked late Friday, slept in, and spent all his waking hours Saturday in the village.

Nick sat up quickly at the sound of my feet on the creaky floorboards.

"You have to share this, Nick. It's your alibi."

"I won't put the wolves in danger, Erin. Who's going to speak for them, if not me?"

"You can't speak for anyone from a jail cell."

Despite my harsh tone, he was unconvinced. "They'll make it public. They'll have to. The wolves will be sitting ducks."

I resisted smiling at the metaphor. "They must have a procedure for keeping an investigation confidential. Once they see this evidence"—I held up the logbook—"and talk to J.D., they'll understand you're innocent."

He glanced up sharply. "I promised him anonymity."

"Before the wolves he spotted became your alibi for murder." But even then, would the nightmare end? Ike Hoover might swear from the top of Mount Aeneas that Nick was no longer a suspect, but people would demand to know why. The whispers would continue until the prison doors clanged shut on the real killer.

Who that might be, I had no idea.

And Christine would still be dead.

"Stay." I headed out front. "Put that down and no one will get hurt," I told Tracy, who'd been about to empty the coffee. She held up her hands in mock surrender. I sprinkled Fresca's spice mix into two mugs and poured hot coffee. "Call me if you need help closing up."

The front door chimed and in walked Dylan Washington, dragging an orange dolly. Its hard black wheels left two narrow white trails of snow.

"The cookbooks," I said. "I completely forgot."

"No worries." But his face said otherwise.

I led the way downstairs and Nick carried the first load

up. Dylan bent for a box and I stopped him. "How's Zayda? She back at school yet?"

He stared into space, eyes hooded, lips thin. "She came back today. She's okay, I guess, but . . ." He met my gaze. "People are butt-heads sometimes, you know? Whispering, staring at her. Pretending she has a gun. One girl grabbed her stomach and fell down, acting like she was shot."

"People are butt-heads," I agreed.

"She wouldn't hurt anybody." He'd recovered his confidence, or at least, his ability to fake it. "Zayda admired Christine. She was excited about the Film Festival. She's got plans. The big film schools are interested in her."

"Dylan, it would help me a lot, to deal with things, you know"—let him think I meant my own emotions, not that I was poking around—"to know why she went out there early."

"She was meeting you. If she was early, she was just excited."

I didn't buy that, but didn't let on. "Did she argue with Christine? We know she went inside—she lost her eyebrow stud—so I'm puzzled why she decided to wait for me outside."

"She—she wasn't thinking." The words came slowly at first, then burst out as his certainty faded. He licked his lips, reminding me of Pumpkin as she gauged her chances of sneaking past Sandburg and beating him to the ottoman. He grabbed another box and started up the stairs. "Gotta get these books across the street before the snow starts."

Nick flattened himself against the sandstone wall as Dylan brushed by. He gave me a questioning look and hoisted a box. I shrugged and picked up another carton, the logbook in my sweater pocket. "We're not done talking, brother."

"I gotta go, Erin. Soon as we get these boxes outta here. Mom made me promise to stop in for dinner, and you know that means showing up early for a drink and a nibble before the main event."

When Fresca frets, she cooks.

"Then let's make it a family affair," I said.

"Explain again why you took it," Fresca said. She gestured toward the gray-veined white chop on the coffee table next to her new martini glass—the one with grass green and royal blue rods twisted together to form the stem. She'd been speechless at the gift—a rare blip for a Murphy girl—and promptly mixed lemon drop martinis. After the other night, I was surprised she didn't pour mine into a plastic cup.

Nick rubbed the magic spot between Pepé's ears, her eyes closed in canine ecstasy. "I told you. It should have been in the church, where there was a security system. So when I saw it in the cottage, I took it for safekeeping."

I wondered. Was this the reason for insisting we meet out there this morning? Had my presence to clean out the place been a cover, so he could search for this?

"I never knew Iggy had any Asian artifacts," Fresca said. "She was famous for loving Western art."

"It belonged to the family. I don't know the history, but Christine said Iggy had let herself be talked into selling one family piece and regretted it, so I took it." He reached for the relic. Unhappy that he'd stopped petting her, Pepé nosed his hand. "Sorry, girl."

My mother glowered. "That was a stupendously, ridiculously, utterly and completely idiotic thing to do."

He flushed. "It made sense at the time."

"Why was it in the house?" I said. "You think that whoever shot her was looking for it?"

"Who got shot?" Landon bounced into the room.

"Uh, nobody," I said. "We were talking about this. It's called a chop. Chinese scholars used them to sign their work."

"'Cause if somebody got shot, sic Hank the Cowdog

on 'em." Head of ranch security, and one of Landon's heroes.

"Because," Nick said, "she didn't want visitors to know she had it. Or a visitor in particular. But who?"

Had Zayda been searching for it? Or had the shooter? Who may or may not have been the burglar.

"Noni, see my dinosaur hat? It's got armored plates like stegosaurs." Landon climbed over Pepé to show my mother his olive green hat, a spine of bright blue fins running front to back.

"Ever since that trip to the Museum of the Rockies, he can't stop talking dinosaurs." Chiara dropped onto the couch next to Fresca and poured herself a martini. "So when the crochet lady brought this in, he had to have it. At this rate, we won't sell any hats. I'll buy them all myself instead."

"Crochet lady?" I said. "The woman who teaches at Dragonfly? Is she working at Puddle Jumpers, too? I thought you made the hat." Double-check Sally's alibi, like a real investigator.

"I made the turtle hat, in class. She made this one. She fills in all over town." Chiara took a sip. "Killer drink."

As one, the Murphy girls' eyes strayed to Nick, who was listening intently to Landon's report on the dinosaurs that once roamed Montana's plains and didn't seem to have heard her.

Dodged a bullet, I thought, and cringed.

"Mama," Landon told his mother as we migrated to the dining room. "I'm going to sit between Uncle and Auntie. Will you be okay sitting by yourself?"

"Thank you, darling. I'll sit next to Noni. And your father will be here shortly."

Jason arrived in time for salad. "Weeknight family dinner. This is unusual." He circled the table, exchanging kisses and fist bumps.

"When Nick called to say Erin was coming, I seized

the chance," Fresca said. "That's the beauty of pasta. Just add more to the pot."

"I've started a new series of paintings," my sister said. "Winter whites. Inspired by the snow."

"Blank canvases? I could paint those." If she could have reached Nick to smack him, she would have.

"First, I painted a stack of white linens on that cane-bottom chair of Gran's," she said. In our half-Irish, half-Italian family, Gran and Granda were the Murphys, and Noni and Papi the Contis. All long gone and much missed. "Next, I'm thinking of the white Haviland plates Jason's Nana left us, or that ratty old bear of Landon's. And Erin, your Milky."

I twirled fettuccine on my fork and smiled. A white-painted cow on wheels Granda made for me. Her teeth hide a drawer, her red leather tongue the pull, and a door in her side opens on a secret cabinet.

"You're getting old, little sister," Nick said. "Your child-hood toys are folk art."

I stuck out my tongue. "Paint a plate of fettuccine Alfredo. In Pondera today, I saw evergreens planted in a galvanized stock tank partly covered by snow. You're always after interesting patterns and shadows and con-trasts. Outside Honeysuckle, the glass gallery. Paint that."

"Oh, that building of Sally's," my mother said.

I reached for my Pinot Grigio, my own winter white. "So, how did Sally get all this property? I thought she was half broke."

"Wherever did you get that idea?" Fresca said.

"She whines about every festival and how much it will cost her. All last summer, she complained that business was terrible, but half the women who came in my shop carried bags from Puddle Jumpers. She's downright nasty about fund-raisers. Never contributes." Hence my shock at discovering she was the patron saint of the program for teen moms.

My mother glanced at Landon, regaling Nick with tales

of what T. rex ate, prehistoric birds, and other dino trivia. "That's just talk. Sally and her cousins are the heirs to the Beckman Timber Company fortune."

I stared, openmouthed, unaware Sally had any connection to the Beckman Timber Company. Long gone, it once owned thousands of acres of western Montana forest, two or three mills, and a plant across the lake that made railroad ties. The timberlands were sold off ages ago, for residential development or to other timber companies.

"Sally's mother and aunt split the fortune. It's an old story—one prospered, the other gambled. Actually, it was Sally's father, Bing Marler, who lost most of the money, in one get-richer scheme after another. Or so I understand. I never knew the man. He abandoned his wife and children when Sally was twelve or thirteen, her brother a year or two older."

"That must have been forty years ago," Chiara said, careful to keep the conversation to the female end of the table. "And she's still livid."

"Runs in the family. Her mother died angry, and broken. Sally's brother, also called Bing, had drug problems. Froze to death under a highway bridge in Denver. I do remember that. Tom and I had just moved back to Montana. Nick was a baby."

"Okay, so she's had a rough life, but why such a poor-mouth?" I took another bite.

"Habit, most likely. Her grandfather diversified nicely, and his grandchildren inherited commercial property all over western Montana. I'm sure Sally doesn't need to work. Her husband left when Sage was little—another long, sad story. There were no places to buy cute things for children around here, so she opened her own shop. I know it's hard to tell sometimes, but she does love the village."

So much for the idea that everyone knows everything about everyone in a small town. Sally was twenty-plus years older than I, her daughter a few years younger. Our families had never been close. There was no reason I should have known her family history, ancient or modern. Except that I felt like I should. Because I'd judged Sally based on my perceptions, and not on reality.

"Noni, may I be excused?"

Landon's question broke into my wonderings. I was surprised to see that the menfolk had already cleaned their plates.

"Dessert?" Fresca mouthed to Chiara, who mouthed back "no." They aren't the sugar police, but they do try to watch Landon's treats. Good idea, since his aunt hands out hand-made truffles and marshmallows like they're, well, candy.

At my mother's nod, Landon bounced up and Nick began clearing the table. "I'll take him home," Jason told Chiara. "You take your girl-time."

"We need to talk," I said. "About the website. I have ideas." They all burst out laughing and my cheeks got hot. "I'm a businesswoman. I'm supposed to have ideas."

"And we love you for it, little sister," Chiara said. "I'll start coffee."

Nick put on his coat and I reached up to kiss him. "Think about it overnight, and we can go see Ike in the morning."

The look on his face signaled that Fresca was listening.

"What was that about?" she said the moment we were alone.

"The chop," I said, telling her half the truth. It was gone. Good. Let him be responsible for it. And for figuring out how to explain to the sheriff why he withheld alibi evidence and stole from a crime scene.

In the kitchen, decaf brewed, its steam perfuming the air. I washed the glasses and pots and pans while Chiara dried.

"The success of Sally's children's shop is ironic, considering what a mess her own family is," she said.

"Some kind of feud with her daughter? There's a grand-baby, right?" I rinsed out the spaghetti pot.

Fresca set out mugs, cream, and spoons—and a jar of her new spice blend. "Sage got pregnant in high school and kept the baby, a boy. The father refused to accept any responsibility. To her credit, she finished school and started college. Living in a house Sally bought her, but still, not an easy road."

And without a program like the one Sally championed. I dried my hands while Fresca poured, and we carried our mugs to the living room.

"But Sage is married. She has a baby girl," I said, tucking one foot under me in the wing-back chair. The picture I'd seen on Facebook. "Not a young boy."

"Such a shame. When the little guy was three or four, he developed one of those nasty brain tumors children sometimes get. Glioblastoma. Fatal."

"Criminy. No wonder Sally is . . ." *No judging, Erin.* My biggest fault. I felt a blow to my chest as if I'd been kicked by a horse, and it wasn't even my family. "So Sage finished college, got married, had another baby?"

Fresca rubbed her throat. "She's a preschool teacher. Sally dislikes the husband, but I think she distrusts men on principle. Hard to blame her."

The Murphy girls sat in rare silence, sipping decaf Cowboy Roast with pumpkin pie spices. In the house my grandparents built, where my parents had raised us. The Orchard and the Merc weren't what held us together, but our love for those shared spaces certainly helped.

My sister leaned down to pet the dog, dark hair swinging forward over the face so like my own. Next to her on the couch, my mother sipped her coffee and met my gaze. Love and loyalty radiated from every bone in her body, and every corner, every nook and cranny in this house.

You're a lucky girl, Erin Murphy. Don't you forget it.

I rubbed my stars, and prayed that I never would.

· Twenty-two ·

Tiny, furious flakes eddied in my headlights as I turned off the highway. The dashboard thermometer read ten above. Our plow driver—not Jack Frost, thanks be— had cleared the long driveway on Tuesday, but you couldn't tell. A good six inches of snow had fallen in the last twenty-four hours, and by the looks of things, that count would double overnight.

Which meant a slippery trek down the hill to check the Big House, aka Bob and Liz Pinsky's place.

I crept down the drive. You'd think the deer would be home in bed, but no. The start of a storm, especially right after darkfall, draws them like mice draw cats.

I circled through the driveway. A bulb had gone out on the front porch. I hit the garage door clicker—making tracks is another trick to making the place look occupied.

"Dang it." Too cold. I climbed out and trudged to the stuck door, easing it up the metal rails. Trudged back to my car and drove into the garage.

The key trembled in my hand. Locks and I have never

gotten along, and the cold made it worse. Truth be told, after what happened at Christine's, I had a serious case of the creepies.

Inside, I slipped off my boots and listened. Quiet. Too quiet? And too cold.

One hand gripping the stair rail, phone in the other, I headed downstairs, all senses alert. The lights had gone on as planned and nothing looked out of place. Paused outside the furnace room door. No hum. Nothing.

I turned the knob and stepped inside. Spotted the problem right away. The pilot had blown out. I found the long-handled lighter and relit it, as Bob had showed me. After a long, breathless moment, the flame appeared with a small, satisfying poof, and the big gray box blazed back to life.

And I let out a noisy sound of relief.

Until I remembered the pipes. The heat couldn't have been off long, but I worried anyway. Detoured into a bathroom and tried first one faucet then another. Running water—music to my ears.

Boots in hand, I padded around the house, my heart beating a little faster and louder than normal. All was well. But it's *weird*, walking around an empty house in the dead of winter.

Gad—another one. Why do so many phrases we use every day evoke death and murder?

I reprogrammed the automatic lights. Replaced the burned-out bulb. Slipped my boots on and shoveled the front walk.

Job done, I perched on the steps and gazed upward. Hard to see the stars through all the snow, but they were there. They are always there. (As my mother says when people grouse about gray skies, it's the clouds that are gray. The sky is always blue.)

I leaned the shovel next to the front door and picked up the old bulb. As if it had flashed back to life, a thought occurred to me. Back inside, I peeled off my boots and traipsed across the warm hickory floors to the library. Bent my knees and ran my fingers over the spines.

Bingo! to quote Ned.

The road had gotten slicker in the few minutes I'd been at the Big House. I tucked the Subaru safely into my carport and carried my bag and my treasure into my cozy haven.

And stopped dead in my tracks.

"What the—?" A white feather floated in front of me. They filled the air, like giant snowflakes. A fine white trail led to the bedroom. Pumpkin crouched in the doorway, tail wrapped around her, the picture of innocence.

Except for the feathers on top of her head.

"Did you two pluck a chicken or kill an angel?" Sandburg sat in the middle of my bed, eyes blazing. When he saw the tabby following me, he started hissing.

"Ahhh. Pillow fight." A deflated down pillow lay on the floor, free of its case and wrung out like a dirty dish rag. I breathed a sigh of relief that the comforter was safe—protected by its cover and an old quilt my Gran had made, tossed on top for extra warmth.

I separated the cats and got out a broom. Quickly realized the folly in that, though the vacuum cleaner didn't do much better.

"Oh, no." A quarter-sized shard of iridescent blue-green glass lay on the rug. Under the bed lay the remains of a small vase I'd bought at the Chihuly Garden at Seattle Center. Not expensive or irreplaceable—not the work of the one-eyed glass master himself—but a sweet souvenir of my city life.

Totally busted.

After the unplanned cleaning spree, I ran a hot bath, scented with Luci's Lavender Valley bath gel, then pulled on my warmest flannel jammies and fuzzy socks. Settled into my favorite chair with a bowl of vanilla ice cream swimming in warm chocolate-Cabernet sauce. I'd left

Pumpkin in the bedroom, but instead of climbing into my lap, Sandburg eyed me from a distance. Apparently I had betrayed him, by tolerating the interloper.

"We'll find her another home, I promise. But we're nice to guests, remember?"

I clicked on my iPad and scrolled through e-mail. Clicked open a note from Kendra, the tea shop prospect, saying she had "decided to pursue other options." In other words, we'd given her a great idea to take to a bigger, hipper town. No surprise. But what spiked my Jell-O was taking the chicken's way out of telling us. I hit reply, thanked her for her interest, and wished her well, then sent a note to my co-conspirators, suggesting they follow up on the remaining leads.

I can be a chicken, too.

Pulled up the Spreadsheet of Suspicion. Added the break-in, and the alibi info for Nick and Sally.

Which reminded me of the crochet lady. I texted Chiara for her contact info. She texted back. I started an e-mail, then decided that a good investigator should not hide behind technology and it wasn't too late to call Crochet Lady.

After reminding her who I was and complimenting her on the cute hats, I got down to business. "Hey, it's hard to imagine summer when it's this cold, but your hats got me thinking. We'll need part-time help May to September, two or three days a week. I hear you're teaching at Dragonfly, and that's great, but if you're available, I'd love to hire you."

"Oh, pooh. Wish I could, but I've already told Sally Grimes I'd work weekends for her. And with the teaching, that's plenty. I'm so sorry."

Sally would try to convince her she'd sell more crocheted hats at Puddle Jumpers than at Snowberry. Probably true, but you can't beat Landon for advertisement. "Fun store. You'll have a great time."

"I subbed for her last Saturday. Helped her open, then

she had an event in Pondera, so I ran the shop myself the rest of the day. Quiet, but that's good when you're getting started."

"If anything changes, let me know. Employees get free truffles." That got a laugh. Nice lady. I wondered if she needed a cat.

In the bedroom, Pumpkin seemed content. At least she hadn't eaten any more pillows. Back in the living room, I poured a glass of Cabernet and picked up the purloined book.

C.M. Russell had been an unlikely looking artist—wild of eye and hair, in hat and high-heeled riding boots, wearing a white shirt with a red sash given to him by the Métis people. His wealthy Saint Louis manufacturing family had sent the teenage Charlie west in 1880, in hopes of taming him and derailing his artistic ambitions.

No such luck—luckily for us. As a young cowhand, he worked clay in his pockets. Left the open range as it was vanishing, to paint the land and life he loved. We make artists work awfully hard to prove their passion and talent. A fortunate few make a living at it. CMR, as people still call him, did—though never easily, and his wife Nancy was responsible for much of his commercial success.

What would they think of the prices his pieces—oils, watercolors, bronzes, even illustrated letters and Christmas cards—brought now? He'd think people had gone plumb loco. She'd think people had come to their senses.

I flipped through the color plates. Lotsa ridin' and ropin',' cowboys and Indians, camp scenes. Stunning vistas in colors folks who've never been out West can't imagine truly exist. They do, especially in the wide-open central Montana plains, where weird and magical sights are everywhere.

In high school, our Montana history class state tour had stopped at the Russell Museum in Great Falls, including the artist's home and cabin studio. Set up as though he'd stepped out for a smoke, an unfinished canvas on an easel and tubes of paint open on a wooden bench, the cabin held a treasure trove of artifacts CMR used as references: guns and arrows, beaded moccasins, sun-bleached skulls, a buffalo robe, and a mounted buffalo head as massive as the one in the Jewel Inn. (The one that I'd refused to sit by when we were kids and went out to breakfast, convinced that its huge golden-brown eyes were following me.)

Much as I love e-mail, wouldn't it be a thrill to receive a letter illustrated by hand? Addressed "Friend Erin," in his customary style, and signed "CMR," with a pen-and-ink drawing of a buffalo skull similar to the one on our license plates.

I sipped my wine, imagining it a cowboy's whiskey.

The last chapters covered Russell's home life and his summers at Bull Head Lodge on Lake McDonald, in Glacier Park. The cabin long gone, the black-and-white pictures conveyed colorful times. When the railroad was new. The Park was new. The stone and timber Lake McDonald Lodge, built by the legendary Northwest architect Kirtland Cutter, was new. CMR carved pictographs in the dining room hearth—destroyed fifty years later in the floods of 1964 that old-timers still talk about.

An epic time.

The pictures of the Russell home in Great Falls matched my teenage recollection: a simple two-story house typical of the early twentieth-century West. No gingerbread, no extravagance. Minimally comfortable by modern standards, with staunchly upright chairs and horsehair couches. No doubt modest compared to his upbringing, but an improvement over bunkhouses and camps. Or maybe not—CMR seemed to have genuinely loved the life of a working cowboy.

Wait. Go back. A photo of the sitting room caught my eye. On the wall, a large black-and-gold tapestry of a pair of cranes.

Where had I seen it before? Not on my high school tour.

And then I remembered: in the church, hanging on the wall opposite the altar, near the rear entry we'd used. Eyes closed, I pictured Zayda huddled beneath it and Nick arguing with a deputy who refused to let him near Christine.

I laid the book aside. Pacing isn't easy in cramped quarters. Behind the door to the bedroom addition, Pumpkin yowled for early release.

The same piece? A copy? Or just similar—tough to compare a black-and-white photo to a tapestry glimpsed briefly. Nick had said the chop was an Asian piece from Iggy's family. Was the tapestry one, too—and had it also come from the Russell home? He'd said she regretted selling another piece. To whom? Had the buyer come back for more?

Well, the tapestry was safe. But it gave me a clue: What else in Iggy's collection might have lured a killer and a thief?

My pacing took me past the microwave, green numbers telling me it was later than I'd thought. So much for my plan to spend the evening browsing for poems and essays the Speech and Drama Club could dramatize, but I did remember to dig out the essay on pie.

Sandburg jumped off the couch where he'd been guarding the living room from invaders and rubbed against my leg. "I'm not sure you deserve treats," I said. "I liked that pillow." Call me a softie, but I tipped a few into his bowl anyway, then did the same for Pumpkin.

"Poor little girl. First you lose your person, then you have to spend all day with that old meanie, and it's winter and you can't go outside. Promise, we'll find you a new owner. This week." It doesn't matter what you say to a cat, as long as you use the right tone.

In the living room, my phone rang. I opened the door and Pumpkin raced past me. "Whoa, girl. Didn't know you had a high gear."

"Sorry to call so late." Adam sounded both tired and keyed-up, a little anxious. "Bunch of us walked downtown for dinner and a beer. Big storm blew in while we were eating and when we came out, we pushed stuck cars for an hour. We were crossing Higgins when a Suburban slammed into a Prius. One of the guys is an EMT and we helped until the ambulance came."

"Ohmygosh. Is everybody okay?"

"Doubtful." His voice shook. "It's a stinking mess down here. I-90's closed."

I consider myself an independent woman. I do fine on my own. But an avalanche of emotion swept down off the hillside and nearly knocked me off my feet. Metaphorically speaking.

My sister was snug at home with her husband and her son. But I heard her anyway: *It's called love, little sister. And you've got it bad.*

"Yikes. Will class be canceled? Can you get home safely?" I settled onto a barstool.

"We're all in the same hotel, teachers and students, so class is on." He made a noise halfway between a laugh and a bark. "Besides, we're all wilderness geeks with rigs full of gear. If we need to go anywhere, we've got snowshoes and skis, avalanche beacons, and a week's worth of protein bars."

He'd be in heaven, kicking and gliding down the trail beside the Clark Fork River on his touring skis.

"Class ends noon Friday," he continued. "Long as I can get out of Missoula, I can get home to you. We can catch a movie."

Was it my imagination, or did his voice hold the same longing as my heart?

I filled him in on the latest developments for the Film Festival. I hesitated before sharing my suspicions about the burglary and the artwork—too vague. Too much like I was thick in the middle of danger, yet again.

Silence on the end of the line when I finished sharing my speculations. He'd sworn he didn't mind my investigating. Encouraged me to use my talents. Had I just given him a chance to change his mind?

"Erin, this is getting scary. Somebody wants something pretty bad. Don't you think—"

"That I should leave this to the professionals? That I don't know how to take care of myself?" Had I misread him that badly?

"I didn't say that. But maybe you're not as prepared for this kind of trouble as you think. Maybe you—"

"Maybe three people wouldn't be behind bars if not for me. Maybe Kim and Ike would have solved those other crimes without me, and without anyone else getting hurt." *Maybe I'm not the woman you think I am. Maybe the girl you crushed on from afar back in college went out into the big bad world and learned a thing or two.*

"Maybe we should talk tomorrow," he said. "When we're not so beat."

"Adam," I said, but the phone in my hand had gone silent.

The stool next to mine gave a soft groan as Pumpkin landed on the burgundy leather seat.

"Oh, girl," I said. "Did I blow it?"

Light glinted off the copper highlights in her green eyes.

From nowhere, a white feather floated into view. It swirled above my wineglass, and danced around the rim. It flirted with diving into the silky red pool, then brushed my fingertips and settled onto the black granite.

Mesmerized, we stared at the feather. "A sign," I told her. "But of what?"

· Twenty-three ·

I stomped my feet and opened the pine green door to Le Panier, the aromas of caffeine and fresh, yeasty bread warming my toes. While Wendy helped another customer, I drooled on the pastry case, as if there were any doubt what I'd order.

"Double shot, *pain au chocolat*," I said when it was my turn. "Any interest in a cat? I've got Christine's tabby, and she and my guy don't get along."

Wendy shot me a look like I'd suggested she chop off a finger, then rammed the coffee holder thingy into place and reached for the milk. Black gold—espresso—dripped into the shot glass.

"Can you ask your staff? She's quite sweet."

The door flew open and Sally barged in. The bakery was the one place where I'd never heard her complain about the cost of things. We all have our priorities.

"It's been a week and they haven't arrested anyone." She barked at Wendy as if I weren't there. As if she hadn't been pointing a finger at my own brother. "I don't know what that Kim Caldwell does all day, up in that office of hers. The office we pay for. And Ike Hoover's no better."

"Four days, Sally. Four and a half. And I can assure you Kim's been hard at work, interviewing witnesses, gathering forensics reports. Checking alibis." I was frustrated, too—with people who whine about things and refuse to help change them. Who whine, whine, and never lift a finger. Okay, so Sally has a secret charitable side, but don't stop me on a roll. "And if you don't quit complaining, and suggesting that my brother had the most to gain, I won't tell her what I know about your alibi. Because you hoped to gain a few things from Christine's death, too."

Though I hadn't worked out exactly what that might be, if not Iggy's money or real estate.

"My—what? I don't need an alibi. I didn't have anything to do with that girl's death."

"Oh, come on, Sally," Wendy said. "Everyone in town knows how ticked off you were when Iggy left her estate to Christine. You griped for weeks. Stood right there and threatened to sue her, to her face, for undue—what's it called?"

"Undue influence," I said. "Taking advantage of someone to get their money."

"I just wanted . . . That little tramp wormed her way into that old lady's life just to get—" Red splotches welled up on Sally's face and throat, and she sputtered like a tractor on the first day of spring.

"She did no such thing," Wendy said, matching Sally's indignation. "Christine was more shocked than anyone at her inheritance. She loved Iggy. You thought everything ought to come to you because you're a shirttail relative. You talk big on family but you don't walk the talk."

Sally had gone as white as bread dough. I helped her sit before she fell down, and drew up another black metal chair.

"You started to say, 'I just wanted.' What did you want?" I spoke gently.

"Why should I tell you?" She wiped the side of her nose with a knuckle.

"Because the more you complain, the more it looks like you're hiding something." Sally's mouth fell open and she clawed the front of her sweater. I pushed on. "But I know you were in Pondera at the baby shower when Christine was attacked. Trish Flynn told me."

She looked as if I'd shot her. "You didn't seriously think I—"

"About as seriously as you think Nick's a killer," I said. "But talk isn't cheap, Sally. It hurts people. Nick lost the woman he loved, and he's had to defend himself to half the town. Prove every step he took on Saturday, be finger-printed, turn over his phone and his boots and I don't know what else." Of course, he hadn't made things easier with his own blackout on the truth.

"You don't know what it's like. You Murphys, you work together, eat together, practically live together."

My heart nearly stopped. Wendy froze, then came to my rescue. "Sally, are you forgetting the hit-and-run that killed Erin's father? No one ever paid for that, and let me assure you, they suffer for it every day."

I dug in my blue bag for a packet of tissues. "Thank you," Sally said, her voice high and wobbly, and blew her nose. Eight-point-oh on the Richter scale, as my sister says of my sneezes.

"You asked what I wanted from Iggy. What I wanted was"—another honk into the tissues—"what she couldn't give me. I wanted my own family back. My parents and my brother. My daughter and my grandchildren, both of them. We were the only family she had left. She should have wanted me to have her things."

I scooted my chair closer and leaned forward, elbows on my knees.

"Isn't the point of family to help one another pursue our dreams? She knew you're fine. You have a thriving shop, a lovely home, and most important, your daughter and granddaughter. And the memory of your grandson. Iggy made a life of art, and of helping other artists. She wanted to help Christine fulfill her dreams, giving her a home and financial security. And Christine was planning to continue that legacy."

"But then she left it all to Nick."

Who felt the burden. "If there are any special pieces—furniture that was in the family, knickknacks you want, I can talk to him."

The door opened and two couples dressed for a day of outdoor fun came in. I stood, realizing I'd abandoned a latte somewhere. Wendy handed me a white bag and a hot paper cup. "I made you a fresh one. Scat before she revs up again."

"I can see the headlines, now," I said. "MURDER SUSPECT KIDNAPS SISTER, FEEDS HER TO WOLVES."

A smile played at the corner of Nick's mouth, a tiny dimple creasing his cheek. I had a good view of the right side of his face from the passenger seat of his Jeep. To be fair, when he dragged me out to the parking lot behind the Merc, he stopped long enough to grab my boots and snowshoes from my car. And he let me bring my breakfast.

"I want you to see what I've been working on. What I'm protecting." He turned at Mountain View and a muscle in his jaw twitched and his throat swelled, skin pale under his winter wind-tan, as we drove past the church and cottage. "So you know what's at stake before you decide to blurt out my secrets to Ike Hoover."

"You don't think Ike can keep the wolf pack confidential? That he won't think it matters?"

His knuckles whitened on the wheel. "I don't know what matters to Ike Hoover."

The anniversary was approaching, and I wasn't the only

Murphy feeling it. Feeling Ike Hoover's fifteen-year-old failure hanging over us.

We drove south in silence, then east onto Rainbow Lake Road. Past Phyl and Jo's place. Left at the swimming hole, onto a snow-covered logging trail that made me glad I'd stopped when I did Tuesday. Kathy's Honda would have high-centered fifty feet in. Above the road, on a snow-covered ridge, stood a weathered log cabin, smoke rising from its stone chimney, a pickup beside it. I craned my neck to peer past Nick at a hand-painted sign, barely visible above a snow drift: REDAWAY LANE.

"Why keep it a secret?" My tone sounded childish, pouty, even to my ears.

"You need to understand what's going on here, Erin."

"Oh, I understand. I understand that you're more worried about a pair of wolves than you are about yourself. That after everything your mother has been through, including being accused of murder and losing her husband to a killer who's still on the loose, you'd rather be accused yourself than breathe a word about wolves in the neighborhood. You weren't around last summer when the fingers were pointing at her, but let me tell you, it was no romp in the woods. I understand that for all your talk about scientific integrity, you're willing to ignore your obligation under the law—you told me yourself that reporting wolf sightings is mandatory. Why? So you can write a journal article ten people will read, and promote your pet theories about—what do you call it? Trophic cascades and how wolves bring back the willows and warblers? I don't care about trophic cascades, Nick. I care about you."

The shoulder belt locked against my chest and flung me backward as Nick stomped on the brake. My head bounced off the neck rest and my shin struck a sharp edge beneath the dashboard. I managed to hold on to my latte, but cold coffee trickled down my bare hand.

Nick slammed the Jeep into neutral and turned on me,

blue eyes dark but blazing. Like the bottom of an alpine lake, or the base of a gas flame. Cold fire.

"You don't understand. These wolves haven't done anything except do what they were born to do. To roam and breed and establish new territory. To play their part in the ecosystem. If one part fails, the whole thing fails. *We* fail. *We* suffer. Every species suffers." He punched out the words. "Jack Frost is harmless compared to some of these—I can't even call them hunters. Real hunters are humane. These people think nothing of taking target practice on a new mother, leaving the pups to starve. They're born blind and deaf, you know, and this is a new pack, with no other females to feed them. These"—he fumbled for a word he was willing to say in front of me—"sons of blockheads think it's fun to wipe out a pack and nail the carcasses to the fence. To set a trap that will kill a dog, strong enough to break a man's leg, and when a wolf trips it, leave him there to die, howling in pain."

I shivered. State authorities prosecute poachers and slob hunters who kill for the sake of killing, leaving the meat to spoil. And everyone in these parts has heard the ravings—drunken or sober—of the rabid wolf haters. But what Nick described made me want to puke.

"Two more weeks, Erin. That's all I need. When hunting season's over, and the den is established, then I can make my report. Any luck, it will fly under the radar long enough for the pups to be born, or even weaned. Then they have a real chance for survival."

He didn't trust Ike Hoover. But he had to share his logs and prove where he'd been—and he couldn't wait two weeks.

"So why is J.D. so worried about confidentiality? Does he think business at the bar will suffer if he's a known wolf-lover? Ned never cares if his opinions scare customers away. Good riddance, he says."

"Ned's got fifty years in the business. J.D.'s only been

here six weeks. He understands the stakes and he's not real keen on getting caught up in controversy until he has to. And he doesn't want crazed men with high-powered guns running all over these woods. But I'm pretty sure that once the pack gets established and I've reported my findings, he'll be a staunch supporter."

I let that sink in. Nick slipped the Jeep back into gear and we drove on in silence. The road narrowed as it looped away from the lake and traversed the ridge. Finally, it ended in a tight turnaround. He told me to shut off my phone, and I remembered that the sheriff still had his.

"Is this where you were when I called, last Saturday?"

He nodded and bent to buckle his snowshoe. We traipsed through the woods, Nick in the lead, scouting for tracks. Not just wolf tracks—the movements of deer, elk, and other wildlife are clues to the wolves' location as well. Every so often, Nick aimed his binoculars on the sky.

We settled into a blind he'd created at the base of a tree, pine and fir boughs our camouflage. Nick made a few notes. I huddled inside my coat, not daring to tell him I was freezing and had to pee.

After spotting two ravens and a golden eagle, Nick crept out of the blind and I followed. He handed the glasses to me. "The scavenger birds are leading us to the wolf kill. I'm going closer. You stay put." He held out his pistol, butt end toward me.

I shook "no." Our dad had taught us all to shoot, but I hadn't held a gun in years. This was not the time to test my reflexes.

Nick abandoned all pretense of stealth, marching into the clearing as gracefully as possible on snowshoes. The idea was to get in and out quickly, using the birds as a gauge of how close the wolves were. As he approached, the ravens flew up into the trees, squawking madly at the intruder. The golden eagle, huge, its face red from feeding, gave him the evil eye, his—or was it her?—only concession to sidestep a few feet away from the fallen deer. Wisely, Nick kept his distance but I knew he was watching the winged predator as he photographed tracks, birds, and carcass, and took a few quick measurements.

Minutes later, he knelt beside me, the ravens swooping back to their find before he'd left the clearing.

"Whitetail. Found the kill Saturday morning," he whispered. "It's still got its nose, so the wolves aren't finished. That's why the birds are so alert."

"The nose? Is that like dessert?"

He signed to shush me as first one wolf then the second entered the clearing. The ravens returned to their roosts, the eagle standing its ground as long as possible before taking flight. "The male," he said of the lead wolf, a majestic long-legged creature, his thick coat a mix of golden brown and gray. His size and the rounded tips of his ears distinguished him from the more commonly seen coyotes. I held my breath in awe.

Behind him came the female, mottled gray on her head and back, her sides and legs white, the straight heavy tail salt-and-pepper. My fingers itched for the phone in my pocket, to take a picture for Chiara's *Winter White* series, but I didn't dare.

We watched as the wolves fed, then ambled back into the woods. If they sensed our presence—and I suspected they did—they didn't let on. They had no interest in us, unless we threatened them. I held myself rock-still, an image in my brain of tagging along with my grandfather Murphy to a farm auction and getting a lecture on not moving a muscle while the auctioneer worked the crowd, lest we accidentally buy a truck or a hay baler.

"Let's get you back to town," Nick said a few minutes later and stood. I took his hand, my knees stiff with cold.

"Now you see what I do." He turned the key in the Jeep's ignition. "Not glamorous. But critical to the survival of the species."

I rubbed my arms and wiggled my toes in my boots. "Hard to believe they're right here among us, and we barely notice."

"It's unusual to have a site so accessible. To me, it proves that humans and wolves can live side-by-side peacefully. They want what we all want: to hang with our own kind and be left alone by the rest."

And enjoy a little fresh venison now and then. We drove by the Redaway cabin. J.D.'s truck was gone.

"You have two other witnesses, sort of." Nick shot me a curious glance, and I went on. "Phyl and Jo hear the wolves at night. They also see you drive out this way too often for coincidence."

He smiled wryly. "Not much gets past those two."

"Not much gets past Ike or Kim, either. They've talked to Phyl and Jo. That's how they knew you were out here Saturday. That, and the rotten cell reception up the Jewel, plus what they get from your phone. Let me tell Kim. Get her to persuade Ike to keep the wolves' whereabouts under wraps. Keeping secrets makes you look guilty, brother. More secrets equals more trouble. It's like compound interest."

Not until he pulled up outside the Merc's back door did Nick speak, turning in his seat to face me. "I can't stop you, Erin. I won't try. Promise me that before you do anything, you'll think about the consequences."

As if I could think about anything else.

· Twenty-four ·

Nick's escapade had almost made me late for my meeting with the drama teacher. Not to mention cold and wet. *Oh, well.* I tossed my gear in the back of the Subaru and zoomed up the hill.

The high school hadn't changed much since my student days. It even smelled the same—hormones and hair spray, with undertones of lemon-scented ammonia. And near the gym, sweat mixed with the dirty-rubber odor of tennis shoes and basketballs. I autographed the visitors' register and headed for the drama classroom. Jaw clenched, I paused to run my fingers over the raised letters of the plaque designating the Tom Murphy Memorial Gym. He'd been going home after a team practice but never made it. I'd been at the Playhouse for a rehearsal when Ike Hoover came to break the news and drive me back to the Orchard.

"Ah, you found us." A tiny blonde in her mid-thirties extended her hand.

Paper banners covered the classroom walls, each illustrated with hand-painted images and lines from poems and soliloquies. "The students created those," the teacher told me. "And they are thrilled at the opportunity to put together a program, short notice and all. These kids thrive on sharing their passion, and community support is invaluable."

She had a class in ten minutes, so we ran through the schedule quickly. The kids had brainstormed with her, choosing poems and dramatic readings focused on food or movies.

"Great choices. Any chance of including this?" I handed her a copy of a page from my recipe binder.

"Pie. Oh, pie. I love pie," she exclaimed, not yet realizing she was repeating a refrain of the essay. "And I know the perfect girl for this piece."

"Great. We're set, then. But what's that one?" I pointed at the final entry on her list, reading "J.C. skit—D.G."

Her eyes sparkled. "Allow me one surprise. I promise, you'll love it."

Famous last words. Like giving directions and saying, "You can't miss it."

I was halfway back to my car before realizing I should have offered her a cat.

"UPS come?" I hung my damp coat on a hook and peeled off my boots.

Tracy nodded. "Brought your sample tins and labels. But no DVD. What if it doesn't get here in time?"

I swore to myself. "I've got a plan, but I'd rather have a movie. Give me two minutes." Bozo had improved enough to stay with a neighbor today, and she was eager to check on him.

Upstairs, I called the distributor for the UPS tracking number—bypassing customer service and going directly to the friendly supervisor—then checked the number. The delivery slotted for today had been rescheduled for Friday. "Weather-related delays," the site said. I picked up the phone and called the copy shop, local shipping headquarters.

"Big mess all over," the manager said. "If it misses the Friday delivery to Jewel Bay, as long as the truck gets to the Pondera hub by noon Saturday, I can run in and grab it."

"Fingers crossed. Thanks."

"Sure," he said. "Wife and I are looking forward to the Festival. We'll do all we can."

And that is why I do what I can for this village.

Back on the shop floor, I sold a few more Valentine's baskets and bags of popcorn. A regular came in to pick up her weekly order. "So glad you carry locally raised beef and pork," she said. "We feel better, supporting our neighbors. And it tastes better."

Exactly.

I unpacked the tins and labels. Good products, good prices. Wouldn't fit our machine—we'd half to fill, seal, and label by hand. Hire a part-timer or do it myself? I had to be careful not to keep Luci from her soap-making. *Don't mess up your own plans, Erin.*

Luci. Soap. I reached for the phone.

"Reg Robbins could make molds for you shaped like wolf and bear tracks, using Nick's casts. I'd recommend earthy scents—sage, cedar, sweetgrass. No lilac-scented grizzly paws."

"How about wild rose? Or huckleberry," Luci said. "And what about cutting soap into animal shapes, like trout and moose?"

Hard to imagine gripping a wet moose in the shower, but I told her to bring me samples and we'd try it out.

"*Yes!*" I said after we hung up. Designing new products is such a high.

Tracy called to ask for the rest of the day off, to spoil her pup and whip up more Valentine's treats. Give me an animal- or business-related excuse and I'm a sucker.

The early afternoon lull stretched on. I straightened shelves, restocked product, and handled the mail. The commercial kitchen stood idle—in season, the jam-maker takes it over on Thursdays, perfuming the entire village with sweet berry scents. Right now, she was peddling her wares and soaking up rays in Arizona. She'd sent me a bag of prickly pear cactus candy, wondering if we'd like to carry it—and true to our mission, I told her if she could make it out of our high plains cactus, you bet.

But finally, I could put off deciding what to do about Nick, the alibi, and the Chinese chop no longer.

I didn't share Nick's distrust of Ike Hoover. True, Ike had not solved the crime that mattered most to our family. But he was a good cop, and a good man. And he kept the cold-case file on the shelf behind his desk.

First, I called the state historical society. The chief curator trotted out to the gallery floor and confirmed my suspicions.

I opened the Spreadsheet. Instead of rows and columns, my sister would use lines and arrows and shapes to illustrate the relationships between facts and people. My brother would make notes and specify coordinates.

Why not combine our approaches? I brought up Christine's place on Google Maps. Kim had said the attack likely occurred five to twenty minutes before death. Nick's log put him on the wolf trail at Rainbow Lake starting before sunrise. My call established he was near there when I found Christine. I zoomed out, searching the ridge above the lakeshore for J.D.'s cabin. The road past the cabin was barely visible through the dense tree cover, but I made out the turnaround where it ended. Clicked on the place mark icon, dragged it into place, and added a label. Could Nick have attacked Christine, fled, and gotten back to the turnaround so quickly?

Pretty tight.

Why did he not see that he had to show Ike and Kim the logbook—or continue living under their suspicions? Chances were they'd find out about it sooner or later, and sooner was better.

Next on the list: Sally. She'd left the village Saturday

at ten thirty, according to the crochet lady, and reached Pondera well before noon. Stayed there all afternoon. She was off the map, and off my list.

Jack Frost. I'd all but crossed him off for lack of motive. Kim discounted motive in favor of evidence. But I didn't have any evidence tying Frost to Christine's killing. Did she?

What if I went back out to interview his neighbors, tracked down his plowing customers, tried to pinpoint his movements? No doubt Kim already had.

Zayda. Her behavior at the scene baffled me. She insisted she'd simply arrived early, gone in, then changed her mind and decided to wait outside. From what I'd observed at the scene, her shock at Christine's injuries had been real.

Both her mother and her boyfriend were as puzzled as I was.

Acting out of character raises questions. But I didn't know her or her character well enough to put those questions into words.

I labeled Christine's place, and dropped another marker at the Georges' house, barely a mile away.

Sat back and stared at map and spreadsheet. Ran through my decision tree yet again. With Adam away—and not so keen on me playing Nancy Drew—and Chiara holed up in her studio, there was no one to bounce my ideas off. I could pout about that, or trust myself.

Sorry, Nick.

Kim's big rig, TIMBERLAKE COUNTY SHERIFF emblazoned on the side panels, stood near the door to the sheriff's satellite office, tucked in an unused space behind the fire department headquarters.

Maroon 5 blared through my car speakers, the lead singer holding on to those notes longer than seemed possible. I'd closed the shop early, certain I knew what to do,

BUTTER OFF DEAD 209

but now that I stood, metaphorically, on the threshold of betraying my family in order to save it, I couldn't do it.

So I did what a good chicken always does.

I crossed the road.

And kept on going. Drove north out of town, then east, winding along the base of the mountains. Jason says a Murphy is incapable of driving a straight line anywhere. We detour down *this* road, take *that* one to see what's there. We stop for historic sites, and drag our friends past personal landmarks. My mother says it's a good trait; it's how she met my father.

Without realizing where I was headed, I found myself in the Jewel Basin, on the same road Adam and I had driven last Sunday.

Adam. My heart sank. Had my pride derailed another chance?

The entries in Nick's logbook confirmed that he was watching packs in the Jewel as well as near Rainbow Lake. Did it matter? He knew, I knew, and Kim knew he hadn't been up here despite what he'd said.

The road led on for miles, curving through drainages and climbing to a popular trailhead. From there, a hiker could plunge into the wilderness or take day hikes into the clear blue alpine lakes—frigid even in August—that dot our rugged mountains. This time of year, even all-wheel drive would only take me so far.

"This is pointless," I said to no one. "Go back before you get stuck."

Even if Kim didn't have the phone records proving that he hadn't been up here when I called, or if Phyl hadn't reported seeing Nick on Rainbow Lake Road, my map project proved his lie wouldn't have protected him. None of his observation sites were far enough from Christine's place.

"That's it," I said out loud. The road was getting slicker by the second and I forced myself to relax my grip on the wheel. "I'm telling her everything I know. I don't care what Nick says." He was digging himself a hole as big as a wolf den, with no chance of escape.

On the way back, I took a different route. True to my family in that regard, at least.

Dense tree cover on this stretch, and I drove on alert, keenly aware that deer and elk would be on the move as twilight fell. Keenly aware, too, that I had a party to throw in not very long, and wasn't dressed for the occasion.

Few people live out here, almost none in February, but instinctively I glanced down each road and driveway, an eye out for other drivers who assumed they too were alone on these roads. On the third road, a woman ran. Jogging in this weather?

I backed up and the figure sprinted toward me. No coat or hat. She stopped ten yards from the Subaru and bent over, bare hands on her knees, panting. Her breath exploded in the air.

"Zayda?" I got out and stood by my car, struck by the sense that she'd bolt if I weren't careful.

She took a few steps toward me, clutching her stomach. *The hell with caution.* I grabbed a spare fleece jacket from my car and dashed toward her. Wrapped it around her shoulders and ushered her into the passenger seat. Blasted the heat. Her teeth chattered.

"Stomp your feet." I wriggled out of my own puffy purple coat and wrapped it around her legs. Handed her my gloves, her fingers so stiff I had to tug them on for her.

"Breathe in through your nose and out through your mouth." Probably not high on the list of hypothermia prevention tips, but it would calm her.

I dug under my seat for a water bottle. "What happened? What are you doing out here?" Miles from home. Even a track star like Zayda would not run far in this weather not properly dressed.

And then I realized where we were. At the end of Larry Abrams's driveway.

"Zayda, what happened? Are you hurt?"

She closed her eyes and shook her head. Shook it violently.

Without saying a word, she protesteth too much.

I locked her in and headed down the long lane. Dylan had said other kids were giving her a hard time. More of that? "What are you doing out here anyway?"

"Nothing. I just had to talk—details for the Festival."

By the time I reached her red SUV, her breath had returned to normal and I thought the worst had passed. No other vehicles except Larry's white Cadillac stood in front of the cavernous log home. "Are you sure nothing happened? Nothing you need to tell anyone?"

"You can't call the police. Don't call the police." She clutched the door handle, ready to run.

"Oh-kaaay." Why would I call the police? "If you say you're okay . . . Keep the sweater for now."

She started her car and I followed her out, driving in tandem toward town. She turned on her road and I kept going.

Places to go, secrets to spill.

· Twenty-five ·

Seventeen was not old enough to make every decision. And I did not believe that Zayda had gone running off into the frigid five o'clock air without coat, hat, or gloves because of "nothing" or "details."

But the puzzle of Zayda George would have to wait. I parked beside my brother's Jeep. "Fancy meeting you here."

Nick opened the gray steel door to the metal building. "After you, little sister."

Turned out he'd been summoned for more questioning. He agreed that I could stay.

That's good of you, I thought. *Since I'm here to save your be-hind.*

"First, your phone." Ike pushed Nick's silver-clad iPhone toward him and Nick slipped it in his pocket.

"Second, complete firearms report came back from the crime lab." Ike rested his hands, fingers loosely entwined, on top of a document in the precise middle of his desk. "As I think we've told you, we recovered a .38 caliber revolver, recently fired, at the scene. Underneath the display cases."

No, you did not tell us that. Not all of it. Kim had refused to tell us where the weapon had been found.

"Ms. Vandeberg was shot with a .38 caliber firearm," he said. "The ME recovered two slugs from the body. I'm sorry if this is upsetting, Nick."

"*If* it's upsetting?" Nick look incredulous. Kim stood guard in her simple but stylish black pantsuit. Arms crossed, she studied us, face giving away nothing.

"The firearms examiner matched them to the weapon we recovered." Ike continued as if Nick hadn't spoken. "From the pattern of gunshot residue on the clothing, she concluded that the victim was shot at a distance of one to three feet. Suggesting that either she knew her attacker, or he—or she—managed to get quite close to her."

I shuddered, afraid to imagine the horror of Christine's last minutes, but unable to stop myself.

"The GSR—gunshot residue—tests of your hands were inconclusive," he said.

"Meaning what?" Nick leaned forward in his squeaky vinyl chair. "They can't prove I shot her, because I didn't. But you don't want to admit that."

Blink and you'd have missed Ike's flinch, it was so slight.

"It was a cold day. The shooter may have worn gloves. Yes"—he said, before Nick could interject—"we took yours and tested them. No residue, inside or out. But the shooting occurred some time before we first made contact with you. You could have worn other gloves and discarded them, or wrapped the gun in a scarf. Simple hand washing removes most GSR."

"You also tested Zayda," I said. Ike kept his eyes on Nick, but I glanced at Kim and read her face: also inconclusive.

"Of course, that's not what's most interesting," Ike said, his baritone cool, almost icy. Kim had told me once, on a ride, that the deputies call him Sheriff Cucumber behind his back. "Again, I apologize for speaking so indelicately."

Nick made a slight motion that told me "apology refused."

"We found three sets of fingerprints on the gun: Ms. Vandeberg's, an unidentified set—some clear, some smeared, and yours."

Never had I been so glad to be sitting. Never had I been so glad for sturdy construction. Because I felt like the roof had fallen in.

Nick slumped in his seat, his face pale. Finally, he spoke, eyes closed, drawing his fingers down one cheek. "You found my prints because I gave her that gun. I taught her how to shoot, last fall after she moved to the church property. Jack Frost is a hothead, and I was worried."

Kim's eyes flicked from Nick to Ike and back.

"Any proof?" Ike said.

Nick paused, remembering. "Just a couple of kids we saw at the shooting range. The one who picked up the books," he said to me. "Looked like he was teaching the girl."

"Dylan Washington." Zayda's boyfriend.

"Find who matches that print," he told Ike, despair turning to anger. "That's your shooter."

"Believe it or not, we thought of that. It's not in the system."

"And you'd rather blame me than track down who it belongs to." Nick's voice rose. "Just like fifteen years ago. When you couldn't find the driver who ran my father off the bridge over Jewel Bay, you tried to blame him."

Ike's eyes darkened. "Reconstruction found no skid marks or yaw marks on the road surface, and was ultimately inconclusive—"

Nick shot forward in his seat, one leg back, ready to launch. "Your favorite word. The reconstructionist said the driver's side damage indicated impact on an angle sufficient to push his car into the guardrail. Pushed so hard he broke through and dangled over the icy water. They didn't find skid marks or yaw marks because the road was covered in snow and ice. You argued he lost control, hit the rail, and spun, causing the left-side damage himself."

I had never heard any of this. I wanted to scream. I wanted to hear it all. I wanted them to shut up.

"I never blamed him, Nick," Ike said, his tone low and controlled. "That was one theory, one possibility we had to consider. But I've never stopped searching."

"Well, I hope you're searching harder for Christine's killer. There's only so much my family can take." As Nick stood, Kim slumped against the wall, her face as gray as the dingy paint.

"Take my chair, Detective. I'm leaving."

"*No.*" I grabbed his hand. "Stop this. You don't have to like him, Nick. But we have to tell them what we know. All of it. Starting with the logbook."

Kim recovered her composure, and perched on the corner of Ike's desk. Nick sank back into his chair. After a long moment, he opened his pack and withdrew the slim green-and-black log. "I was working Saturday, as I told you. But not in the Jewel."

"We know that," Kim said. "The phone records show you were somewhere near Rainbow Lake when Erin called you."

"My sister," he continued, "followed me Tuesday morning—"

"You knew?" He hadn't let on.

"Borrowed car, borrowed hat—lame disguise. She'd begun to suspect that I wasn't in the Jewel when she called me, after she found Christine. Yesterday, she confronted me, and today, I took her out there to show her what I found. I've been tracking a pair of young gray wolves who've taken up residency in the woods above Rainbow Lake. They've mated, they're getting ready to build a den. My field notes establish everything." He laid the book on Ike's desk. "Saturday, I turned my phone back on when I got back to my Jeep. Erin called less than five minutes later. My GPS coordinates will match your cell tower records."

"Anybody see you?" Ike said. "Notes can be created after the fact, and wolves aren't reliable witnesses."

My brother's ears smoldered.

"He took pictures," I said. "The camera notes the time and date. Or are you going to say those can be faked, too? But there is a witness. Tell them, Nick."

He breathed out heavily through his nose. "I promised my source anonymity, for his own protection. You know how crazed some people get over wolves. Can you keep this under wraps?"

"Can't promise till I hear what you have to say, but we'll do our best."

After a long hesitation, Nick relayed J.D.'s report of spotting the wolves. Reluctantly, he agreed to leave the log to be reviewed as evidence. He handed over the card from his camera, showing the dates and times he'd photographed tracks, the kill, and the wolves, but also the metadata, so they could convince themselves that the info hadn't been falsified.

We were all exhausted when Nick said one last thing. "Don't blame my sister. She's been urging me to tell you. In fact, you came here to tell them yourself, didn't you?"

I peeked at the time on my phone. "Partly. Also, I figured out what the thief was after. Sort of. But the Film Festival starts in forty-five minutes and I'm a mess."

"Better talk fast, then," Ike said. But his eyes held a twinkle.

That was a challenge I could handle. I whipped through my theory: The burglar and the killer were the same person. He or she knew Iggy had a valuable art collection.

"So far, nothing new," Kim said.

"Iggy's family—actually, her husband's family—had a long relationship with Charlie Russell and his wife, Nancy, and other artists of the era. I think the killer was after a piece that once belonged to the Russells. Maybe a gift to them—an item that didn't stay in the Russell house or studio, or go on display in the museum. There's a photograph of the Russell house that shows the black-and-gold crane tapestry that hangs in the back of the church. I'm sure it's the same. Nick's identified another piece of Christine's that we think may have belonged to the Russells as well."

Nick set the chop on the desk. We left out the part about him taking it. Tampering with a crime scene and all that.

"This morning, I called the state historical society. The Rings visited the Russells at Bull Head Lodge, when David Ring, Iggy's late husband, was a boy. They signed the cloth screens the Russells used as a guest book. Kim, you remember seeing them, on our high school tour."

Wordless, she nodded.

"Lrss," Christine had said. "Shop" and "lrss."

"Russell was famous for writing illustrated letters to family friends, especially to the children. I think Iggy had a letter Russell wrote David, and someone—I don't know who—wants it. Someone who's been digging into Russell history, hoping for a big find. We—you—need to identify those people and track them down."

"You think that person went to the church to try to convince Christine to sell, and when she refused, shot her with her own gun?" Kim said.

"They struggled. That's how it ended up under the display cases."

"How did this person get in?" she asked, her tone doubtful.

"How do you propose we identify these mysterious collectors?" Ike asked.

"That, I'm not sure," I said to Kim, and then to Ike, "both Iggy and Christine died before finishing the inventory. It may be listed there—or not. I'm hoping she consulted an appraiser or an art expert, since she planned to leave some of the collection to the Art Center. The chief curator at the historical society is new so he didn't talk to her, but he promised to check with his staff."

Ike made a note. "We'll start there, then talk to her lawyer and the Art Center. And bring me that photograph of the tapestry." He glanced at his watch. "Tomorrow. Your public awaits."

"Thanks. You coming, Kim? Kyle will be there—his GTO is in the documentary."

"I—don't think so. Too much to do here."

"One more thing," Nick said, and I gripped the arms of my chair. "That is the original stone chop, but there's a copy. Iggy had a bronze casting made, with a patina that resembles stone, to keep after she donated the original. I'm pretty sure it was in the display case in the church, and I'm willing to bet it's missing."

The corollary of Fresca's Law of Acting As If is to completely ignore the possibility that you might be sorely undressed. My mother, however, does not recognize that corollary, and gave my stretchy black cargo pants and lime green fleece turtleneck a disapproving look from top to toe when I entered the Playhouse lobby for the opening night reception.

I smiled brightly. At least I'd found a floaty turquoise scarf in my office to dress it up, and a change of footwear. I'd fluffed my hair in the bathroom mirror, and successfully scrounged in the bottom of my bag for a pink lip gloss.

No matter. In Jewel Bay, plenty of folks—especially the male of the species—consider fleece jackets and hiking pants dress-up clothes.

"This is so much fun," the owner of Village Antiques told me. "What a great idea!"

"Christine's brainchild," I said, and she touched my arm, her eyes soft.

"Great food." Her husband, the town pharmacist, gestured with a half-eaten cheese pastry.

"I'll drink to that," said Donna Lawson, the liquor store owner, raising a glass.

The lobby sparkled. A jazz trio played movie themes. Older folks pointed at Larry's posters, reminiscing about movies they'd seen. Others studied the display showing off the Film Club goals and projects, and chatted with Club members, dressed to kill.

Criminy, Erin, enough of the morbid clichés.

The Bijou sign added the perfect retro-hip touch. I headed for the buffet and was reaching for a crostini when my sister grabbed my arm.

"Erin, where have you been? Big problem. The toilets are backing up."

"Crap," I said.

"Exactly," she replied. "Two kids are mopping up, and Ned's on the case." As a veteran barkeep, Ned Redaway knew a thing or two about old plumbing. He was also a veteran of the board of directors that runs the community-owned theater, and had been involved up to his eyeballs in the latest renovation. The one that expanded the restrooms and cost a bundle.

At that moment, Ned emerged from the women's room, wiping his brow with a red bandanna. "Sorry, girlie. I think the sewer line is froze."

"Frozen? But those lines are buried."

"Cold as it's been, sh—sorry. Poop freezes. Can't do nothing about it tonight."

Seriously. My next project ought to be a petition to repeal Murphy's Law. "We'll block the doors." We muscled garbage cans into place as barricades. I jumped onto a painted bench and clapped my hands for attention.

"Thank you all for coming out tonight to celebrate the Food Lovers' Film Festival, and to support the Jewel Bay High School Film Club." I clapped again, and the audience applauded and raised their glasses. "Unfortunately, the weather is complicating things. Seems the sewer line is frozen."

Chuckles and groans from the crowd.

"Obviously, we can't ask you to hold it the entire evening, so Snowberry Gallery will keep its restroom available until the screening starts. And the antique shop across the street?" The owner waved her hand, signaling agreement. "If you get desperate during the show, Applause and Chez Max are the closest restaurants, both open this evening. Thank you for understanding. There's more to eat and drink, and in a few minutes, we'll move this show into the theater."

Odd that the freeze hadn't affected the neighboring buildings—yet, anyway—but no time to dwell on that.

Ned offered his hand and I hopped off the bench. "Girlie, you got a knack for solving problems, by jingo."

"Thanks, Ned. This town keeps me in practice." My stomach reminded me that I'd been aiming for food when the fit hit the shan. I retraced my steps and wolfed down two crostini and a cheese pastry. I grabbed a glass of Prosecco and mingled, thanking donors. Nothing happens in Jewel Bay without donors.

So I made the rounds, mingling, chatting, sipping, and thanking. And trying to ignore the sticky patches under my armpits.

"Good job." I snared a taste of sushi. Max had made three types of rolls, working the paddlefish caviar in after all. Wendy beamed, the white chef's toque she wears for special occasions bobbing. "Everybody loves the food."

I stood at the edge of a small circle gathered around Larry Abrams and sipped. The bubbles tickled my nostrils, and I suppressed a sneeze.

"Collectors save history," he said. "Or bits and pieces of it. Some things people instantly recognize as worth preservation. Journals from the Lewis and Clark expedition, for example. The gifts they gave the Indians. Amateur archaeologists still search along the trail for physical evidence."

"Didn't they find a military button a few years ago?" Donna said, "Near a possible campsite?"

"Wish I could find that missing cache." The pharmacist chuckled, referring to a bit of Lewis and Clark lore.

Across the room, Zayda George stood on tiptoes, scanning the crowd. She'd piled her blond hair high and wrapped the knot in an orange band that matched her stretchy pink-and-orange top. Cute look, frazzled expression. Maybe I could talk with her tonight and figure out what had happened this afternoon. Figure out whether her parents needed to hear about it. Or the police, as she'd implied, then insisted otherwise.

"If your ancestors had lived near the trail," Larry said, "they might have found buttons, or pill bottles, not knowing the stuff had any connection to the Corps of Discovery. Eventually, they'd have buried the finds with the rest of their garbage, or left them gathering dust in an outbuilding. Or their kids would have tossed the stuff. Admit, most of you think we savers are a bit crazy, but after we've done the legwork and spent the money, you're impressed. The way you're all oohing and aahing over my posters."

He had a point. Though I lack the collector gene, I was learning to appreciate those who have it—whether for things they love, like my mother's martini glasses, or items of cultural significance, like Larry's posters.

"For some of you, they bring back memories or evoke another time," he said. "But without guys like me, they'd be lost. Languishing in the back rooms of junk stores in obscure towns, where they mildew and crumble, wrapped in plastic and stuffed in a bushel basket in the corner."

He was beginning to sound like a scold, in front of people we'd invited here to thank. "Larry, I—"

"Umm, sorry, Erin. Larry, we need you backstage." Zayda broke in. "There's a problem with the screen."

His brows drew together sharply and he strode off without a word, Zayda beside him, her hands flying as she spoke.

"No worries," I called out brightly, then said "'Scuse me," and trotted after them, winding between clusters of film lovers. *What now?*

They hustled down the side aisle of the theater to the stage, where Dylan and Dana stared up at the towering white projection screen. Two huge flaps of the silver Mylar backing hung loose. I gasped. I didn't know how much we'd paid for the new gear, but the screen had not been cheap.

And it was absolutely essential, tonight and every night this weekend.

"What the hell happened?" Larry stepped back, then moved closer to examine the flaps.

"We don't know," Dylan said. "We turned on the projector and realized the screen was all messed up. We ran down here and this is what we found."

The trio and their advisor examined the damaged screen. My phone said eight minutes to our scheduled start time.

"Well, there's no time to fix this right. Lower the pipe and get me some duct tape." Larry could be quite the bulldog.

The kids stood silent, flushed and uncertain, then Dylan moved toward the rail assembly on the side of the stage and Dana reached for the bottom of the screen.

"Zayda, check the ticket office for duct tape. I'll see if we have some at the Merc." I sprinted up the aisle, the girl behind me, then dashed outside and down the street. The cold air smacked me in the face and froze my nose hairs.

I found a big fat roll behind our front counter and sped back to the Playhouse. Zayda stood outside the office, hands empty, looking ready to cry. I held up the tape in triumph, not pausing.

The big screen lay on the stage like a flat, dead whale.

Breathless, I handed Larry the tape. He peeled the end loose and stuck it on Dana's fingers, handed the roll to Dylan, and motioned the boys to back up, glancing from tape to screen as he eyeballed the length needed. He whipped a knife out of his pocket and sliced it off.

"This may not be pretty," he said as he knelt at one end of the long slash. "But it's all we can do for now." Dana crouched at the other end, and they lowered the tape over the rip, Larry gently smoothing it into place.

Beside me, gripping the roll, Dylan crossed his arms over his torso, shoulders curving forward.

"Glad to see Zayda's calmed down."

He glanced up, clearly puzzled. "She's fine. What are you talking about?"

"She wasn't fine at five o'clock, when I picked her up running on the road out by Larry's place."

Even in the dim light, he looked pale.

"One more strip." Larry wiggled his fingers. Dylan held out the roll of tape and they repeated the procedure. "Okay, raise the pipe. Slowly. How did this happen anyway? It didn't rip by itself."

No reply.

"Let's get a move on," Larry shouted. "We're late."

My right eyelid twitched as Dylan tugged on the rope that hoisted the pipe up to the ceiling.

"Fingers crossed," Zayda said as she joined us. My thoughts exactly. We held our breaths and watched the screen as Larry and Dana guided it back into place. As the tape held.

"The images may be blurry, but better than nothing. We might be able to borrow a screen in Pondera. I'll make a few calls tomorrow. No time to test this thing," Larry said. "Let's get this show on the road."

I dashed back to the lobby, sweatier and stickier than before. No visible signs that the throng had noticed the delay, except for a wide-eyed glance from my sister, helping Wendy refill appetizer trays. In the ticket office, Zayda flicked the lobby lights twice and I pasted a smile on my red face as the guests filed past me into the theater.

As Larry had said, the screen had not torn itself. I was no judge, but the tears looked like cuts. Slashes. Deliberate damage.

Simple vandalism, or a targeted crime? And who—or what—was the target?

"Thank you," I whispered in the general direction of the stars. The damage had been repaired, at least temporarily, and no one had been hurt.

But I had one more question: How long could I reasonably wait before calling Deputy Kim Caldwell?

· Twenty-six ·

"The silver screen. A night at the movies. I'm so grateful to all of you for braving blizzard warnings and backed-up pipes to help kick off what I hope will be the First Annual Jewel Bay Food Lovers' Film Festival." Applause from the movie lovers and festival supporters who filled most of the theater's four hundred fifty seats—a stellar turnout for opening night. "Without you, there would be no festival. And there would be no festival without our dear friend, Christine Vandeberg, the force behind the dream. You all know, I'm sure, that she died unexpectedly last weekend, leaving me to fill her shoes. It's such an impossible task that I had to wear these."

I lifted a leg to show off my red cowboy boots, a lucky find underneath my desk.

"We are muddling on, as I think she would have wanted. I hope you all forgive us when things go wrong, because they already have."

They laughed, thank goodness. "For this inaugural event, we've chosen five films that explore the role of food in our lives, and the lives of those who grow, cook, and serve it. Each celebrates the discovery of truly good food and its power to transform our lives, to bring people together, to ease tensions. To express emotion. Our Saturday night special is a double feature, with a performance by the high school Drama Club at intermission." Applying the adage that "what you think about, you bring about," I ignored the possibility that *Chocolat* might not arrive in time.

"Complimentary popcorn, cookies, and soft drinks will be available all weekend. Other food and drink will be available at the concession stand. Proceeds support the Film Club, a hardworking group of high school students. Tonight, the kids debut for us their short documentary, *Auto Biography: Classic Car Collectors and their Driving Passion*, delving into a special obsession: the love of old cars. Here to tell you more is club president Zayda George."

Zayda climbed the short steps to the stage. I handed her the mike, then headed up the aisle as she described the project. I paused, listening, as she mentioned the antique Rolls-Royce rally that came through town last summer and sparked the kids' fascination with fascination, as Zayda put it.

After one last glance at the audience and the girl onstage, I pushed through the door and out to the lobby.

In time to see my old friend slash nemesis slash partner in rooting out crime march in, boot heels echoing in the space that minutes ago had been a flurry of hugs and handshakes and conversation as the cabin fever that grips our community every winter finally broke. Criminy, but a lot was happening fast these days.

Judging from the black pants and jacket she'd worn this afternoon, a little rumpled now, Kim hadn't been home since I left the sheriff's office.

"Plenty of good food left." I gestured to the tables. "Help yourself."

"I'm not sure I should be here," she said.

"Why not?" I handed her a plate. Applause from the theater signaled the end of Zayda's introduction. We both picked out a few appetizers, me listening distractedly for sounds of the film. When the theme music started, I took an éclair in celebration. "Yeah, so you didn't buy a ticket. I'll sic the kids on you later for a donation."

Which reminded me that I hadn't decided what to do about the Zayda incident. Telling law enforcement would only hone their focus on her. And I didn't want to put her through that unnecessarily.

"Come on. Film just started," I said. Kim pointed to a sign reading NO FOOD OR DRINK IN THEATER and I rolled my eyes.

We sat in the back row, nibbling on contraband, as Jewel Bay came to life on the screen. I'd seen a rough cut a few weeks earlier, when Larry and the kids pitched their idea to debut it as part of the Festival. Christine and I had both loved the idea. We'd also loved getting a ready-made team of enthusiastic volunteers. They'd done a super job showcasing local collectors and restorers. Show us a side of ourselves that we haven't seen before and you've got a hit.

But I hadn't paid much attention to the details.

On screen, we saw an elfin man in his early seventies, hair still dark, describing the Hudsons he'd restored. A woman and her son relayed their passion for the muscle cars of the 1960s, and how working on them together had brought them closer. The kids had found a Model A club and a pack of classic 1950s Chevys.

Then a familiar image from Caldwell's Eagle Lake Lodge and Guest Ranch filled the giant screen: a gambrel-roofed barn, a high peak over the hayloft and long sloping lines spread wide. Weathered gray-brown siding, recently rechinked. A century old, Zayda as narrator told us, predating the guest ranch.

Cut to inside, where the camera rolled slowly down the center aisle, past hand-hewn posts and beams, and panned the horse stalls. My favorite chestnut mare, a sweetheart named Ribbons, stood patiently in one, her buddy Kintla, a tall gray-and-white Appaloosa, in the next. The sight spurred an urge in me to ride out into the hills, to shake off the winter cobwebs and catch a good, deep breath of spring. *Soon*.

Then the camera zoomed in on a dark corner of the barn. The last stall held a shadowed shape. Kyle's plaid-shirted arms came into view as he carefully drew a cover off the car.

"Here's my baby." He stroked the hood. Light entered the frame, exposing the GTO's bold red-orange paint and racy lines. The camera picked up the figure of the man, moving steadily in on his face. A happy face, filled with an uncomplicated joy. "This car and I, we've been through a lot together."

Beside me, Kim shifted, jaw tight, arms gripped across her chest.

The camera followed Kyle as he circuited the car, picking out the highlights he described: deep bezels that held the headlights, air vents on the hood, eyebrows above the fenders. He raised the hood and the camera zoomed in on an engine so shiny it might have been cleaned with silver polish and a toothbrush.

"My uncle had a similar model and I adored it. Worked my tail off at the Lodge for extra money. Finally, I'd saved enough, and my uncle and my dad and I went to a car auction. Found this old wreck. A buddy and I repainted it. Spent every hour we had on it."

"What makes this car special?" Zayda, offscreen.

"Speed. Freedom. The open road. Behind the wheel, nothing can stop you. Unconditional love, because a car, you know, it only asks that you take care of it and in exchange, it will do purt' near everything you ask." Interior shots accompanied his words. The camera operator had done some fancy angling.

"Family kept it for me when I went in the Army. Gave me something to come back to after I got shipped to Iraq. Yeah, I have my family and career—I always intended to be a chef in civilian life, and hoped to work here at the Lodge. That dream came true. But a guy needs something he loves to do that doesn't demand anything from him except his attention."

"You park it next to the horses for extra horsepower?" Zayda asked. "How about a ride?"

"You bet. Runs great, despite its bumps and bruises. I've still got a little body work to do." The camera closed in on Kyle, his hand pointing to several long scrapes on the front-left quarter panel.

Beside me in the dark, Kim gasped.

· Twenty-seven ·

The screening ended and applause began. I popped up and headed for the lobby. Pushed through the double doors and Kim helped me latch them open. No time to ask what she thought of the movie.

"Thanks for coming. So glad you came," I said over and over, smiling and shaking hands with donors and guests.

"Great job those kids did," the minister said.

"Makes me want to find an old Hudson to restore," her husband said.

"Don't you dare!" She smacked him playfully on the shoulder.

And so it went—compliments for the kids, the food, and the festival, and wisecracks about frozen pipes and backed-up toilets.

"You called the sheriff?" Larry's attention shifted from me to Kim in disbelief. Club members stood behind him in the nearly empty lobby. "But we don't even know—"

"Oh, no. Deputy Caldwell came to see the film."

"Don't know what?" In a flash, Kim was back on the job. That quick switch officers constantly do has got to be killer on the nervous system.

Larry opened his mouth but I cut him off. "Nothing. Speculation about somebody plugging up the sewer lines on purpose. Pranking us. Odds are, it's a frozen line. Fingers crossed that it doesn't affect other buildings."

Kim glanced from Larry to me. "Okay. Which one of you kids is collecting donations?"

Zayda produced the jar, and Kim tucked in a twenty. She gave us all one more appraisal, then left the theater.

"Why didn't you want her to know the screen was cut?" Larry said when the door closed behind her.

"Do you want her to shut us down on opening night? If one more Jewel Bay festival is tainted by murder, this whole town might as well pack it in. No more tourists. No more vacationers. No more village." I waved my hand, sweeping them all away. "I don't know what happened to the screen, and we all need to keep our eyes open. But let's not jump the gun."

Dylan and Zayda exchanged nervous glances. "What about that guy?" she whispered.

"What guy?" I said. "When?"

"It was nothing," Zayda said quickly. Worry—or fear—darted across her face, her topknot wobbling. "Just this guy walking through the alley Wednesday after school. He asked a bunch of questions about what we were doing. Then he left."

My forehead wrinkled. "Short guy, chubby, my age or a little older? Bright blue parka?"

Dylan shoved his hands in his pockets. "It was nothing. Just 'hey' and 'what's going on?'"

I had wondered when I spotted him what brought Danny Davis to Jewel Bay—and the alley behind the Playhouse—in the middle of the afternoon. Had he gotten inside somehow and damaged the screen?

He had no connection to the Film Club kids or Larry Abrams. At least, not that I knew.

But what if I'd been wrong about Christine being killed for a piece of art? What if the real reason was to stop the Festival? Jack Frost had pointed at "the guy with the fancy car." Danny rented fancy cars—Porsches and BMWs—and coveted them. What did he drive?

Don't be silly, Erin. Why on earth would he want to disrupt the Festival?

"I guess we're set then," Larry said. "Now all we need is that last movie."

I raised two crossed fingers.

Twenty minutes later, the last plastic plates and glasses stuffed into trash bags, the lobby swept, Chiara and I sank onto a painted bench. "Oh," I said, recognizing the abstract dashes and swirls. "Did Iggy paint this one?"

Chiara nodded and handed me a bottle of Prosecco that still held a few swallows, her eyes twinkling in the downlight. "Hieroglyphics on drugs. I always wondered what she was smoking out in that church."

"There are rumors about her neighbor, Jack Frost." I took a swig and passed the bottle back. In sync with her new paintings, my sister was a vision of winter white in creamy white leggings, a cable-knit fisherman's sweater that hit her mid-thigh, and a cordovan leather belt that matched her boots, an off-white silk gardenia in her dark bob. "Loved Iggy dearly, miss her like crazy. Never did quite understand the art."

"Ditto. Great job tonight, little sister. I'm not loving the outfit, but your cat scratch has healed nicely."

"Bad enough that Mom's chief of the fashion police. Now you, too?" I leaned back, eyes closed. *To tell or not to tell?* I blew out a breath and made a decision. "I took some incomplete thoughts for a drive this afternoon. Ended up rescuing Zayda George from I'm not exactly sure what, then ran into Nick at the sheriff's office."

Chiara listened without comment as I relayed the Zayda incident and Nick's anger at Ike. My voice got hotter as I said I'd never heard the speculation that our dad's fatal accident might have been his own fault, not a hit-and-run. How much it hurt—in my chest, my stomach, my jaw—to know that my family had hidden the truth, in the guise of protecting me. How I thought we were so close—Sally thought we were so close, everyone did—but I'd been wrong. If my family wasn't the safe haven I'd always believed, just the masters of acting "as if," then who was I?

She let out a long sigh and gave me back the bottle. One swallow left. I drained it. The cool bubbles slid down my throat, a reminder that sweetness and light live on, even when the night seems so dark.

"About Zayda, no clue. But about Nick—no one was hiding anything from you, Erin."

I leaned forward, gripping the now-empty bottle in both hands. "You thought you were protecting me back then, and I get it. I was a kid. But I haven't been a kid for a long time. I don't want protecting. I want honesty."

"It's not that simple, or that complicated." She hugged herself, the white gardenia bobbing. "After a couple of days, Mom sent you back to school. The three of us were at the house, making funeral plans, when Ike came out. I can still picture him. Fifteen years younger, but Ike never changes. They worked 'round the clock, but they had nothing. No witnesses. All that ice and snow meant no marks on the road and no decent tire tracks. What the ambulance and tow truck didn't destroy, the weather did." She traveled back in time, remembering. "All they had to go on was the angle of how he hit the guardrail, and a paint smear on the front left side of his car. They sent it to the state lab for analysis, but they didn't have any results yet.

"Ike wondered out loud about other explanations. What if there hadn't been a second car? Might Dad have lost control and slammed into the guardrail himself? Could the impact have spun him around? Ice and snow are unpredictable.

"Nick came unglued. Mom and I had to talk him down. But he got over it. At least, I thought he did."

But the memory of Nick's explosion had triggered Ike's doubts about my brother's temper.

"So, no hiding. No covering up. Just no reason to tell you about a brief, embarrassing blowup. The tests on the paint samples came back later, but it was an after-market paint, and they never identified the car. Not as far as I know, anyway." She wrapped an arm around me and brought her face close to mine. It was like looking in a mirror that reflected a different world. "Maybe we do sometimes forget you're grown-up now. But you are who you always thought you were, Erin. You're smart, and determined, and loyal."

I sniffed back tears. "You make me sound like Sparky the Border collie." Our childhood dog. Technically Mom's—a birthday present, quickly given one of Dad's many nicknames for her.

"Well, you are a little bossy, like Sparky. Like all the Murphy women. You are my best friend as well as my favorite sister—"

"Your only sister. Don't try to sweet-talk me out of being mad." I rubbed my left eye.

"Whatever it takes. Hey, I understand how you feel. Christine's death has Nick all nervy and on edge, and the past came roaring out of the blue. But now I'm a mother myself, so listen to me: Protecting one another is what family does. We don't always get it right, but it's part of the job."

I leaned in and held her tight.

B ack in the Merc, I plucked an éclair out of the box of leftovers Wendy had given me. Changed my boots, scooped up my bag and iPad, and headed home.

Nine o'clock. The sky had cleared, and stars pierced the dark chill as if God had flicked on the high beams. I zipped my coat, parked at the cabin, and wrapped the scarf around my neck twice. Grabbed the Maglite from the glove box and strolled down to the shore.

As caretaker, I've got full run of the place. Super-sweet in summer, when the lake sparkles, the gravel beach perfect for swimming, kayaking, or just sitting. Bob and Liz are fabulous hosts and between deck, sloping yard, dock, and beach, their parties rock. The forest is special in summer, too, its many-greened canopy dappling the fragrant duff with sun and shadow.

But winter casts its own magic spell. On sunny days after a storm, the bluebird sky defies description. Defies any mood, too—it's nearly impossible not to tilt your head back for the sun's kiss.

Avoiding the icy drive, I trod the wooded path, feet snug in my hiking boots. Stood on the shore and gazed up, opening my arms and twirling like Landon in his Superman cape. It's good to have a five-year-old in your life, for inspiration.

His mother had given me much to think about. I brushed snow off a stone bench and perched, gloved hands in my pockets.

What a mess. Despite my caution to Larry, the screen damage did worry me. A string of unrelated crimes seemed unlikely. No question in my mind that the murder and break-in were related. But the evidence—as I knew it, and if I included motive, again as I knew it—appeared to rule out both Sally Grimes and Jack Frost. A week ago, I'd have cheerfully blamed either one of them. And while I was even less fond of Frost after he'd waved a gun in my general direction, I realized that in assuming I knew all about Sally, I had missed the most crucial things about her. What drove her—good and bad.

And I'd nearly missed her alibi.

How did the screen damage fit in? Danny Davis's presence in the alley was odd, but could be an innocent coincidence.

My breath formed puffy white clouds in the air. Across the lake, a band of lights shimmered where houses huddled near the shore.

I understood why Ike had zeroed in on Nick. By lying about where he'd been, my brother had made himself easy to doubt. The fingerprint report on the murder weapon raised more questions. And the history—Ike's perception of him as a hothead—formed a trifecta of suspicion.

Ike Hoover perceived Nick as a man with a temper, and took that as a sign that he was capable of killing in the heat of the moment. Nick's theory that the attacker had turned on Christine—with the gun Nick gave her—reinforced Ike's suspicions: Nick could have been that attacker.

In reality, Nick was mostly calm and collected. Stubborn. Determined.

A Murphy.

But he was also a man capable of sitting long hours in a hollowed-out snow cave, hidden by branches, waiting for four-legged predators to stroll by. If he wanted to kill—if he wanted the inheritance, as Sally had suggested—he'd have planned it.

How could I get Ike to understand that Nick wasn't a wild-eyed lunatic, just a man raw with grief? And that Christine's murder had not been planned. I suspected that the killer had intended a theft, and gotten a shooting. I was beginning to appreciate that a good cop has to be a good psychologist, too. Difference is, he—or she—has to use what they learn to solve crimes, not personal problems.

These crimes had become mighty personal for my family.

Icy waters lapped the lakeshore. While some evidence pointed to Nick, other evidence ruled him out. Perplexing as that was, the same could be said for Zayda, the final suspect on my list. She'd been fingerprinted the same time as Nick—the unidentified prints were not hers.

I closed my eyes, listening to the waves. Instead, images of Christine filled my mind: At the Art Fair in August, laughing as I chose a painting. Last Friday, leaning over the pool table to take a shot, laughing up at Nick when she missed. Plucking a french fry from the basket.

Glowering at Jack Frost. Bleeding on her studio floor.

Pain stabbed the back of my throat. I swallowed, with difficulty, but it wouldn't go away.

Criminy. What a week. What if I was on the wrong track, thinking the break-in and murder were related? The damaged projection screen suggested that someone wanted to stop the Festival. Which meant that Iggy's art collection—now Nick's, via Christine—had nothing to do with anything.

The screen slashing might be simple vandalism. I just didn't know yet.

No. That was too much coincidence.

With one last look at the night sky, reflected in the waves as if in a broken mirror, I pushed myself up and headed back up the trail.

Was I on the wrong track in another way, too? Believing I needed to investigate all these events, and believing that the right man—any man fool enough to love me—would go along?

I reached in my pocket for my phone. Then it rang. I smiled up at the sky, guessing the caller even before seeing the name.

Too much coincidence.

"I've been asking too much of you," I said. "I do stuff that worries the people who care about me, and then I don't want to hear about it. I'm sorry."

"I'm sorry, too," Adam said. "I blew it the other night. I got upset by things that had nothing to do with you, and let my protective side go into overdrive."

My cabin beckoned. "The stars are gorgeous and I miss

you. But Adam, I need you to understand that this—this drive to investigate, to solve the problems that threaten people I care about, that threaten this village—it's part of who I am."

"I know." The gentleness in his voice enveloped me. "I meant what I said the other night: I love that you use your head to follow your heart. If I'm ever in trouble, I want you on my side."

He paused and I wanted so badly to put words in his mouth.

"I love you, Erin. That means I worry about you, and I want to keep you safe. But more than that, I want you to follow your passions."

Took the words right out of my mouth.

Not until later, after we said good night, after the cats had staked out positions on opposite sides of the living room, glaring at each other and at me, while I sat in the chocolate brown chair, the Spreadsheet of Suspicion open on my lap. Not until then did I remember something he'd said once that might be the push I needed to solve this case.

"You know us fanatics," he'd said. "Whether it's painters or cooks or backcountry skiers. We'll do nearly anything for that high."

The same logic applies to collectors—and investigators.

·Twenty-eight·

I marched straight through the Merc and out the front door, greeted by the rumbling engine of the utility truck parked in the alley next to the Playhouse. Few things justify disturbing a peaceful Friday morning in the village, but emergency sewer repairs definitely qualify.

A man in a heavy tan coverall with a county patch on the breast pocket rewound a thick cable on a spool on the back of the truck. Farther down the hill stood a plumbing company van.

"Hey, there. What's the news?" I shouted over the noise.

"Some idiot stuffed part of a theater curtain down the backstage toilet. In the actors' restroom, where nobody saw it. Backed up all the plumbing in the building and messed up the sewer lines."

"On purpose? So they aren't frozen after all?" Relief rushed through me. "I'm running the Film Festival this weekend. Will we have working toilets tonight?"

"If I have anything to say about it." He pushed a big

square button on the side of the truck and the crank rewinding the snake stopped.

"Thanks." I waved. He raised a gloved hand in acknowledgment. Silently, I blessed the plumbers, electricians, heavy-equipment operators, and other hardworking men and women who keep some semblance of order in our crazy world.

I shivered, and not just from the twenty-degree morning air. If the utility operator was right, the sewer line had been damaged intentionally. Sabotage—ugly word.

Last night I'd made an act of dismissing Larry's comment about vandalism, to keep Kim off our tail. I'd only said maybe the plugged toilets were a prank because, from where I stood, I could see the blocked-off restroom doors. I'd had no reason to think the sewer lines had been damaged intentionally.

Apparently, I can think like a criminal when circumstances warrant.

But not well enough. Try as I might, I could see no connection between the rack and ruin at the Playhouse and the death and destruction at Christine's.

Best not to contemplate such things on an empty stomach. I headed up Front Street to the Jewel Inn. Mimi pointed to a table and mouthed "Be right with you." A waitress brought two steaming mugs and I ordered quiche Lorraine to go.

"Zayda did a great job last night," I said a minute or two later. "Both as MC and as narrator of the film."

Mimi's wan smile stopped short of her blue eyes. "The kid's nuts about movies. She's been sweating over her film school applications for ages. I just hope this whole fiasco doesn't throw her off stride."

Murder is more than a fiasco. But it's not an easy word to say.

"She back in class? Routine helps, but kids can be cruel. Unintentionally, but . . ." As I remembered so well.

"She went back Wednesday. My day off, so the kids and I had breakfast together at home. She and T.J. argued over who would drive, so I solved the problem by dropping them off myself."

I smiled. With a teacher dad, driving to school had rarely been an option, unless one of us had practice or a late rehearsal. Like the night he died.

"She told me about the damage to the screen. Erin, what is going on?"

"Don't know." The heat from the coffee had not yet thawed my suspicions. When the cats and I had studied the Spreadsheet last night, Sandburg wondered if one of the kids had tried to sabotage the screening, out of resentment or feeling overshadowed by the others. Trying to connect the Playhouse vandalism to Christine's murder and break-in, Pumpkin favored an outsider theory. Why, none of us had a clue.

"Mimi, something weird happened yesterday. Besides the damage to the screen and the sewer lines." I briefed her on my conversation with the utility operator, then told her about running into Zayda—almost literally—out by Jewel Basin.

She fell back in her chair, both hands to her mouth. "Larry? Did he—do you think he—?"

"No idea. It's possible, though I've never heard any rumors about him behaving inappropriately toward students. Why would she have gone out there?"

Mimi shook her head, eyes wide. "This whole thing is so bizarre. She won't talk about any of it, and that's not like her. She's a great kid, so responsible. Yesterday, a couple of kids made shooting gestures at her in the hall, miming the hanging rope. Laughing like it's all a big joke. Had her in tears. She's never held a gun in her life."

Nick had seen Dylan with a girl at the shooting range, teaching her to shoot. They could corroborate Nick's testimony about taking Christine to the range. Still not proof, but consistent with his claim that he had given her his gun.

Did their trip to the range mean anything else?

"Mmm. If I get a chance, do you want me to ask Larry

why she was out at his house? Subtly. Or talk to Deputy Caldwell?"

She paled, no doubt at the prospect of giving Kim more reasons to look closely at Zayda. "Let me talk to Tony first." She stood and picked up our mugs. "Merchants' Association meetings start March first. Breakfast, here. And I talked with another prospect for the teahouse."

I knew the man she named, a grocery deli employee. Dorky guy, nice enough, but hard to imagine him rocking the village vibe. "Great. Hey, one more thing. I need a home for Christine's cat. Cute cat. Great with people and other animals." *Fibber.*

But Mimi was already halfway to the kitchen. "Full house. Two kids, two dogs, a lizard, and a hamster."

The waitress emerged carrying my breakfast in a box. As I pulled on my coat, the antelope mount above the hostess stand appeared to be watching me. Ready for Mardi Gras, in his beads and Groucho Marx glasses.

"You get any brilliant ideas, party boy," I said, "give me a call."

"What is all this and where is it going?" Tracy whipped toward me the second I crossed the threshold, her beaded kitty cat earrings swinging madly.

"Oh, geez. I wasn't expecting you until next week," I told the delivery man. He'd already off-loaded one huge packing crate, another strapped to his orange metal hand truck. My fingers flew to my hair as if of their own free will. "We haven't cleared space—can they go right here for now? Move that display case and the table like so?" I pointed, he nodded, and Tracy's gaze swung between us.

"But what are they *for*?" she said.

"The antique red hutch is for our tea and drink line. This—see the temperature controls?" I pointed as the delivery man cut down the cardboard box, revealing a sleek commercial glass-front case, slightly used but good as new. "This is for Tracy's Truffles. You've outgrown that countertop display."

Tracy stared, mouth open, fingers entwined in her long black skirt.

"I don't want you to leave, Trace. If you decide to open your own shop, I'll be your biggest fan. But you are part of the Merc. I want you to stay, even if it means hiring someone to work the floor so you have more time in the kitchen. Please. Weird truffles and all."

Her right earring caught the light from the white ceiling pendants. "You have to admit, those chamomile-bee pollen chocolates are pretty tasty."

The delivery man wrinkled his nose. We laughed, and she threw her arms around me. "Erin, this is exactly what I wanted. I knew when I saw how willing you were to help Luci. It will be a big change—huge—but you always say in business, the name of the game is change."

"And give the customers what they want." I gestured toward the artisan truffles in their too-small case. Tracy chimed in, and we recited in unison: "And what they don't know they want—yet."

We spent the next hour juggling inventory and hatching plans for Tracy's new products. And sharing theories about the vandalism.

"The Playhouse Affair," I said. "Sounds like a bad movie from the 1940s. It's got to be related to what happened at Christine's. Otherwise, too much coincidence. But I don't see *how*."

Tracy wiped the last packing dust off the red hutch. "Coincidence is when other people don't tell you their plans."

I paused, mid-sweep. "That's brilliant."

"I read it on a tea bag."

The front door opened as I bent over, snorting with laughter.

"This looks like a fun place," the customer said.

Running the credit card on her purchases twenty minutes later—now *that* was fun.

"Don't forget the dog treats," I reminded Tracy during a burst of enthusiasm over lemongrass ginger truffles and chai sipping chocolate. "Remember that woman who called from Calgary about your gluten-free dog cookies? When the website's up to speed, those will be best-sellers."

Early afternoon, I found myself glancing out the window far too often for a glimpse of a man in a brown uniform. When he finally arrived, the DVD box in hand, I kissed him.

The color of the UPS logo triggered another thought. "Sea salt chocolate caramels."

Tracy made a note, grinning from earring to earring.

I grabbed my coat and hat—snow was falling straight down and piling up—and crossed the street, carrying the precious DVD and a box of popcorn and seasonings. The utility truck and excavator were gone. Ned Redaway raked disturbed dirt and snow back into place.

"Gol darn it, dag nab it, girlie. What some people won't do."

"Will the plumbers have the inside damage repaired in time?" I brushed a fat flake off my eyelashes.

"They say they will. And I didn't have to threaten 'em twice. If I find out who did this, girlie, I'll throttle the son of a gun."

But what I wanted to know was why.

To my surprise, Dylan greeted me at the Playhouse door and took my box. "I got out early to set up. The Festival is my senior project. Academics and community service."

"Perfect. Look what came. Can we check it out, make sure it's right this time?"

His forehead wrinkled and he glanced at the floor, then made a decision. "Yeah. Larry doesn't like us messing with the projector by ourselves—it's expensive. Digital, wireless. But it's not as complicated as he thinks it is."

My mom says kids—anyone under forty—understand

computers and electronic gadgets telepathically. Maybe
so, but these kids understand a heck of a lot more than I
do. That's the difference between interest and passion.

In the control room, Dylan turned on the projector and
I squinted through the darkened windows at the stage.
From here, the damage wasn't visible, but I'd seen last
night that the images were no longer as crisp as they should
have been.

"Still wondering how that happened," I said.

Dylan bit his lip and dropped the disc. In my mind's
eye, it smashed into a million pieces. That had to be worse
than breaking a mirror—seventy-seven years bad luck for
everyone within seven miles.

He swore, fumbling as he picked it up, blew off the dust,
and inspected it quickly, then slipped it into the projector.

A French village appeared on the hastily repaired
screen, townspeople climbing the steps to church, greeted
by the smarmy mayor, le Comte de Reynaud. I felt a rush
of giddiness, as if I'd just eaten two Flathead Cherry truffles and washed them down with a triple espresso.

But before I could leave, I needed to make sure Dylan
and Zayda would corroborate Nick's story. "Dylan, you
took Zayda to the shooting range last fall, didn't you? Do
you remember seeing Nick and Christine?" He nodded.
"You've got to tell the sheriff. It will make a world of difference for Nick."

"Erin, can I ask you something?" His voice a notch too
high, he stared out the window, then turned to me, his face
a collage of confusion and fear. "They don't really believe
Zayda killed Christine, do they? I swear, she didn't. Not
that your brother did, but I finally figured out why she went
out there early."

A door opened out front.

"You have to understand. We all love making movies,
but Zayda—she's on fire." The words stumbled out. "It's
like it's in her blood. She'd die if she thought this couldn't

be her career. She knows stuff Larry doesn't know. But she needs—"

Footsteps approached and we froze.

"What's going on?" Larry Abrams said. He flicked on the light.

I blinked furiously in the sudden brightness. "You startled us, that's all. The film arrived. The right film, thank goodness."

A scowl and a look of relief crossed his face at the same time, as if coming from opposite directions and meeting in the middle.

"I thought, just this once—" Dylan began, but Larry silenced him, saying "Good. Glad to hear it."

Think fast. "Dylan, I've got another box—"

"Later, Erin. The kid's got work to do."

"You bet. Later." Halfway out the door, I glanced back at Dylan. The kid who'd decided it was better to spill someone else's secret than to keep it, only to be stopped short.

Later.

· Twenty-nine ·

A dam strode in the Merc's front door about two seconds before I headed out the back. No way would I show up stinky for my own party two nights in a row.

"Oh, little darlin'," he said. "Long, cold lonely winter."

Here comes the sun.

After a long, delicious kiss, I took a step back, hands on his arms. "Roads okay?"

"Rotten. Plows can't keep up. Snowing and blowing like mad." At my frown, he added, "Didn't know how crummy it would be until I was halfway home."

"Glad this shindig is mostly local." I rubbed my lucky stars for a safe evening.

We made plans to meet at the Playhouse. Adam had never seen any of the movies on the menu, but swore he was game for all five—though I made clear he could bow out any time.

Unwilling to sacrifice another pillow, I'd separated the cats that morning. But the log wall between them didn't dampen the high-decibel yowling that greeted me.

I scooped up Sandburg and rubbed the sweet spot above his nose. "You been yelling all day? You'll give yourself sandpaper throat." A few treats in his bowl soothed his nerves and I opened the bedroom door. Picked up Pumpkin and repeated the routine. Set her down and took a shower.

Only after I got out did I realize that I'd left the bedroom door open. I wrapped my hair in a towel, cinched the belt on my robe, and peeked out.

No cats.

Crept into the living room like fog. Frowned. *Where were they?*

"You little stinker." I grabbed a sponge and wiped up Sandburg's spilled water. His kibble lay scattered on the tile entry floor. He crouched by the overturned bowls, hissing.

"How did a butterball like you get all the way up there?" I hauled a step stool into the laundry room and hoisted Pumpkin out of the wicker basket perched on top of the cabinet above the dryer. She bared her teeth at the enemy as I carried her past him. "You're lucky we didn't both break our necks."

So much for dressing in leisure. I pulled on a red ribbed wool sweaterdress, black tights, and my red boots. In a bow to the weather, I donned a black knit cap, red trim around the edges. No point letting Landon have all the hat fun.

The cats tucked into their separate quarters, the door between them shut tight, I went to the movies.

Show up five minutes late, and the fun's already started. That's Jewel Bay for you.

The Bijou sign twinkled and I sent a silent greeting to Christine. *Good idea.*

Wish you were here.

In the lobby, aromas of popcorn, warm cookies, and wet wool competed for attention. My mother and sister wore 1940s post-war skirted suits, in honor of Julia Child's arrival in Paris. Chiara had coaxed Jason into a period suit and skinny tie, but no amount of Fresca's magic could have persuaded Bill to trade in his fleece pullover and hiking shoes twice in one week.

The Georges, the Washingtons, and other Film Club parents came in together, several of the women in costume. Donna Lawson rocked a perfect red Chanel pant suit with black-and-white spectator pumps. I did a double take: Heidi Hunter, owner of Kitchenalia and my mother's closest friend, in a vintage black-and-white checked two-piece dress worthy of Lauren Bacall, a black beret atop her dark blond hair, her ever-present diamond tennis bracelet glistening. Arm in arm with Reg Robbins, ex-NFL star turned art potter, tall, dark, and well-muscled, grin as broad as the valley views from his hilltop studio.

"Are they together? As in—*together*?" Heidi ran through men like water through a sieve. Reg avoided most village social events, and kept his personal life, well, personal.

The feather on Fresca's green beret bobbed. "And it just might work."

Kyle Caldwell came in with the Lodge baker, the brunette he'd met for pool Tuesday night. Tracy and Rick arrived, Nick and Adam behind them. Hugs and kisses all around. We joked about Rick and Nick and rhyming names. Adam sweetly inquired after Bozo.

Rick kissed my cheek. "You look wonderful. Tonight's bittersweet, but you're in charge. How can it fail?"

"Thanks. Did Tracy tell you what we're doing in the shop?"

"Perfect solution." He beamed. "Just don't give the chocolates so much space you don't have room for flour and oats."

Ah, staple foods versus specialty items, the daily table versus the tourist trade. The tension never strayed far from our conversation—a big reason why our fledgling romance had met a quick end.

The main reason, snowflakes glinting on his dark curls

and the shoulders of his parka, bent his head toward Tracy as she chattered about truffles and dog treats. Adam caught my eye and winked.

I smiled back, then looped my arm through Nick's, leading him away from the door. "So glad you came. It will be a hit and a tribute. I promise."

Fresca approached, arms open, Chiara behind her carrying wine for me and a beer for Nick.

"Thanks, Erin." He kissed the top of my head and let them take charge of him.

Without Christine to handle MC duties, I'd delegated the job, to give the kids experience. Tonight's honors went to the girl with multihued red hair. I popped into the theater as she finished sound check and she flashed me a thumbs up.

Back out front, the kids took positions at each entrance, ready to pass out programs. No sign—or smell—of plumbing problems. I surveyed the growing crowd. *Half the town. Yes.*

Including Deputy Kim Caldwell, standing near the ticket office eating popcorn.

Breathe, Erin.

The lobby lights dimmed. *Showtime.*

"Erin, there you are." Dylan slid to a breathless stop in front of me, Zayda close behind him. "I went out to shovel the side steps, so they're clear for people who leave that way. And I saw that guy again."

"The guy you saw Wednesday?" *Danny?*

"Sorry. We didn't tell you the whole story last night— we thought—and then I meant to tell you this afternoon, but I chickened out. The guy we might have accidentally let in. Who might have cut the screen and damaged the plumbing."

My brain heard, but didn't quite compute.

"He's out back, by the breakers. Come on." Dylan sprinted for the theater—the quickest route.

I shot Kim a panicked look and tore after him.

Down the side aisle we flew. Dylan pushed the door open and I followed, Zayda on my heels. The clang of metal on metal deafened me.

"Danny! Stop! You'll electrocute yourself." The stocky man ignored me, swinging the snow shovel wildly at the olive green transformer box.

I grabbed for his arm, but he danced out of reach.

"I don't care. I deserve it. Whatever you think of me, I'm so sorry." He flailed at the box, blinking as tears ran down his plump red cheeks and into his eyes. Whatever he hoped to accomplish, we had to stop him.

With the advantage of youth over size, Dylan lowered his shoulder and rammed him. Danny staggered backward. The shovel flew out of his hand. Zayda scrambled for it, nearly going down on the slick slope.

"It was an accident," Danny said, words blurred by the scuffle. "I never meant to hurt him."

"What are you talking about?" Slashing the screen and damaging the pipes clearly were not accidents. Neither was hammering away at the power supply for a theater holding more than four hundred people.

As if regretting his incomprehensible apology, Danny found a second wind and launched himself toward Dylan. At the same moment, the side door opened and Kim stepped out. Locked in a struggle, the two men fell into the junipers alongside the building.

Black metal glinted in Kim's hand.

Danny stuttered to his feet, blinded by tears and rage.

"Danny, stop or she'll shoot," I yelled. How could I stop him? A blank paver, left over from the last remodel when blocks stamped with donors' names were used to pave the front walkway, lay by the door. One had flown through the Merc window last summer, and using another now felt like justice. Sweet, dangerous justice.

Just stun him, I told myself. *Slow him down.*

Cracked, the paver fell into pieces in my hand. What

next? Danny lowered his head to charge me, the nearest body. Channeling my nephew's superheroes, I yanked off my black hat and flung it in his face. At the same moment, Zayda slammed his knee with the shovel and down he went, yowling like my cats.

"Just kill me," Danny said, in between screams. "Because I killed him."

"Him? Who? What are you talking about?" I panted for breath. "The only person dead is Christine."

"You?" Kim said, sounding incredulous. "You were with Kyle?"

"What is going on?" I felt like a bobble-head doll, eyes and ears swinging between two people conversing in a foreign language.

Kim pulled handcuffs out of some hidden pocket and snapped them on Danny's wrists. "Help me haul this idiot somewhere safe."

I stuck my head inside the theater, putting on my biggest fake smile. "All under control. Let the real show begin."

Muttering into her radio, Kim dragged Danny by one arm, Dylan tugging the other, up the sloping alley. The smooth soles of his city shoes slipped on the packed snow, slowing them down.

City shoes. No snow boots with their heavy treads for Danny. He was not the cottage burglar.

At Front Street, Kim gave me a questioning look.

"Playhouse office?" I grabbed the door.

"Go find Kyle," she commanded, and I obeyed.

Ten minutes later, Ike Hoover, in civvies, strode into the already crowded office. Two uniformed deputies stood guard outside. Cuffed to the chair, Danny squirmed under Kim's glower. Eyes wide as saucers, Dylan and Zayda flattened themselves against the wall as if they wanted to disappear into it.

This whole chaotic mess baffled me. Why on earth did Danny Davis give one fig about the Food Lovers' Film Festival?

"He knows what you did, Kyle," Kim said. "He's been covering for you all these years."

"Did what?" Forehead creased, Kyle studied her for answers. "Covering for what?"

"Fifteen years," Kim said, her voice strained but determined. "It was your car that pushed Tom Murphy into the bridge. You hid it in the barn so no one would see the damage. They never matched the paint, but—"

My mouth fell open. Ike gripped my upper arm and steadied me.

"Yeah. You and your hot rod, you hit the coach's car. Sped away like a coward." Danny spat out the words, eyes bulging, mouth twisted.

"Ohmygod. It was *you*. You killed Coach Murphy." Kyle's blue eyes blazed in fury.

"No, Kyle. It's time to stop all the lies," Kim said.

Kyle stretched out a long arm, pointing at Danny. "The lies started fifteen years ago. When this piece of . . . garbage borrowed my car. You said you scraped a tree. I should have known." He turned to me. "Erin, I'm so sorry. I never put it together."

Danny started to speak but Kyle spun around, using his ex-Army officer's control. "Shut your trap. You've done enough damage."

Realization filled Ike Hoover and he stepped forward, arms stretched, palms out. "Enough." His stern focus rested briefly on each of us, then settled on Danny Davis, now quiet. Danny dropped his gaze to the floor. "If I understand correctly, Davis, you took Kyle's GTO for a drive. You struck Tom Murphy's car on the bridge. You sped on past as his car spun and slammed into the guardrail, killing him."

Kim covered her mouth with both hands, her blue eyes the only color in her face.

"You drove back to the Lodge," Ike continued. "Later, you told your buddy you'd had a minor accident with a tree. You did not tell him you'd hit another car and run."

Danny nodded almost imperceptibly.

Ike turned to Kyle. "You and Davis had already graduated. You'd enlisted, but you were at the funeral—I remember the parade of Tom's former student athletes shuffling past the coffin and down the reception line, greeting Mrs. Murphy and her children."

"Shipped out two days later," Kyle said.

Kim made a strangled noise.

"You have something to add, Detective?" Ike said.

"But I thought—I saw—" Tears filled her swollen eyes. "I was at the Dairy Queen. I saw the car go by. I thought you went in the Army because you felt guilty. To escape responsibility. But I never said anything, because you were my cousin. Oh, God, Erin, I'm so sorry." Her attention shifted from her cousin to me to the real culprit. "But it was you driving. Not Kyle."

Danny's chin quivered and his nose dripped.

"You thought—"Kyle's voice shook in disbelief. "All these years, you thought I killed Coach Murphy and ran away? He was my *coach*. You know what that meant to me. I've never gotten over it. None of us have."

Except Danny Davis, who raised his head to watch the Caldwell cousins come to a reckoning.

Everything I had never understood about my friendship with Kim and its unexpected change after my father's death became clear. Her harshness toward Kyle, so evident last summer. She had misunderstood what she'd seen back then, and I'd misunderstood her response.

Counting on my red boots for confidence, I took a deep breath to steady myself. "So why go after Christine? Why try to stop the Film Festival?"

"Christine? That girl who got murdered? I had nothing to do with that." Danny sniffed back teary snot, his face a runny mess. "At Red's last week, when you said your car was in the kids' movie, I knew I had to stop it. I've always been afraid"—he paused for a huge, grotty sniff—"that somebody musta seen. A witness who would see the car and put two and two together."

"And get four instead of three, like I did." Kim cradled one elbow, her other hand clutching her lapel.

"That's why you offered to buy the car," Kyle said.

"Waaaait a second," Ike said. "What do you mean, he tried to stop the Film Festival?"

"Uh, Sheriff." Dylan cleared his throat. "I—we didn't report what we saw because we felt like idiots and we thought we'd get in trouble. But he—Danny? He was the guy hanging around here Wednesday afternoon." Dylan explained that he and Zayda had chatted with Danny in the alley, when they delivered the programs, display boards, and other Festival supplies. Danny offered to help; they declined. He peppered them with questions about their documentary.

Zayda's turn. "We tried to be polite and listen and stuff, but it was weird. Like why would this guy who didn't know any of us care? But he quizzed us about the cars and which ones made the final cut. Said he was an old carhead and the GTO he was trying to buy might be in the movie."

"But we screwed up," Dylan said. "We left a brick—not exactly a brick. What do you call 'em? From the pile by the back door?"

"Pavers." Kim and I spoke at the same time.

"Right. I jammed a paver in the door to hold it open, while we were going in and out, but we got distracted." He blushed, broadcasting what the distraction had been. "He must have snuck in and slashed the screen."

"What time?" I said.

Zayda punched her phone. "It was right after my mom called. Three forty-seven."

"That fits when I saw him in the alley," I said, remembering the red-faced man in the blue parka puffing up the hill.

"Back up. Explain what happened to the screen," Ike said, and Dylan explained. "You messed up the plumbing, too?" Ike asked, and Danny nodded.

"That's why you tried to buy my car," Kyle said to Danny. "So you could get rid of it. And no one would ever know."

"But why come back tonight?" I said to Danny, although it probably violated a million rules to interrogate a suspect directly. The rules no longer mattered to me.

"Like you said. To stop them from showing their film."

"But it aired last night." He'd seen the old schedule taped to the door, not knowing we'd moved the documentary up a night.

I have never seen one of those giant Snoopy and Superman balloons that fly in Macy's Thanksgiving Day Parade. But if one of them snagged on the Empire State Building and sprung a leak, and deflated all over Fifth Avenue—in my mind's eye, that's how Danny Davis looked as he realized the futility of all he had done to save his sorry hide.

Ike opened the door and called to the deputies. "Take Mr. Davis to Pondera and book him on felony mischief, three counts, and assault on young Mr. Washington. I'll file the negligent homicide report myself. It will give me great satisfaction. Ask dispatch to send over the crime scene crew."

They nodded and hauled their prisoner out.

Ike turned back to the rest of us, one burden visibly lifted, another descending like night. A serious case of the shivers gripped me.

Kim looked like a good horse rode hard and put away wet.

"I expect the crime scene is a mess, with everyone who's been on and off that stage." Ike threw a sharp look at the kids and me. "We'll do the best we can, for the courts. But no reason to alarm the public. As long as nobody goes back stage, we can wait until the movie ends."

After all Christine's work and mine, I'd completely forgotten about the movie.

· *Thirty* ·

Ike also wanted to wait until after the movie to share the news of Danny's arrest and confession with my family.

"No," I said. "No more secrets. No more protecting people by holding back the truth, even for an hour."

And so I'd crept into the darkened theater and come out with Fresca and Bill, Chiara and Jason, and Nick. And Adam.

Worry clouded my mother's lovely features. "Darling, are you all right? Who was that awful man?"

"Fresca," Ike said, taking command, "we've made an arrest."

"In the murder?" Nick said, and Chiara wrapped an arm around him. "Justice for Christine?"

"No." Ike's low, gravelly voice broke. "In Tom's death. Justice for Tom, finally."

All eyes focused on Fresca. Not until I sensed the warmth of Adam's presence behind me did I realize I'd been holding my breath. We all had. For fifteen years.

Ike relayed the sordid tale. How Danny Davis had snuck Kyle's beloved sports car out for a spin, lost control on the ice, and struck my father's car. Sent it careening into the bridge, the impact slamming the driver's side into the rail, killing a good man all but instantly. "He was driving too fast, of course. It was negligence, not deliberate, but still homicide."

His words sank in. Fresca extended her arms and enveloped the three of us.

"I never knew, Fresca," Kyle said. "I swear. He told me he'd taken the car earlier in the day. Not that night, or I might have guessed. He said he'd hit a tree and offered to help me fix the damage, but boot camp started two days after the funeral . . ."

"It's all right, Kyle." Her soft, firm voice filled the silence between us all. "I don't blame you."

"Blame me, Fresca," Kim said. "I heard the crash. I saw the car speeding away. I didn't see the driver. I—I assumed it was Kyle. If I'd only spoken up, the truth might have come out years ago."

Fresca extended a long, manicured hand and Kim gripped it like a lifeline, until Kyle drew her to him and held her tight. I had never seen my old friend cry, not even at my father's funeral. I touched her shoulder and kissed her damp cheek.

At the sounds of moviegoers outside the ticket office, I sprung to life. Acting "as if," I summoned the strength and mustered the muscle to go thank the villagers, my friends and neighbors, for coming out.

"Wonderful. Just wonderful," said a villager. "I adore Paris!"

"When are we making Julia Child's *boeuf bourguignon*?" Rob Burns asked his wife, the former Bunny Easter.

"Sunday," Bunny replied, "if you're chopping onions."

"This was perfect." Donna Lawson clapped her hands

together in front of her chin, her dark eyes shining behind her glasses. "I can hardly wait for next year."

"Wouldn't have missed it," Heidi said, extending a hand. Behind her, Reg beamed. "I've seen *Julie and Julia* half a dozen times, and it always makes me happy. Such fun to go out to the movies for a change. But where did you all disappear to?"

A long sigh, my "acting as if" smile slipping slightly. "Long story. We'll fill you in later."

But not until the lobby was empty and the deputies toting black cases of crime scene gear had commandeered the stage did I remember that for all the revelations, for all the relief, we were no closer to the truth about Christine.

Thank the stars for Wendy, *pain au chocolat*, and double espresso. I could not have powered through Saturday morning at the Merc without them.

I love hearing "good job," "can't wait for tonight," and "what a great idea" as much as anyone, but after last night's emotional reeling, my eyes stung and my feet dragged, weighted down as if by lead.

Or feedbags full of popcorn.

Turned out our little "just for us townies" celebration had tempted visitors from all around the valley and beyond to venture out, despite the weather. "Oh, we just love Jewel Bay," went the refrain. "You throw the best parties."

Killer parties.

The door chime rang all morning, keeping Tracy and me hopping. We boxed chocolates, bagged soaps and lotions, offered tastes of wild chokecherry jelly. Sold oodles of linguine, tomato sauce, and artichoke pesto. More than a few customers brought in empty baskets and left with them full of carrots, onions, and squash from Rainbow Lake Garden, buffalo jerky, and creamy goat cheese. And popcorn and seasonings.

At noon, Rick brought Tracy lunch and a Bozo report. He offered to get a bite for me, but a break would do me good. "You stay. Serve popcorn, chat up your products," I said. Tracy shone in his presence and he shimmered like wheat ripening in an August sunset breeze.

I grabbed the festival notebook, planning to take one last gander at Christine's notes, flipping the pages as I walked. *Criminy.*

Outside, my thick sky blue fleece was not quite warm enough. Hard to believe that a few short months ago, it had been summer. Christine and Iggy had shared a booth at the Art Fair, right in front of our store. Christine's painting hung upstairs in my office, a forever memento.

How would I remember Iggy?

Eyes closed, I raised my face to the sun. "Auntie," I heard and opened my eyes. Landon stood on top of the snow berm in front of the gallery, Superman cape flung over his winter jacket.

I crossed the street and scooped him up, his breath as sweet as the feel of his arms around my neck.

"You're sad, too," he said, with the perceptiveness of the very old and the very young.

I set him on the sidewalk and crouched in front of him.

"Mommy's sad," he said, voice and face solemn. "She and Daddy talked all night. She cried. They don't know I saw them. Is it because of Christine?"

I swallowed hard. How to balance honesty with my sister's right to determine how much he knew? "Partly. But mostly, it's about your grandpa. Your mommy's dad, and mine, whom you never knew."

Round eyes stared at me. "He died. A long time ago."

"Yes. And we got some news last night about it, and it made us sad, for now. But we'll feel better because we know." How much he understood, I could only guess.

"Let's get a cookie," he said. "And we'll feel better now."

No contesting that logic. I poked my head in the gallery

to tell Chiara where we were going. In Le Panier, we ordered cookies and a glass of milk, and a portobello panino. We ate at a mosaic-topped café table, Landon's legs swinging as he told me all the goings-on at kindergarten.

"And Mommy says she's going to keep my painting forever, as part of her collection, so when I'm a famous artist, she can sell it and retire on the profits. Auntie, what are profits?"

Two teenagers, deep in conversation, charged up the sidewalk across the street.

"Landon, we need to go." I hastily rewrapped the uneaten half of the sandwich.

"But I wasn't done telling you about school."

"Sorry, little guy. Make it up to you later." I deposited him at the gallery, and took off for the Playhouse.

"The first movie starts in an hour," I told Zayda. "We can get out there and back and he won't know a thing. Tell him your mom had an emergency at the Inn and you had to go help."

"If we get caught—"

"Then we have to make sure we don't." Brave words. But I finally knew what had happened to Christine, and I couldn't prove it without Zayda.

"Your mom says competition for film school is stiff. You need a reference from him. But he wouldn't give you a good one unless you helped him, would he?" I steered the Subaru onto the highway. My young passenger's cheeks flushed and she squeezed one hand with the other. *Bingo.* "Unless you let him into Christine's studio."

"He said he needed to talk to her, that he would just go in with me. But then he made me leave, shoved me out. Locked me out. I swear, I never thought he'd hurt her. Or steal anything."

So that was how she'd lost the telltale eyebrow ring.

And that was "the job" Larry had referred to last week, when I'd overheard her talking to him.

"He said he'd make sure every application I made got scuttled. That I wouldn't get a janitor's job at a film studio if I didn't help him. What will happen when he finds out I double-crossed him?"

I turned up the Jewel Basin Road. "He's a killer, Zayda. And you can make sure he's punished."

Her jaw quivered and she bit her lower lip, stilling it.

"Look in the notebook. In the very back," I told her. At an old lady's handwritten partial inventory. Had Christine put it there so she could talk to Larry about the items he wanted? The items he'd hounded Iggy for.

Had killed Christine for.

"Ohmygod," Zayda said, bent over the pages. "Hey, you missed the driveway."

Another long drive ran parallel to Larry's. It hadn't been plowed in weeks, the owners no doubt sipping gin and tonics in a golf course condo on Kauai. I parked the Subaru heading out, for a quick getaway. We'd slip over the property line, in and out like thieves in the night.

Or like what we were: thieves in the broad daylight.

Zayda punched in the security code. Squinting, clenching my teeth, I waited for the alarm to blare in our ears. But all was silent. You'd think a smart guy would know better than to let a smart kid watch when he disarmed his fancy system.

"Downstairs," she said, and I followed, gloved hand on the rail, feet slow, as I took in the splendor of what Larry called his "little log home."

"Hurry," she urged. But how could I hurry past this glory? An oil painting of two young Indian men, one holding a pipe, the other a drum. J. H. Sharp. Seriously? Joseph Henry Sharp?

"C'mon," Zayda said, rushing past glass-front cabinets chock-full of railroad china, antique firearms, beaded moccasins, and more. I didn't dare dawdle.

Zayda charged down a hallway lined with 1950s Great Northern Railroad calendars and stopped in front of a wood-paneled door, an electronic keypad beside the frame. "In here. I saw them Thursday, when I came out to beg him for the reference." She punched in a code and nothing happened.

Tried a second time. Nothing.

The oxygen seemed to have gone out of the air. "Breathe," I told her. "Three times, slowly."

Charmed on the third try, the lock clicked and the brass doorknob turned. We stepped into another world.

The past is a foreign country, the saying goes. And so, apparently, is the heart of the rabid collector.

In pride of place on the nearest wall hung a beaded cradleboard, an object I'd only seen in museums. Next to it, a beaded sash, more moccasins, a knife sheath. Quillwork? A glass-front bookcase held antique pistols. In another, I recognized two Russell bronzes. On the other shelves, more bronzes depicted Blackfeet Indians and rodeo cowboys.

In the corner, a well-worn brown leather chair, brass trimmed, sat next to a brass floor lamp, the paper-thin hide shade painted with red and yellow primitive figures. Behind it hung the brass gong Adam had mentioned.

Ah. Another Asian piece from the Russell house? Was that the piece Iggy had sold, to her regret?

Larry Abrams's private office. The one where he kept his finest treasures.

Zayda stood before an oak rolltop desk. Slowly, she breathed in and out three times, then slid open the tambour top—an S-curve, the rarest kind—exposing tiny drawers with brass pulls, open cubbies, and letter slots, even a pair of pencil rests. Wearing her gloves—*good girl*—she slid open a drawer and withdrew a chop with a lion's head and a packet of letters, yellowed by age and tied with a thin scarlet ribbon.

"Letters Charlie Russell wrote to David Ring when he was a boy," she said. "And Christmas cards from his protégé to David and Iggy. She wouldn't sell them, and neither would Christine."

I scanned the room, one wall, then the next, and the next. "Is it all stolen? Is this—ohmygod. Is this why he sits on the boards of all those little museums and historical centers all across the state? He donates minor items and everyone praises him as a great patron of small-town culture, but he's using them to get access—"

"Hush!" Zayda whispered. "He's here. We have to get out."

We scurried back down the hallway, pausing every few feet to listen. "We'll sneak through the main gallery and out the back," she said. "What if he's reset the alarm?"

"Then run like stallions."

We almost made it. If antique rugs lay flat, we would have flown out the back door, across the snow-covered lawn, and into the woods. But Zayda's clunky boots were no match for the Persian rug on the gallery's smooth floor. She tripped and fell, face down, with a sickening thud, clutching the packet and the chop. The copy of Nick's original, valuable in its own right.

"Stop right there."

My fingers grazing the door handle, I froze at Larry's command. Turned slowly at the snick of the hammer being drawn back on the ancient black pistol in his hand. Single shot? How good was his aim? Dare I chance it?

The heavy boots on his feet caught my eye, and I knew they'd match the treads found in the cottage and the woods.

On the floor, Zayda groaned. Rolled over, clutching her leg. "My ankle. It's broken." She tried to sit, touched her heel to the floor, and screamed.

Larry let his gun arm drop as he focused on the girl, writhing in pain. I grabbed a framed piece from an easel near the door. Barbara Stanwyck gripped Ronald Reagan's arm as I brought the poster for *The Cattle Queen of Montana* down on Larry Abrams's skull.

· Thirty-one ·

"Not that I don't appreciate you solving crimes for us, Erin," Ike said dryly after his deputies hauled Larry off to jail, "but I do wish you'd call me before following up on your brilliant ideas."

"Would you have believed me? Or Zayda? That a respected member of the community—big shot, Art Center board member, Hollywood zillionaire—was a killer and a thief? That he blackmailed a teenager into doing his dirty work and nearly got away with it?"

While the uninjured Zayda—her theater talents were not all behind the scenes—trained Larry's gun on him, I'd called 911. Then I'd quizzed our would-be captor as he sobbed, not for killing Christine, but for the loss of his movie poster. The poster from the sole movie he could recall his father ever taking him to see.

"His Rosebud," Zayda now explained. "Like Orson Welles's character in *Citizen Kane*." Larry's entire career—all the movies he had helped make, in more than forty years in the industry—and all his collections circled back to that childhood love of Westerns, spurred by the memory of a single afternoon in a Brooklyn theater called the Bijou.

He hadn't meant to kill her. But when he slipped the stolen bounty into his pocket, she'd caught the movement reflected in the glass on a painting. She'd pulled out the gun Nick had given her. They'd struggled. It had gone off. The smeared prints told the story.

"Rosebud. Now I guess I've heard everything." Ike was obviously not as keen on movies as the teenager sitting next to me in Larry's living room.

The casual visitor would have been mightily impressed by the collected works of modern Western artists and twentieth-century masters. But only those few—fortunate or not—who visited the inner sanctum saw the real treasures. Like Adam and Zayda, they were awed but largely unaware of what they'd seen.

Unable to brag about his stolen treasures, yet unable to keep them to himself, Larry couldn't resist showing off. And, I realized, it was his fancy car—that big white Cadillac—that Jack Frost had seen at Christine's.

"You'll need experts," I told Ike. "To make a complete inventory, then compare it to lists of stolen objects from around the West. Some museums may not even know their items are missing, their own inventories and security systems are so inadequate."

"Why steal from Christine?" a detective new to the case asked. After Danny's arrest last night, Ike had ordered Kim to take a few days off.

"He knew she planned to give the bulk of Iggy's collection to the Art Center, where he could see it, but not get his own hands on it," I said. "If he took what he wanted before she knew what she had, there would be no trail. He didn't know Iggy had left a partial inventory that listed the letters. After she died, he saw another opportunity. He ransacked the cottage to see what else he could find, but I scared him off."

"With no inventory, Christine could not have proven what he'd done," Ike said. "Clever. Since she didn't trust him, he used you, Ms. George, to worm his way into the church."

"He promised me no one would get hurt. He was my advisor. I trusted him. It was a mistake I will always regret." The anxiety that had enveloped Zayda for the last week had vanished.

She had, as the saying goes, collected herself.

Red-and-white bag of popcorn in hand—classic butter-and-salt flavoring, thank you very much—I dropped into the seat next to Kim. In the back row of the Playhouse, on the aisle, where we'd sat the other night during the documentary. Where we'd sat as kids, when we worked as ushers in the summer and watched aspiring professionals perform.

"Saturday night at the movies." I offered her popcorn. "I am not getting up until this Festival ends."

Even in the dim light, I could see Kim smile. She wore jeans and boots, and a classic cowgirl shirt with pearl snaps. She'd lost the pastiness brought on by last night's shock, but she needed a good dose of sunshine.

By mid-February, most northwest Montana denizens resemble ghosts. And this had been a particularly brutal winter.

"Can you believe I've never seen *Chocolat*?" she said. "I work too much."

"Ten-four."

But before the movie came the last-minute high school production. The perky teacher-coach took the stage to cheers from the young in the crowd. *Coaches*. My chest tightened. The good ones linger long after they're gone.

First up, a girl I didn't know read my piece on pie. "Pie, we love pie," went the refrain and the audience repeated it with singsong delight. I felt myself grinning widely, a hand on my rumbling tummy. Then the red-haired girl gave a dramatic reading of a poem called "Making Tortillas." I could almost feel the wet corn between my hands as she clapped, pressing grainy meal into "thin yellow moons . . . finding their shape." Could almost feel the heat of the griddle, hear the grease sizzle, smell the tortilla cooking.

As promised, the hit of the night was the coach's surprise. Dana, the tall, skinny Film Club member I knew as Dylan and Zayda's sidekick, had us splitting a gut as he re-created Dan Aykroyd's famous *Saturday Night Live* skit, impersonating Julia Child.

Laughter never felt so good.

Also as promised, I stayed put during the brief intermission before the second feature. So did Kim. I spotted Adam with a friend on the other side of the theater and waved.

When the crowd in the aisle thinned, Kim spoke, facing forward. "As a cop, I ought to lecture you on not telling me what you knew—or suspected—when Larry suggested that the damage to the screen had been deliberate vandalism. You deliberately steered me away. But as your friend, I get that you didn't trust me. You haven't trusted me for a long time. I hope someday, you'll trust me again."

Not a promise I could make yet. *Soon.* I reached across the armrest and squeezed her hand. And noticed she wore the silver and black onyx bracelet I'd given her in high school.

Long about the moment when Alfred Molina playing le Comte, the mayor determined to drive the passionate, sensuous Vianne out of town, breaks into her shop and falls asleep after gorging himself on forbidden chocolate, understanding struck. For most collectors—obsessives like Larry excepted—collecting grows out of passion. Whether sparked by love and memory, like my mother's fondness for handmade martini glasses or Kyle's fervor for the GTO, it touches something deep inside. Something good—beauty, excellence, devotion.

Even preservation, as Larry had so fervently argued Thursday night before the documentary aired.

I lack the drive to collect. But my own passions—for food and family, retail, and this village—fill the same yearning.

And they never need dusting.

I did leave my seat at the end of the movie, to pass out chocolate hearts wrapped in red foil for all and red roses for the women—valentines, courtesy of Tracy and the florist. Kim lent a hand, in what seemed like a genuine show of community spirit.

Afterward, she told me the rest of the story. "In our neighborhood canvass around Christine's place, we finally developed enough evidence to establish what we've long suspected: Jack Frost was running a major grow operation on his property. The Northwest Montana Drug Task Force executed a raid this afternoon and took Jack into custody. His wife's away, but they'll get her, too."

I let out a low whistle. "The tension between him and Christine?"

Kim nodded. "She reported her concerns to us several weeks ago. She and a few neighbors started jotting down license plate numbers. We got those notes and ran down the owners. Put together a good case."

She hadn't been free to tell me. The world can be so simple, and so complicated.

"We also confirmed regular sightings of wolves down at the lake and of your brother driving by. J. D. Beckstead corroborated Nick's story, as did others.

"But we didn't have a clue about Larry Abrams's role in Christine's death until you called us. We'd wondered about the art angle—the murder occurred in a painter and collector's studio, after all—and your information about Russell made the connection a real possibility. But if you hadn't figured out Zayda George's role, and earned her trust . . ."

"Earned it? I kidnapped her and cajoled her into breaking and entering. But thanks." We embraced, awkwardly, and headed for the lobby. "Hey, do I get an honorary badge now?"

"Maybe Landon will lend you his Hank the Cowdog star."

"Ohmygod. I can't believe it. Did the earth stop spinning?"

Adam peered over my shoulder. "What's wrong?"

I pointed. Sandburg and Pumpkin lay on the ottoman by the fireplace, curled around each other like a Halloween version of the yin and yang symbol.

Sandburg opened an eye. Pumpkin mewed. Then both cats went back to sleep.

Adam slid a small black box out of his pocket.

"I didn't get you anything," I said. For years now, Valentine's Day had been little more than a time to sell chocolates and Champagne so other people could celebrate.

His dark curls danced. "Doesn't matter. Open it."

Inside lay a fused-glass heart in shades of red on a black cord necklace.

I raised my face for a kiss, sending a silent "thank you" to the plow crews who'd brought Mr. Right safely home to me.

Sunday afternoon. The Playhouse was packed for the final movie, *Ratatouille*, chosen for its family suitability. And because it's one of my favorite movies ever, foodie or otherwise, and what's the point of running a film festival if you can't share your faves?

Sunday dinner at the Orchard may be a family tradition, but we're flexible when it comes to food and celebrations.

After the final credits, the Murphys and friends joined the Georges, Washingtons, and other Film Club families for an Oscar dinner at the Jewel Inn. Their new chef wasn't scheduled to arrive until April first—fingers crossed for that one—so Tony did the kitchen honors.

And they were magnificent.

Mimi handed me a huckleberry martini. One sip sold me. "To die for," I said, then flushed purple as the berry.

"I guess I'm glad you missed my call yesterday," she said, "or we wouldn't know who killed Christine, and my daughter might still be under suspicion."

"Sorry about that. I was too busy chasing down crime to check my messages." I sipped, and snared a mushroom-goat cheese appetizer from Zayda's tray as she made the rounds.

"We met with the final tea shop prospect," Mimi said. "The one from the grocery store."

The one I'd thought a waste of time to consider.

"He's perfect," she continued. "He brought samples to the interview. Sweet and savory scones. Scrumptious sandwiches. Jewel-studded iced petit fours. The most gorgeous fruit plate. And of course, tea. He's the one, Erin. He understands the village and he says he can open in the old tavern by May fifteenth."

After he power-washes the place with industrial-strength cleaners.

The Inn's front door opened, and my heart sped up as if it had just been injected directly with Italian roast.

Sally Grimes, smiling tentatively. I had sent her sweetheart to jail, and she smiled at me. Behind her came Sage, and Nathan holding Olivia. The toddler's calm eyes embraced everything, and her pink-and-purple dress had come straight from Puddle Jumpers.

Sally extended a hand. "Erin, thanks to you and Zayda for putting an end to this nightmare. And thank you and your brother for showing me what family really means."

After a week that had me questioning at times how much I knew about family, her words left me speechless.

"I understand now that Larry was using me to get at Iggy's collection. I won't pretend his betrayal didn't hurt me, deeply. I've had a lot of betrayal in my life, and I let it blind me. I didn't see that he was using my own anger— my anger with Iggy—to manipulate me." Her eyes glistened, but her gaze didn't waver.

I opened my mouth but she held up a hand. "Nick came by last night. He brought—" She put her hand on her chest. "He brought the antique bassinet he found in the church basement. My great-great-grandfather made it. Olivia's too big, but it's perfect for her dolls and stuffed animals. Until there's another baby in the family."

"The walnut secretary is yours whenever you want it," Nick said, coming up beside me. "And you and Sage can come out and choose whatever you'd like from the family things."

Color me stunned.

Sally took a deep breath and let it out slowly. "It's a wake-up call, is what it is. A chance to break the cycle of anger and betrayal that's gripped my family for too long. I understand now that my daughter's life is her own, not a chance for me to get a do-over. And I want to be in their lives. More than just sending cute baby clothes at Christmas and on Olivia's birthday."

Careful not to spill my martini, I hugged her.

I actually hugged Sally Grimes.

Zayda and her brother T.J. circulated with trays of crab salad on cucumber slices and eggplant-tomato meatballs. We ate, sipped, mingled, and chatted—the perfect end to the Festival.

That and knowing two men were in jail for a very long time. I glanced at my mother, still pale from the shock of finally learning who had killed my father. But she radiated a peacefulness that reached out and embraced us all. The peace of finally knowing.

"That was generous," I told Nick.

"I don't need those things, and they matter to her. The Russell items will go to the museum in Great Falls. I'm keeping the copy of the chop. The rest of Iggy's collection will go to the Art Center. I'm counting on you to throw the party you promised. Sally agreed to fund the security upgrade. All she wanted was a little acknowledgment that she was part of the family."

That's all most of us want. And when we're kept in the dark—intentionally or not—we feel excluded. I'd learned to trust my heart on that one.

"And she'll support Christine's plan to endow a scholarship for high school art, film, and drama students," he continued. "Turning pain into a positive."

"What about the property?"

"I haven't decided yet. But if you want the cottage—" He glanced across the room at Adam, listening intently to Landon. "Your cabin's pretty small."

The warmth crept up my throat. "Long as I don't have to live next door to Jack Frost."

"Jack feared change."

"And that the cops would find out what he's been growing back there."

"That, they have." Nick's grin reminded me of Adam's. In some ways similar and in others very different, these two men of mine.

"So you don't think he hates wolves as much as he feared discovery?"

"No, he hates them. They represent destruction of an old way of life, a life of being left alone, and flaunting society's rules. Our laws."

"People are going to find out about your fledgling Rainbow Lake pack."

He nodded. "I've talked with the wildlife managers. Since it's a breeding pair, they're prepared to move them, if necessary."

"Good work. If I move in to the cottage, brother, I think I'll find me an artist to sculpt a wolf out of salvaged auto parts."

He howled.

Tony, in his white apron, emerged from the kitchen and tapped a glass with a spoon. Mimi whipped off the baseball cap he always wears while cooking, exposing his bald head. "Dinner in two shakes," he said. "But first, a toast to the First Annual Jewel Bay Food Lovers' Film Festival!"

Cries of "hear, hear" and "cheers!" rose to the timbers.

"'First annual' has a nice ring," Bill said.

I threw up my hands. "Don't look at me. Besides, the Festival depends on the Film Club. Shouldn't a decision wait for a new advisor?"

"We've already talked to the drama coach," Dylan said. "She's in."

Before I took my seat, Landon asked me a question. "Auntie, what's a poor mouse?"

For the second time in a week, I sloshed my martini, and I swear, it was my first. But it's hard to take seriously a question about mice from a five-year-old dressed like the Cat in the Hat. In honor of Dr. Seuss's approaching birthday, Chiara had made him a tall red-and-white hat and an oversized bow tie, and drawn whiskers on his little cheeks.

"At dinner at Noni's," he went on, "you said somebody was a poor mouse."

The light went on. He'd misheard my description of Sally as a poor-mouth. "That is what Sandburg and Pumpkin have been dreaming of all winter: A poor mouse to chase."

Satisfied, he ran off to sit between his father and his noni.

"Good save," Chiara said.

"That outfit is adorable. You should make a line of children's costumes."

"I'm learning from you, little sister. No products that aren't consistent with the gallery's mission."

"Sell them at Puddle Jumpers," my inner imp said. "Sally would be thrilled."

My sister rolled her eyes. "You are incorrigible."

I looked up at the antelope in his beads and Groucho glasses and winked. "I hope so."

·····

The Food Lovers' Film Festival Guide to Food and Drink

·····

COCKTAILS WITH THE MURPHY GIRLS

Huckleberry Martinis

HUCKLEBERRY VODKA:

Commercial huckleberry-flavored vodkas are available. Erin prefers to make her own. This drink is similar to a Cosmopolitan.

3 ounces vodka
3 ounces huckleberries, fresh or frozen

Pour vodka over berries in a mason jar or mortar; mash the berries with a fork or a pestle and let sit at least one hour.

(The berries can be steeped up to a week.) Strain before using.
Makes 3 ounces huckleberry vodka.

   3 ounces huckleberry vodka
   2 ounces triple sec
   1 ounce lime juice
   1 cup ice cubes

Combine ingredients in a cocktail shaker. Shake until the
outside of the shaker is frosty or your hands are cold. Strain
into two chilled martini glasses. If you prefer a sweeter drink,
add ½ teaspoon simple syrup to each drink.

SERVES 2

Huckleberry Margaritas

Serve on the rocks or blended, with salt or without.

HUCKLEBERRY TEQUILA:

   3 ounces tequila
   3 ounces huckleberries, fresh or frozen

Pour tequila over berries in a mason jar or mortar; mash the
berries with a fork or a pestle and let sit at least one hour.
(The berries can be steeped up to a week.) Strain before using.
Makes 3 ounces huckleberry tequila.

   3 ounces huckleberry tequila
   2 ounces triple sec
   1 ounce lime juice
   1 cup ice cubes for on the rocks, two ice cubes for blended
   lime wedges

On the rocks: Combine ingredients, except lime wedge, in a cocktail shaker. Shake until the outside of the shaker is frosty or your hands are cold. Strain into two glasses. Serve with a lime wedge.

Blended: Add first three ingredients to blender with two ice cubes. Pulse and pour into glasses. Serve with a lime wedge.

If you prefer a sweeter drink, add ½ teaspoon simple syrup to each drink. For salted rims, shake salt onto a saucer. Run a lime wedge around the rim of each glass and dip the glass into the salt.

SERVES 2

• • • • •

AT HOME WITH ERIN

The morning after a night out, relax at home with Erin and the cats.

Erin's Sunday Morning Scones

⅓ cup or more chopped pecans, toasted (see below)
1 cup unbleached, all-purpose flour
1½ cups whole wheat flour*
¾ cup flaxseed meal
2½ teaspoons baking powder
½ cup brown sugar, firmly packed
½ teaspoon baking soda
½ cup (one stick) butter, cut into small chunks

1 cup buttermilk
zest of one orange
⅓ cup dried cranberries, soaked in hot water to plump and
    well-drained
cinnamon sugar** or raw sugar to sprinkle as a topping
    (optional)

Preheat oven to 300 degrees.

Toast the pecans for 10 minutes at 300 degrees, shaking the pan once or twice during baking. Don't overbake; the nuts will continue to brown and crisp as they cool.

Raise oven temperature to 375 degrees.

In a large mixing bowl, or a mixer or food processor, mix the flours, flaxseed meal, baking powder, brown sugar, and baking soda. Add the butter and mix or pulse until the mixture looks like large crumbs. Add half the buttermilk and work in, adding the rest as the dough starts to pull together. (Erin likes to use a food processor to mix in the butter and buttermilk more easily.)

If you're using a food processor, transfer the dough to a large mixing bowl. Add pecans, zest, and cranberries.

Cover two baking sheets with parchment paper. Flour a large cutting board. Form the dough into a log. Cut the dough into five equal pieces. Use your hands to shape the first piece into a circle, about half an inch thick. Cut into four equal triangles and transfer to the baking sheets. Repeat with the remaining pieces. Sprinkle with cinnamon sugar or raw sugar if you'd like.

Bake 18–20 minutes, or until lightly browned.

MAKES 20 SCONES. THESE FREEZE BEAUTIFULLY.

King Arthur's unbleached white whole-wheat flour will give these scones a lighter color and texture that is particularly yummy, but if you can't find it, regular whole-wheat flour works fine.

** 1 teaspoon cinnamon to ¼ cup white sugar is a tasty combo. Erin stores the mix in a small airtight container, as it keeps well and is extra-tasty on scones, buttered toast, and oatmeal.

Fennel and Blood Orange Salad

Erin likes this as a complement to sautéed scallops or shrimp, or a salmon burger.

¼ cup hazelnuts or walnuts, toasted (see below)
1 medium-to-large fennel bulb
juice of 1 lemon
salt and freshly ground black pepper
2 large blood oranges (the Cara Cara, a red-fleshed navel
  orange works well)
1 small shallot, peeled and cut into paper-thin slices
10 mint leaves, chopped
2 tablespoons extra-virgin olive oil
1 tablespoon fennel fronds, chopped, for garnish

Preheat oven to 300 degrees.

Toast nuts for 10 minutes in a 300-degree oven, shaking pan occasionally. (Don't overbrown, as nuts will continue to darken after toasting.) Cool. If you use hazelnuts, roll them between your hands, to remove any loose skins; discard the skins—they are bitter. Coarsely chop the nuts and set them aside.

Slice off the root end of the fennel and discard. Trim the stems, saving a few fronds for garnish. Slice bulb thinly, using a sharp knife. (Some cookbooks recommend starting at the flat bottom side, but Erin thinks it's easier to rest the bulb on its side, which is fairly flat, and slice from the end, using the stem end to hold the bulb.) Toss the slices in a mixing bowl with lemon juice, salt, and pepper.

Remove peel and pith from oranges. Cut the oranges in half crosswise, and use a small serrated knife to cut the sections from the membrane and add the sections to the seasoned fennel. Squeeze juice from the orange halves by hand or with a juicer, and add juice to the seasoned fennel. Add the shallot, mint leaves, olive oil, and chopped nuts, and toss gently. Serve alone or on a bed of greens, and garnish with the fennel fronds.

This salad can be made ahead; add the mint and fennel fronds before serving.

SERVES 4

Chocolate-Cabernet Sauce

Perfect on top of ice cream or cheesecake, after a hard night of sleuthing.

1 cup heavy cream
1 tablespoon unsalted butter
½ teaspoon vanilla
2 tablespoons Cabernet Sauvignon
½ pound semisweet chocolate, broken into pieces for easier melting (Erin likes Scharffen Berger's baking bars)

Heat the cream, butter, vanilla, and wine in a small saucepan over medium heat. Add the chocolate and stir until smooth.

Makes about one pint. Erin stores the sauce in a pint jar in the fridge, and warms it for serving by setting the jar in a bowl of very hot water.

Pumpkin Spice Coffee Blend

Created by Fresca, in honor of the newest member of Erin's household.

- 2 tablespoons ground cinnamon
- 2 teaspoons ground nutmeg
- 2 teaspoons ground ginger
- 1½ teaspoons ground allspice or cloves, or a blend
- dash of ground cardamom
- 1 teaspoon dried orange or lemon peel

Mix ingredients together in a small bowl and store in a jar or tin with a tight lid. For a pot of drip coffee, add ¼ to ½ teaspoon of the spice blend to the ground coffee. For a single cup of espresso, drip coffee, or French press coffee, use ⅛ teaspoon to start, until you know how much tastes just right to you.

If you like to sweeten your coffee, turbinado sugar goes well with this blend; add it to the spices or to your cup. Feel free to experiment with the amounts and add other spices, such as a vanilla bean or whole cloves. Trust your own taste buds, and have fun!

· · · · ·

FROM TRACY'S KITCHEN

Tracy's Cocoa Nib Hot Chocolate

Seriously smooth and rich. Try adding a dash of cinnamon or chili powder to the dry ingredients. A splash of Kahlua, Peppermint Schnapps, or Bailey's Irish Cream will add an extra kick.

¼ cup cocoa nibs
2 cups whole milk
6 ounces 65 percent to 70 percent bittersweet chocolate, finely chopped
⅓ cup sugar
¼ teaspoon kosher salt
¼ cup water

OPTIONAL:

¼ teaspoon ground cinnamon
or
¼ teaspoon ancho chile powder

Pulse the cocoa nibs in a spice grinder or a small food processor until coarsely chopped, three or four times. Pour nibs into a 1-quart saucepan and add the milk. Cook over medium heat, stirring, until milk reaches the simmer stage, just below a boil, about 160 degrees. Remove from heat and let steep for 30 minutes.

Meanwhile, combine the chocolate, sugar, salt, and water in the carafe of a 1-liter French press. Set aside.

After steeping, reheat the chocolate milk mixture until it begins to simmer. Pour into the carafe through a mesh strainer. Set aside for 1 minute, while you rinse mugs with hot water. Stir cocoa to combine the chocolate and milk. Pump the plunger of the French press 10–15 times to froth and aerate the cocoa. Serve immediately.

SERVES 2

• • • • •

CELEBRATING THE MOVIES!

Jewel Bay Critter Crunch

8 cups plain, popped popcorn (If you're using an air popper, this is about 1 cup of raw kernels.)
½ cup raw, unsalted peanuts
½ cup raw, unsalted almonds
6 tablespoons butter
3 tablespoons light (clear) corn syrup
¾ cup brown sugar
¼ teaspoon vanilla
¼ teaspoon baking soda
1 cup semisweet chocolate chips

Preheat oven to 300 degrees. Spray or grease a baking sheet.

Pluck all the old maids (the unpopped kernels) and skins from popcorn and pour popcorn into a bowl. Add nuts and stir to mix.

To make caramel, combine butter, corn syrup, and brown sugar in a small saucepan over medium heat. Cook and stir until mixture boils. Continue cooking at a low boil for 4 minutes. Remove from heat and stir in vanilla and baking soda.

Pour caramel mixture over popcorn and stir to coat. Spread onto greased cookie sheet, and bake for 10–15 minutes (10 for chewy, 15 for crunchy). Remove from oven and add the chocolate chips. Stir slightly, until the chocolate begins to melt. Cool and eat.

MAKES ABOUT 8 CUPS.